I0542547

# Holiday Hearts

## A Valley Ridge Romance

## Mary J Hicks

**MJH Publishing**
Marietta, OK

Copyright © 2017 by Mary J Hicks

All rights reserved. No part of this publication may be reproduced, distributed or transmitted in any form or by any means, including photocopying, recording, or other electronic or mechanical methods, without the prior written permission of the publisher, except in the case of brief quotations embodied in critical reviews and certain other noncommercial uses permitted by copyright law. For permission requests, contact the publisher.

Printed in the USA

www.maryjhicks.com
marehicks4@gmail.com

Publisher's Note: This is a work of fiction. Names, characters, places, and incidents are a product of the author's imagination. Locales and public names are sometimes used for atmospheric purposes. Any resemblance to actual people, living or dead, or to businesses, companies, events, institutions, or locales is completely coincidental.

Holiday Hearts/ Mary J Hicks -- 1st ed.
ISBN 978-0-9963488-2-9

*To Myron L. Hicks, whose unconditional love and support gave me the freedom to be me. He is ever on my mind and alive in my heart.*
*To Greg, and his family—the wonderful people he's brought into my life.*
*And to Gayle, who keeps me smiling.*

*Let the words of my mouth and the meditation of my heart be acceptable in Your sight, O Lord, my strength and my Redeemer.*

~PSALM 19: 14~

# CHAPTER ONE

# Autumn Days

As Lauren stood in the middle of the large family room, she couldn't for the life of her remember what she was there for. Absentmindedly she adjusted the waistband of her too tight jean-leggings and reminded herself not to wear that pair again until after the baby came. She racked her brain until Winslow and Winnie padded into the room, giving her their, 'Where have you been?' look.

Ah—dog brushes!

With relief and renewed purpose, she charged toward the antique cedar chest that held the dog's toys and grooming tools. Tumbling among the toys, some tattered beyond repair, she tossed items left and right until she found Winslow's black brush. Eyeing several of the ragged toys in her hand, she hesitated a second before dropping them back. Now wasn't the time to purge the dog box of ruined toys. Not finding Winnie's pink brush, Lauren closed the box.

They'd have to share Winslow's.

"Come on, guys." She snapped her fingers and led the dogs to the library, a place of solitude. Sitting cross-legged on the floor, she motioned to Winslow and he happily plopped where she patted the rug in front of her. She applied the brush to his soft black and white coat. Winnie settled on the floor to watch and wait her turn.

The dogs loved the attention and the warmth from Winslow's body, coupled with the steady rhythmic brushstrokes, provided a relaxing therapy for Lauren. The task freed her thoughts to wander. She hadn't been able to concentrate all day for thinking of Jackson.

He'd been distracted the last several evenings and again at breakfast.

She'd fought the urge to quiz him before he left for the gallery; it hadn't been easy, but holding her tongue never was. The brush moved back and forth while her thoughts did the same over the last few days. What *was* troubling Jackson? Nothing came to mind. She breathed deeply and expelled a sigh. "There you go, bud—all finished." Winslow gazed up at Lauren, his eyes questioning, *is that all?* Winnie's tail wagged happily as she rose to take Winslow's place. They knew the routine.

Thirty minutes later, as she was finishing with Winnie, as if her thoughts had guided him to her, Jackson walked into the room. Lauren glanced up at his drawn features. Her chest tightened. Something was wrong. She made the last few strokes through Winnie's soft coat and reaffirmed her resolve to let him bring it up first, whatever it was.

He ambled across the room to her and the dogs.

After watching briefly, Jackson extended his hand. Lauren clasped it, unfolded her legs and allowed him to pull her to her feet. Pretending not to notice his melancholy expression, she said, "The dogs are overdue their grooming—the shaggy little critters!" She laughed as Jackson knelt to ruffle their fur. "They both have appointments tomorrow morning."

"And about time," he said. "You guys are a bit scruffy." After a moment Jackson stood and gathered her into his arms. "I missed you today."

Lauren twined her arms around his neck, buried her face against his chest and spoke softly "I missed you too. You should have called me. I'm always agreeable to coffee at the Cat In Paris."

"I know. I thought about it, but the gallery was busy and I hated to leave."

Comforted in the protective circle of their arms, Lauren held Jackson tight; willing him to know that whatever troubled his mind, they could work it out.

She thought back to a few days ago when he and his business partner, Matt, had disagreed about the contract of a new artist for the gallery. But the disagreement hadn't seemed serious, and they'd both laughed about something moments later.

Jackson exhaled wearily.

"Would you like an iced tea before dinner?" Lauren reluctantly moved from his arms.

"Sounds nice. May we have it on the patio?"

"Of course. Go ahead and relax, I'll be right with you." Jackson liked to sit on the patio in particular when he had something on his mind.

As Lauren left the room, she glanced back. Jackson wandered toward the French doors that led out to the patio, one hand in his pocket and the other slowly raking his hair. If he didn't open up soon, she would ask what was wrong—in spite of sounding like a mother hen. She smiled when Jackson's aunt asked *her* if anything was wrong as she went to the fridge. "No, Aunt Willa, just thinking. Have you seen Brooke since she got home?"

"Only briefly. She went straight to her room without her usual milk and cookies." Aunt Willa raised her brows. "Probably on the phone." She chuckled.

Lauren filled two glasses with crushed ice and poured the tea. "I hope she's not coming down with something." Fleeting doubts of being a good stepmother for Brooke still hit Lauren now and then. "It's not like Brooke forgetting to check on baby to see how much he's grown in a day." She and Aunt Willa shared a smile before Lauren headed to the patio.

It occurred to her that it was odd for Brooke and her father to be acting strange at the same time. Jackson had called Aunt Willa and told her not to pick Brooke up after school, that he'd run by for her. Why the change in plans?

Jackson chose to sit in the corner of the stone patio that caught the first shade of the evening. The countryside around Valley Ridge showed signs of an early fall; the leaves drifting now and then from the trees were tinged with gold. The ancient Elm branches overhanging that corner of the patio moved softly in the breeze. He sat in the shade with his arms folded, head back on the chair, eyes closed. She hated to disturb him.

"Here, sweetheart," she said softly. When he opened his eyes, she handed him the frosty glass and sat in the chair next to him. "A tiring day?"

"Yeah, I guess. How was your day?" He swirled the glass gently for several seconds before taking a swallow.

"It was good. I only gained two pounds." She smirked ruefully.

He smiled as if he hadn't really heard. Not like him. She hesitated. "Jackson—is anything wrong?" She sat her glass on the patio table and touched his arm. "Have you and Matt argued? You guys always talk through your differences, neither of you ever hold—"

He took a deep breath. "Yes, something is wrong, but it's nothing to do with Matt."

"Can't you tell me?"

Jackson studied the glass in his hand. "Mrs. Flowers called yesterday. Brooke got in trouble at school." He took another swallow of tea, peering at her over the rim of the glass before he placed it on the patio table. "I was with a client and couldn't get away at the time, so I made an appointment to talk with her this afternoon."

"Why didn't you tell me?" She stared and tightened her hold on his arm. In Lauren's heart, her young stepdaughter came close to being a perfect child. Not waiting for an answer to her first question, she said, "Could there be a mistake?"

Jackson leaned forward and placed his forearms on the tops of his knees. He twisted the wedding band on his left hand as he often did while thinking. "No mistake. Brooke admitted her part."

"Her part?" Lauren leaned forward.

"It seems that Mandy and Brooke decided that a fellow student received good grades this semester because her mother bribed the teacher."

"What?" Lauren hid a smile.

"It's not funny."

Jackson's severe expression quickly squelched her urge to smile. "No, it's not. But I'm sure they didn't mean any harm." She was quiet for a moment. "What did they do?"

"During recess, they slipped back into the classroom and searched the teacher's desk."

Lauren sobered. "Oh." She rubbed Jackson's back and leaned her head against his shoulder. "Still, it's not the end of the world, just a childish prank." She breathed relief. "I've been worried about you. I thought something bad had happened."

"I'm sorry you worried, but this *is* bad. Brooke has always been a good child." He glanced at Lauren. "I couldn't believe it at first. She's growing up too fast."

"Yes, children do that. Don't you know I worry *more* if I don't know what's going on?" She was quiet. "I suppose that's why Brooke's gone straight upstairs the last two evenings. Was she terribly upset?"

"Yes, of course, and very sorry." He placed his hand over Lauren's. "I know it's not the end of the world, and I should have told you first thing, but I needed to think about it. I'm concerned." He patted her hand and sighed.

"Will she be expelled?"

"Oh, no. Mrs. Flowers just wanted us to know what the girls had done. They'll probably clean chalkboards for two weeks." He reached for his glass and took another deep swallow. "I've seen this coming for some time. Mandy's a good child, but she's adventuresome and reckless. I worry about her influence on Brooke." He pulled Lauren to him. "What can we do? They've been best friends since first grade." Jackson groaned. "We can't make them stop being friends— can we? Should we?"

"I don't think that would be wise. Mandy is spirited and curious about things, but she's never done anything really bad. This seems out of character even for her." They sat in silence several moments before Lauren spoke. "This incident could make Brooke and Mandy see firsthand what happens when you act without considering the consequences." Lauren paused. "I'm sure they'll think twice before pulling a prank like that ever again."

"I hope you're right. I can't believe Brooke hasn't spoken to you about it?"

Lauren smiled. "She's probably embarrassed or afraid it would be bad for the baby if I got upset. She's very protective." Lauren pulled away from Jackson to better see his face. "I still can't believe you didn't share this with me."

"I told you, I needed to think about it, and I didn't want you to worry, sweetheart."

"If I remember correctly, you're the one who lectured me about the need to share our problems."

"I'm sorry, maybe I overreacted. It threw me a curve."

Jackson's troubled expression suddenly reminded her of an exchange she'd witnessed on the schoolyard. "I'm curious, have you heard either of the girls mention a new student?"

He slowly shook his head. "Not that I recall, why?"

She was thoughtful. "One day last week as I waited for Brooke, she and Mandy came through the school doors laughing and chattering as usual. But as I watched, another girl, one I didn't recognize, joined them." Lauren pursed her lips. "They appeared to be arguing, but I dismissed the thought as it was unlikely."

"That is odd. Mrs. Flowers said Brooke got along well with the other students." He grinned. "Brooke's mentioned in conversation that Mandy is bossy; maybe she bossed the wrong person. You think the other girl may be involved as well?"

"I don't know. But I remember thinking the incident was odd. I may speak with Mandy's mom, see if she's noticed anything."

Lauren snuggled up to his arm and placed her head against his shoulder. "Remember your dad telling you not to worry out of turn? Let's practice his advice—and if anything like this happens again, you'd be justified in separating the girls for a while. You might discuss that possibility with Brooke. She would hate to be separated from her best friend."

Jackson closed his hand over Lauren's. "That sounds like girl talk. Would you do it?"

"Sure, if she comes to me. I may enquire about the new girl too."

Jackson's brows went up, he gave her a thoughtful look.

They both turned when the French doors opened and Brooke stepped outside and ambled tentatively toward them. She went to her dad and put her arms around his neck.

Jackson patted her shoulder. "I told Lauren."

Brooke began to cry softly. Moments later she left her dad and came around to fall into the chair next to Lauren. "I'm sorry, Lauren."

Lauren gathered her into her arms, Brooke hid her face and sobbed, "I'm not going to be friends with Mandy ever again!"

Jackson's wide-eyed gaze met hers over Brooke's head and Lauren saw her own surprise mirrored in his eyes.

"Oh, Brooke, it's not wise to make a decision like that right now—do you think?"

"I hate her!"

"Hate is a strong word. You and Mandy have been friends since first grade."

Brooke shook her head. "I didn't want to look in Mrs. Flowers's desk, but Mandy said we had to." She glanced up briefly before ducking her head again. "Mandy said we had to search the desk to get evidence. But I was scared."

Lauren brushed the hair back from Brooke's face and prayed for the right words to help Brooke understand about responsibility, but without the lasting sting of condemnation that Lauren experienced as a child.

"I suppose it was easier to go along than to say no, wasn't it?" Lauren coaxed. "What would Mandy have done if you had refused to help search Mrs. Flowers's desk?"

Brooke drew away from Lauren and glanced down at her folded hands.

Lauren gently pressed for an answer. "Mandy was probably scared too. She might not have gone ahead if you had refused to help her. What do you think?"

Brooke kept her head down. "She had to . . . be-cause . . . she had to get evidence."

Lauren hugged Brooke close. "If you two are tempted ever again to solve a mystery, come to your dad or me before taking action."

Jackson cleared his throat and stood. "Well, I'm sure nothing like that will ever happen again with you and your friend—"

"She's not my friend anymore." Brooke kept her head down. "I hate her!"

# CHAPTER TWO

# The Letter

When night finally gave way to morning, Lauren was relieved, but still tired as she slipped off the bed. She'd slept very little and she knew Jackson hadn't either. The evening before they'd managed a somewhat constructive conversation with Brooke at the dinner table, even though she went to bed vowing she was no longer Mandy's friend.

Later, Lauren filled Aunt Willa in on what had happened at school.

She glanced across the room where Jackson slept soundly and quietly pulled on her robe. He needed to sleep as long as possible. She carefully closed the door to their bedroom and headed downstairs to the smell of freshly brewed coffee.

She wandered into the morning room looking for Aunt Willa. "Oh, there you are," she said as Jackson's aunt came from the kitchen.

"Good morning. I had a call to make and thought I'd do it before reading my paper. I'm stiff this morning." She arched her back. "Too much gardening yesterday."

Lauren smiled. "Claude will be upset with you, that's his job."

She chuckled. "I think I'll take it easy this morning."

They moved to the serving bar.

Lauren poured their coffee and glanced toward the stack of mail from the day before. It lay unopened on the antique desk where the housekeeper placed the mail and newspapers each day. Lauren browsed the assortment and handed Aunt Willa her paper.

"Thank you, dear." She settled into her chair with a sigh. They had two subscriptions to the local paper. Jackson and his aunt liked to read at the same time.

Lauren's gaze lingered on a pale silver envelope. It sparked a familiar excitement in her heart as always. The handwriting whisked her back to childhood. The lettering was more refined now, but still as bold and uninhabited as always. She took a seat in one of the large chairs in the morning room and glanced up when Jackson quietly came into the room. In a few moments he took the chair opposite hers and placed his coffee on the side table.

"Good morning. Did you survive the night?"

"Good morning, and yes, I did. I tiptoed out hoping you might sleep a bit later."

"I was awake." His glance caught the envelope. "Anything interesting?"

She smiled. "This letter might prove interesting."

He rattled the paper. "Is that yesterday's mail?"

"Yes. With everything going on, I didn't open it."
She tapped the silver envelope against her hand. "This
is from my cousin in Colorado. I only hear from her
every few years."

"I didn't know you had a cousin in Colorado."
Jackson lowered the paper. "You've never mentioned
a cousin."

"Really? I have two cousins there. It seems like
they live in another world. I suppose in a way, they
do." She leaned back in the comfy chair and sipped her
coffee. "We didn't spend much time together as children. Mother always said it was too far for me to travel
alone and she could never get away. But the cousins
came to New York occasionally." Lauren sighed. "I
loved those visits. I wonder what Max is up to."

Jackson made an impatient sound. "Open the envelope and find out." He tilted his head and looked
puzzled. "Where in Colorado does Cousin Max live?
And what does this cousin do?"

Lauren's smile turned to soft laughter. "Max lives
several hours outside of Durango, in a place called
Riverbend, and Max does whatever Max pleases."

He went back to his paper, mumbling, "I suppose
he never gets bored." His eyes peered over the top of
the paper when Lauren smothered a titter of laughter.

"Sorry, I'll explain later." She studied the pale
sheet of paper and after reading for several moments
she looked up. "Max is coming for a visit!" Lauren ran
her hand gently over her rounded stomach. "She asks
if it would be convenient through the Thanksgiving
holiday."

"She?" Jackson lowered his paper.

"Oh yes, that's why I was laughing, Max is a girl. She's a year older than me. Her mother was my mother's younger sister, Aunt Jane."

"May I ask why a mother would name her daughter Max?"

"She didn't. Max was named after our Great Aunt Max, who was named after her great grandfather, Maximillian Stewart Quinn. The family called her Max. Mother said it was a sad thing when Aunt Jane allowed herself to be talked into sticking that name on an innocent baby. She didn't blame Max when she got old enough to threaten anyone who dared call her Maximillian. Like the aunt she was named for, Max refused to answer to anything but Max."

"What did your great aunt think about that?"

"She was very elderly and died before Max and I were old enough to know her. But she would have agreed since she too, preferred to be called Max."

"You have two cousins? Who's the other one, Harry?" He grinned.

"No." Lauren smiled. "Whitney."

Lauren rose from her chair and wandered to the windows, her back to Jackson as she spoke over her shoulder. "Whitney is the youngest. She's two years younger than Max. But she always acted older."

Jackson rattled the paper into a neat fold and got to his feet. "I'm glad they're coming. It'll be nice to have more family at Thanksgiving." He strolled to the windows to stand beside Lauren. "And Brooke will look forward to meeting them."

"It will only be Max. Whitney can't get away. When they were eleven and nine, their parents died in a small plane accident." Lauren said quietly, "I remember like it was yesterday when Mother and I flew to Colorado for the funeral." Lauren sighed. "The girls were raised by an uncle and aunt on their father's side."

Jackson gave her a warm hug. "I'm sorry. You girls had a rough time, didn't you?"

"It was a bad time. Mother turned even more inward. She and Aunt Jane had been very close while growing up." Lauren turned from the window. "Aunt Jane's marriage caused a rift between them. I never understood why, but that was long ago." Lauren rubbed her forehead. She'd not had a headache in months, but now one lurked.

"Are you okay?" Jackson trailed her back to the chairs.

"Uh-huh, but it just occurred to me, this is the first of September." She glanced up from where she'd sat in her chair. "Thanksgiving is barely three months away with so much to do."

Jackson eased into the big chair across from hers. "Like what, except look forward to the holiday and the big party?" He tilted his head.

"Everything will have to be perfect now that Max is coming."

"But you're always saying that everything *is* perfect. Is this Max high-maintenance?"

"She's probably the least high-maintenance person you'll ever know." Lauren tucked the letter into the pocket of her robe. She hadn't bothered to tell Jackson that Max wanted to talk about something. And she didn't plan to tell him that as a child, Max had found trouble wherever she went.

Lauren's mother had called her a wild Indian and wouldn't allow Lauren to spend any part of summer vacations at the Quinn home. The fact that her younger cousin, Whitney, was a perfect young lady didn't help any, because Lauren idolized Max, and she had happily gone along with any scheme her older cousin dreamed up. No matter how much Whitney, the rules-keeper, begged, and threatened to tell their parents, Max charged headlong into trouble.

The recent problem with Brooke and Mandy made it a bad time to share with Jackson that Max had been another Mandy when they were kids.

Jackson got to his feet and tucked the paper under his arm. "Well, I'm off to work. Don't worry about Thanksgiving. Aunt Willa and her help are on top of it." He leaned to plant a kiss on top of her head and headed to the door where he paused. "You think Brooke will patch things up with Mandy? She shouldn't blame her entirely, she had a choice too." He shook his head, glanced at her again and said, "I'll drop the dogs off at the groomers if you can pick them up this afternoon."

"Oh, thanks, honey! That would be a great help. The groomers will call me when they're ready." She smiled at him. "And, Jackson, don't worry about Brooke, it's going to be okay."

He nodded and called the dogs.

She pulled Max's letter out of her pocket. It saddened her that she and her cousins hadn't stayed close over the years. She wished they'd made the effort. Quickly she re-read the part she hadn't mentioned to Jackson—that Max was a bronze artist, that she sold originals and copies to collectors and wholesale to gift stores.

Max had written that lately she'd noticed something odd from one of her buyers. A man who owned a gallery in New York regularly purchased twelve cop-ies of the same piece from the gift shop in their hotel in Durango. Whitney, an architect, has an office on the second floor of the hotel. Out of habit she watches over the sales of Max's bronze pieces.

Whitney became curious about the purchases and questioned why the buyer didn't purchase wholesale, since he qualified as a wholesale buyer. For the last eight months this buyer had ordered twelve copies of a small horned toad once a month. He always ordered online and around the fifteenth of the month.

Once when they were out of the toads, the buyer selected a small bunny and ordered twelve, at the same cost, same time of the month.

Max wrote that on a recent business trip to New York, Whitney made a point of visiting the gallery. The owner wasn't there and neither were any of Max's bronze pieces. Were horned toads that popular in New York City? The hotel gift shop in Durango was lucky to sell that many in a month!

Lauren slowly folded the letter. Something about the tone of Max's letter triggered an underlying appre-hension. It had been so long since she and Max had spoken; Lauren hadn't realized that Max was a suc-cessful bronze artist. She'd just assumed that Max dabbled in the craft as a hobby.

Max had never wanted anything except to manage the sprawling ranch her father had left. Having lived there all of her life, she'd hated the time she went away to school. When Max had finished school and returned to the ranch, she vowed never to leave again.

Lauren glanced at her watch, bit her lip for a sec-ond, and hurried upstairs to the studio. Digging in the deep drawer of her desk she found the old address book she'd had for years. The ranch number wouldn't have changed—Max used to say that nothing ever changed at the ranch, and strangely, that thought comforted Lauren.

She dialed the number. "Yes, hello, is—may I speak to Max?"

"No, sorry. Miss Max not here. I take message, yes?"

"Do you know when she'll be back?"

"Sorry, no. I happy to take message."

"Yes. Please tell her that her cousin, Lauren, called. Thank you."

"Thank you. She get message."

Sharply disappointed, Lauren slouched into one of the chairs by the windows. A tap sounded on the open door. Lauren glanced to see her lifelong friend Clair, standing there.

"Am I interrupting anything?"

"I'd have to be doing something to be interrupted." Lauren indicated a chair. "I haven't even dressed. Come sit. I need to talk."

"Oh? What about?" Clair strolled into the studio and sat opposite her.

"Do you remember long ago when my cousins from Colorado used to visit for several days at a time? I was ten or twelve the last time . . .?"

"Vaguely. I remember the one called Max as a fun child. You got in trouble every day that she stayed with you." Clair laughed. "Your mother disapproved of her character. Too bad you girls couldn't have lived closer." Clair settled into the chair and crossed her legs. "She didn't come as much after her parents were killed. Whatever happened to her? I can't remember the sister."

"Whitney was the sister. Max is a bronze artist."

Clair's brows went up. "Really? I didn't realize you'd kept in touch. What did you want to talk about?" She gazed at Lauren.

"My cousin. We haven't really kept in touch, just a card with a note every now and then. But I got a letter from Max yesterday. It's odd in this day and time to write letters; who still does that? Why not text or call?"

"Oh, not so odd, some people still like the nostalgia of corresponding through letters. I still do. So, what did this letter say?"

Lauren chewed her lip and gazed at Clair. "You never write me—"

"I see you all the time, silly girl. And you don't appreciate the lost art of—"

"Yes, yes I know—never mind." They laughed. "Clair, you have good instincts, so instead of telling you the contents, I'd rather you read it and tell me how it strikes you." She handed the letter to Clair. "I'll run downstairs and fix us a tea tray while you read."

"O-o-o-k-ay . . ." Clair's green eyes widened with interest.

Lauren took her time with the hot tea and scones. She gave Clair time to read the letter. When she returned upstairs and placed the tray on the round footstool between their chairs, Clair gazed out the large windows with the letter folded in her hand. She looked at Lauren.

"My first thought was why a wholesale buyer would order from the gift shop and pay retail prices?

Max could be making light of something that she may really be concerned about. But why would she think you'd know anything about a situation like that? Do you think that's why she wants to come visit—to ask your help in some way?"

"I don't have a clue." Lauren poured the steaming tea. "A gallery paying retail for bulk was what caught Whitney's attention in the first place." Lauren shrugged. "If the guy in New York is paying for the merchandise, why would they care how many horned toads he buys or what day he orders or what he does with them? I feel the same as you—something more is going on that Max is not telling."

"Will you encourage her to come for the holidays?" Clair nibbled a scone.

"Of course! I look forward to seeing Max again and for her to meet Jackson and Brooke. Brooke will love her free spirit—maybe too much." They exchanged a sobering glance.

"Well, it'll be fun for Brooke to meet Max, a real cowgirl." Clair grinned. "And Drew, too. My sweet, cowboy loving husband will be impressed!" Clair sipped from her teacup and sat it on the table. "I remember when Max was little. Dad thought she was so cute in her boots and western shirts with the little pearl snap buttons."

Lauren laughed. "Mother couldn't believe Aunt Jane allowed her to dress however she wanted to." Lauren sobered. "As a mother myself, I may learn to appreciate Mother's concern about Max's character."

Clair nodded and raised her brows. "Uh-huh, the worm turns."

Nodding, Lauren said, "Something like that." Extending her hand to Clair, she retrieved the letter, unfolded it and read the lines where Max wrote that she'd like to arrive in Valley Ridge the Saturday before Thanksgiving. "I'll plan a dinner party and invite everyone so Max can meet our friends." When Clair didn't respond, Lauren glanced her way. "What?"

"I didn't say anything." Clair popped the last of a scone into her mouth.

Lauren sighed. "Well? Don't you think a dinner party is a good idea?"

"Of course I do. It's just that we'll have to wait so long to find out what's going on." Clair grinned. "And I'll be dying to know."

"I do believe you're every bit as curious as Miss Brooke is."

"Yes, I suppose so." Clair laughed and stood. "Come with me to the gallery. I have to make a delivery. We can talk while driving."

"Okay. Jackson dropped the dogs off at the groomers so I'm free until three-thirty when I collect Brooke from school. Clair, don't mention any of this to Jackson."

"I'll not say anything, but doesn't he know your cousin is coming?"

"Of course he knows that . . . just not the other stuff."

"I won't utter a word, but I don't understand why you'd care."

"I don't really know, instinct I guess. I don't want Max to get off on the wrong foot with Jackson. He— he worries about the baby and me."

"Really? I hadn't noticed undue worry."

"Oh, truthfully, it's not me or the baby. I'm healthy and fit and the baby seems to be, too." Lauren glanced at Clair. "I hadn't planned to say anything about it, but Jackson is worried about Brooke." Lauren stacked the teacups on the tray.

"Brooke?" Clair paused from plumping the pillow in the chair she'd just vacated. "Why on earth is he worrying about Brooke—she's the model child!"

Lauren got the tray, and balancing it above the slight baby bump, led the way downstairs.

"In most ways, I agree. But her best friend is a year older than her, and though that has never been an issue before, Mandy's now twelve going on sixteen."

"I must be missing something. How does Mandy have any bearing on Max?"

"You remember how Max had a way of finding trouble as a child—and from her letter, I suspect she still does. Mandy is the same type personality. Trouble has a way of seeking her out and Jackson's aware of that." They'd made their way into the kitchen where Lauren began loading cups into the dishwasher. She debated if she should confide in Clair.

Clair leaned her backside against the counter next to the dishwasher. "Oh—like what?"

Lauren hesitated briefly. "Mandy and Brooke got in trouble at school. They suspected their teacher was bribed into giving a certain student higher grades." Lauren rolled her eyes at Clair's repressed smile. "I know, but it wasn't funny when Mrs. Flowers called Jackson about Brooke's part in the fiasco."

"Brooke's part?" Clair's brows lifted.

It was Lauren's turn to hide a smile. "Mandy loves drama, so naturally, she connected a gift of chocolates from the parent to the teacher as a bribe. It seems that days before grade cards were passed out, the student's mother brought Mrs. Flowers a box of candy. Later the student happily showed Mandy and Brooke, as well as other students, her grades which were much better than usual."

Lauren led the way to the morning room with Clair trailing along. She plopped into one of the large chairs and motioned Clair to the other one. "I'll run upstairs and dress in a minute, but I need to sit for a moment."

"Are you okay?"

"Of course. Just tired and lazy; I didn't sleep much last night."

"Oh, not good. Well, back to Brooke, how did she get involved?"

Lauren laughed. "The same way I always did with Max. Brooke went along with Mandy's scheme to search the teacher's desk for clues of foul play." She shook her head. "Those girls watch too many mystery shows—they were caught, of course."

"Oh goodness! What happened?"

"Mandy confessed her suspicions to the teacher."

"Uh-oh, I bet that didn't fly! I wasn't aware that Mandy was such a precocious child. The times I've been around her, she seemed intelligent but. . . ." Clair frowned. "What happened?"

"Fortunately, Mrs. Flowers is a gentle, wise woman. She kindly explained to the girls that the parent was only showing her appreciation to Mrs. Flowers for recommending a good tutor for her daughter—which accounted for the student's higher grades." Lauren smiled and glanced at Clair. "Jackson's concerned about Mandy's influence on Brooke." Lauren sighed. "It could be more serious the next time Mandy gets an idea that leads to a sleuthing mission."

Clair nodded. "Of course, things could get out of hand, but Mandy is so likeable."

"Yes, another trait she shares with Max. That's why I'm concerned about the impression Max could have on Jackson. He's already concerned—and describing Max would be like describing Mandy." Lauren rested her hands in her lap. "I want him to at least give Max a chance." Lauren stared out the window, lost in thought until Clair made a sound reminding her that she was still there. Lauren sighed. "You read in her letter that she asked me to meet her in New York to check something out, since I know the city better than she does." Lauren tucked her hand protectively under the slight curve of her stomach.

"Does Max know you're five months pregnant?"

"No, she doesn't know about the baby—anyway I haven't told her."

Clair bristled. "Promise me right now you'll not go anywhere or do anything without Jackson's full knowledge—promise me!"

Lauren laughed and waved a hand, dismissing her. "Clair, don't be silly!"

"Silly or not, I'm serious."

"Don't start worrying, she won't be here for several more months. I just want Jackson to meet Max and get to know her." Lauren chuckled.

Clair laughed. "The Max I remember was different, even as a child—different but charming." Clair smiled. "Besides, a high mountain cowgirl is expected to be different."

Lauren nodded slowly. "Yes. That's my concern. I just hope she's not too different."

"You and Max neither one are kids anymore. Max has probably matured into a cautious, sensible woman—like yourself," Clair said, tongue in cheek.

"You read her letter." Lauren suppressed a flicker of excitement.

Clair's eyes grew round. "On second thought, whatever happens, it might be wise to go ahead and explain Max to Jackson before she arrives."

Lauren shook her head, the dark ponytail swung furiously as she widened her eyes. "Absolutely not! I won't even consider it. He'd start censoring before she even gets here."

# CHAPTER THREE

# Holiday Plans

Later in the afternoon, while driving into town, Lauren decided to swing by the groomers and get Winslow and Winnie before picking Brooke up from school.

Her mind wandered again to Max's letter. Brooke would love Max. Lauren shushed the small voice reminding her that Max was fun and unpredictable—and Brooke was impressionable. Visions of trouble kept nagging. "Ridiculous!" she muttered.

Max was an intelligent, educated woman and meeting her would be good for Brooke.

The Pampered Pooch Salon was downtown Valley Ridge, and while she was there, she'd run by the bookstore and pick up the book Jackson had ordered. Lauren paid for the book and was headed toward the exit, when through the glass door, she saw her friend Ally, approaching from the sidewalk.

After Jackson's good friend and business partner Matt, married Ally Parker, she had quickly fit into Lauren's circle of friends. And now, as she struggled with the baby carrier toward the bookstore, Lauren reminded herself that soon she would be lugging a carrier around too.

She hurried to open the door. "Hi, Ally! Let me help." Lauren held the door wide until the two were inside. She followed Ally across the bookstore to a large, plush chair where she placed the carrier and began to uncover the baby.

"Thanks for helping." She glanced at Lauren. "How cute you look! This is the first time I've seen you in maternity clothes." Ally beamed as she made the baby comfortable. "Even though you can still get away without wearing them."

"Thank you. Yes, I do keep stretching my old clothes over my growing body." Lauren laughed. "But I ran into town with Clair earlier this morning, and I thought I'd better make an effort. It pleases Brooke when I wear maternity clothes, so I took time to dress motherly. She's afraid her friend Mandy, doesn't really believe there's a baby coming to our house."

Ally laughed. "Well, you look wonderful. How is Clair?"

"Thanks, I feel good, and Clair is fine. Drew will be joining her this weekend."

"When are those two moving to Valley Ridge full time?" Ally asked.

Lauren shrugged. "They might as well." She and Ally chatted about the amount of time their friends spent in their country *cottage.*

Lauren leaned over the carrier and crooned to Eli. "Isn't it scary how fast he's growing!"

"It is! Matt can hardly enjoy him for worrying about it." Ally laughed and took a deep breath. "If I'd waited another year to have a child, it might have been too late—this is very tiring!"

Lauren agreed. "I keep reminding Brooke she'll have to be my full-time helper."

"You're lucky to have a helper." Ally pushed her hair behind her ear. "I'm fortunate to have Polly too."

"For sure you're fortunate in finding your house-keeper."

Ally glanced at the baby. "Polly's more than a housekeeper. Thankfully, she loves helping with Eli as well." Ally took a deep breath and relaxed. "And where are you off to?"

"Oh, picking the dogs up from the groomers and then on to school to get Brooke."

"Speaking of Brooke, how are the art lessons coming along?"

"Just great. Her school activities cut into our time, but we make it up through the holidays and summers."

"Yes, the holidays, they'll be here soon—my favorite time of the year."

"Speaking of, I have a cousin coming to spend Thanksgiving with us, and I'm having a dinner party to introduce her to our friends."

"Oh, how fun! When does she arrive?"

"November the nineteenth. It's a while yet, just keep the day open for us." Lauren glanced at her watch. "I'd better run get the dogs and hurry on to school."

The mention of Brooke made her chest tighten, they still had issues to resolve, but hopefully a day at school would help Brooke's attitude toward Mandy.

Like Jackson said, Brooke's arm wasn't twisted, she'd made the decision to go along with the scheme. Lauren recalled the stricken expression in Jackson's eyes when Brooke had declared for the second time that she hated Mandy.

"Lauren, are you okay?"

"Sorry, I . . . I was remembering the errands I have left."

"Well, it was good to see you. Come have coffee one day next week—we need a visit."

"I'd love to, Ally! And by the way, I saw Matt this morning. He's looking good."

"Yes, he's happy."

With a smile and another glance at her wrist Lauren said, "His happiness shows. What day next week would you like to coffee?"

"What about Tuesday afternoon, one o'clock—is that okay?"

"Great, I'll be there." She leaned over Eli's carrier and kissed a fat little knee and told him bye, then to Ally, "I'll see you later."

Ally smiled back. "Looking forward to it."

Driving to collect the dogs, Lauren thought about Matt's happiness. Jackson was probably cautioning him to enjoy this time with Eli—because little babies grow up. The incident with Brooke had put him in an odd mood. As they'd prepared for bed the night before, Jackson commented again on how fast Brooke was growing up. And he'd been quiet all evening.

Lauren hadn't slept well the night before and had checked the clock at midnight, before finally falling asleep. Driving along, she suddenly remembered the dream she'd had the night before. She'd dreamt that Brooke was angry that the new baby was a boy. In the dream, Brooke had insisted they take it back and get a girl baby, and then she had run screaming into the woods, saying she hated the baby. Lauren had woke in a sweat and slipped out of bed to make her way downstairs to the kitchen for a glass of cool water.

As she drove to the groomers, she wished the troubling dream had stayed buried in the mysterious layer of the brain where unpleasant dreams reside until eventually fading from memory.

Reaching across the passenger seat for a bottle of water, she twisted the cap off and took a long drink.

The Pampered Pooch wasn't busy; maybe she wouldn't have to wait for the dogs.

"Hi, Lauren! Your guys are ready. We were just about to call you. Kara is bringing them out. They've been prissy all afternoon—proud of their looks!" The owner, Kathy Woods, laughed and rang up the charges for Lauren.

They shared a laugh about dog behavior, along with another owner who nodded and agreed that her poodle did the same thing.

In less than ten minutes she was back in the Range Rover with the dogs—next stop, school. She said a prayer that she would know what to say to Brooke—words to help her through this unhappy period of hurt and anger with her friend.

Lauren would allow Brooke to take the lead—in case she wanted to talk about how it went with Mandy. She was glad she'd picked the dogs up first, having them along might ease the tension.

She pulled along the curb, waiting her turn into the pick-up lane. The line moved slowly, as usual. Finally, she pulled to the stop and scanned the crowded walkway from the main entry. Lauren hadn't realized just how nervous she was about Brooke and Mandy.

"Winslow! Come—" Lauren stopped tugging on Winslow and stared out the window. Coming down the walk, heads together, Mandy and Brooke giggled and compared papers as if nothing had happened. Lauren went limp with relief. "Oh wonderful!" she whispered. The dogs had made it to the front seat as Lauren put the passenger window down.

Mandy waved and called, "Hi, Lauren! Winnie's pink bow is cute."

Lauren waved back. "Thanks, Mandy! She thinks so, too!"

The girls laughed and whispered together once more before Mandy ran off to get her bike. Brooke opened the door and climbed in, giggling and hugging the dogs.

"Wow—they do look pretty!" Brooke touched the pink bow in Winnie's topknot.

"When I picked them up, Kathy said they'd been prissy all afternoon—they know when they look pretty. You can put them in the back now."

Brooke wrestled each dog over the seat, one at a time.

"I know how they feel. When you and dad got married, I felt pretty all that day, but it was nice when I put my old clothes back on."

"Oh, Brooke, you delight me. I couldn't have said it better. I guess that's why we have special clothes for special occasions." She glanced at Brooke. "But really, every day is the most special of all, right?"

"Uh-huh!" Brooke peered up at Lauren. "Do you suppose that's why we just have Christmas and

Thanksgiving once a year, but regular days all the rest
of the time?"

"That makes sense. It would get tiresome if every
day was Christmas, and we had to dress up. Let's run
by the gallery for a minute. I need to check on something, okay?"

Brooke mumbled, "Okay."

They walked into the gallery laughing about
something the class clown, David Holt, had said to the
teacher. Jackson's questioning gaze went from Brooke
to Lauren. With a slight shake of her head and a smile,
Lauren answered his question and said, "Hello, guys."

Matt and Jackson returned the greeting, always
happy to see the girls.

Jackson had worried all night about Brooke saying she hated Mandy. He'd mentioned it this morning
before he left for work. Lauren wanted him to know
everything was okay.

Brooke went straight to her dad and without a
word put her arms around his neck. She stayed in his
comforting arms longer than usual.

Finally, words came, muffled against his neck. "I
love you, Dad."

"I love you, too, Pumpkin." His eyes met Lauren's, and he knew everything would be okay. Unaware they'd brought the dogs in, Jackson startled
when Winnie suddenly barked.

Brooke pulled away from her dad's embrace and
laughed. "Winnie's jealous, Dad! She wants you to
notice how pretty she looks. She has a new bow!"

Jackson bent over and scooped her up to his lap.
"My goodness, a little attention at the beauty parlor

works wonders." He smiled when Brooke giggled and reached for Winnie.

"I'm going to show Maggie."

Brooke looked upon Maggie, the gallery's top salesperson, with new respect ever since Maggie announced her engagement to Levi. It was obvious that Brooke and her friend, Mandy, had a colossal crush on the handsome Levi Brickman.

"Maggie's gone." Jackson said, "She's with a client. Take a picture with my phone and send it to her."

"Okay." She took the phone and wandered toward the break room with Winnie in her arms and Winslow tagging along.

Matt called after her, "Don't hurt Winslow's feelings; he looks pretty too."

They heard Brooke giggle, and she called back, "I'll take his picture."

As soon as she was out of sight and hearing, Jackson motioned for Lauren to move closer and whispered, "What happened at school today? Did you see Mandy or Mrs. Flowers—"

"All is well. I'll tell you later." When Jackson tried to continue, Lauren touched her finger to his lips before she turned to a smiling Matt. "I ran into Ally and Eli at the bookstore. He's growing so fast!"

Matt chuckled. "He is for a fact. Ally buys new clothes every few weeks."

Jackson said, "It's scary to think that in a few years we'll have first-graders!"

They were lost in thoughts of how fast time was passing and how the holidays would be upon them soon, and how it would be Eli's and the new baby's first Christmas, when Brooke came into the office with both dogs trailing her.

"Lauren, I have homework. I need to go home."

"Yes, dear, I'm ready. Collect the dogs. We'll see you at the house, Jackson." She told Matt bye and gave Jackson a happy, everything-is-okay smile and breezed from the office.

"I'm glad we went by the gallery. I wanted to see dad." Brooke said shyly.

"I'm glad too. And I know for a fact your dad is always glad to see you."

Brooke cocked her head. "You too, Lauren. Dad likes to see you as much as me."

Lauren laughed. "I agree. He likes to see us both—but maybe you just a wee bit more." The next few minutes were followed by lighthearted back-and-forth banter of who Jackson liked to see the most. The fun exchange gave Lauren the courage to ask how the day went with Mandy. "It seems that you and Mandy are still friends, yes?"

Brooke ducked her head. "Yes. Mandy is my very best friend. I was just mad yesterday." She gazed up at Lauren. "I didn't mean it . . . what I said about Mandy."

"Of course not. You girls have been friends way too long to let something come between you." Lauren paused. "I was surprised, I've never heard you say you hated anyone—"

"I said it because Mandy said it first."

Lauren took her eyes off the road for a second. "Mandy told you she . . . the same thing?"

"Uh-huh. At school."

"Did you say it back to her—at school?"

She shook her head. "Just to you and Dad."

"Good for you, sweetheart—I'm glad you didn't say it back to Mandy."

She nodded. "Me too. In play period Mandy explained everything, and I'm not mad."

"Oh, Mandy explained everything? Can you share it with me?"

Brooke sighed. "Well, it was really Mrs. Flowers's fault. Mandy said she should be glad we were trying to expose cheating at school . . . and not get mad at us."

Expose cheating . . . that was not a phrase either of the girls would use. Lauren struggled to stay calm. She took a steadying breath and gripped the steering wheel, at a loss for words. She had to have time to think on this new direction the situation had taken. And pray that Brooke didn't share that bit of information with her dad over dinner.

# CHAPTER FOUR

# Growing Pains

Lauren's relief that everything was okay with Brooke and Mandy had been short-lived. The conversation with Brooke on the way home from school opened a whole new situation. She managed to hang on to an appearance of normalcy long enough to get home and have a short visit with Aunt Willa.

Brooke chattered and enjoyed the customary after-school snack. But as soon as Lauren could, she fled upstairs to call for backup.

In times of stress, calling Clair Weston was a natural reflex. Clair had been the one to help and advise Lauren since she'd been an eight-year old living in an elegant New York townhouse with her mother, yet alone in the world.

Lauren settled into the big chair in the studio and pressed Clair's number. "Oh, I'm so glad I caught you!" Relief loosened her grip on the phone.

"I'm glad you did too. Drew and I were just talking about you guys this morning. I was thinking about staying over longer than planned—and he'll drive out day after tomorrow for several days. Oh, I'm sorry, I suppose you had a reason for calling other than hearing my itinerary. So, what's up?"

"Remember what I told you the other day?" Clair must have needed to briefly search her memory; while she did so, Lauren prompted her. "You know, about Brooke and Mandy?"

"Oh yes, of course. How did that work out?"

"In one way, okay, but another problem followed the first." Lauren hesitated. "I need advice and that's your specialty." Lauren laughed as Clair began hedging.

"I may not be the person to advise you about children."

"I don't know why not, you raised me, look how well I turned out."

"No comment."

"I'll ignore that. When will you be free?"

I'm driving out Thursday—tomorrow. Drew can't make it until early Sunday." Clair was quiet for a moment. "I take that whatever it is, you're not telling Jackson." Her voice took on a note of disapproval.

"Not yet and no lecture, please. I'll explain when you get here."

They said their goodbyes and ended the call. Lauren put her head back on the smooth cool fabric of the chair and closed her eyes. She listened to the faint murmuring of conversation between Brooke and Aunt Willa from downstairs. The sounds drifting up from below were soothing, safe and comforting.

She settled deeper into the cushiony chair, allowing her thoughts to drift back to when she and Clair first met and years later to when Clair married Drew.

She opened her eyes to Jackson's smiling face. He had knelt beside her chair and was softly calling her name. "Aunt Willa sent for you. Dinner is waiting."

"Oh, goodness! I didn't mean to fall asleep. I was speaking to Clair one moment and the next you're waking me. What time is it?"

Jackson looked at his watch. "It's 5:57 to be exact."

Lauren stretched. "No wonder I feel so refreshed—I slept almost two hours."

"It's little wonder. We didn't get much rest last night. After dinner I want to hear all about Brooke and Mandy's making up. Maybe we'll all get our sleep tonight."

"Well, I'll tell you what I know about it. At least they are still friends." She glanced at Jackson. "Have you spoken with her about . . . anything?"

Jackson pulled her to her feet. "No, and that's okay. I'm just glad it's over. And I don't expect we'll have anymore of that kind of thing." he smiled and patted her shoulder. "Thank you for being there for her."

Lauren nodded and hoped she could help Brooke understand that Mandy's thinking was not the proper attitude for two young girls who'd pulled the stunt she and Mandy had pulled.

Lauren clasped Jackson's hand as they went down the wide stairway side by side, but her thoughts were miles away. How could she tell him that neither of the girls felt they'd done anything wrong, that Mandy had convinced Brooke they'd been the ones wronged?

The next morning, Lauren was up early again. She hoped to have some quiet time with Aunt Willa. But as she poured coffee, the phone in the morning room rang. "I'll get it!" She said, and with coffee in hand she hurried to answer the phone.

"Hello." It was Nicolas Conti, the gallery owner in Florence who represented her work. She smiled and set her cup on the desk blotter. "Nicolas! I was just thinking about you the other day." She carried the phone across the room and sat in the chair next to Aunt Willa. For several minutes she listened.

After several furtive glances at Jackson's aunt, Lauren rose and wandered over to stand at the floor-to-ceiling windows.

"I'm honored to be chosen, but let me think about it, Nicolas. Yes, I remember when you suggested the possibility, but I didn't think it would really happen—and it's so soon! You know how Jackson is about the baby. He's over protective—" Lauren was glad Aunt Willa couldn't hear the other end of the conversation, and that Jackson hadn't come down for coffee yet.

"I'll talk with Jackson and get back with you—yes soon." She laughed. "I do remember we have a contract and what it says." Excitement made her light-headed. "It was good to hear your voice, too. Good-bye." She walked across the room to replace the phone just as Jackson entered the morning room with his paper.

He poured a steaming cup of coffee and said good morning to his aunt, then turned to Lauren. "And who's responsible for that big smile on your face this morning?" Jackson sat in his chair.

"It was Nicolas, from my gallery in Florence." She retrieved her coffee from the desk and took the chair opposite him.

Jackson scanned the paper. "What did Nicolas have on his mind—he's sold all your paintings and nagging for more?"

"No. He . . . he called about the Italian Exhibit. You know, the big exhibit and show of the year. International press and all that hoopla." She hesitated. "The committee chose me for the feature artist."

Jackson dropped the paper to his lap and gave her his full attention. "That's wonderful! You deserve the honor—I'm very proud for you!" He smiled at his aunt and glanced back at Lauren. "When does the exhibit occur—isn't it pretty soon?" He tilted his head, and a question came to his eyes when she sighed and averted her eyes.

"In four weeks."

He frowned. "That is soon! Are you not pleased about it?" He folded the paper and tossed it aside.

Lauren stood and moved to the windows again. With her back to the room she said, "I'm very pleased—it's just that he . . . Nicolas insists that I be there for the show." She didn't dare turn around. There wasn't a sound in the room until suddenly, Jackson stood at her side.

"Nicolas insists?" He waited.

"Yes, he says it's imperative that I attend the show. And I do understand how important it is for the featured artist to be present. Patrons and collectors like to meet the artists. It's good PR." Her tone pleaded for understanding.

Jackson ran his hands through his hair and cast a glance at his aunt as she quietly departed the room. "Lauren, I understand the importance, I give art shows, too. But I'd rather you not plan on going over there. Not this time, please. The baby's due soon. If something went wrong. . . ." He paced in front of the windows. "Maybe it would be best to pass on this show and plan to do the next one, don't you think?"

Lauren slipped her arms around his waist and made him look her in the eye. "In the first place I may not be given this opportunity again, and it's still four months before the baby is due. I can fly to Florence, spend four days and be back home with nearly three and a half months before my due date."

"I would rather you didn't."

"Jackson—please! This is important. Nicolas will see to it that this show gets top billing over anything else this fall." She laid her head against his chest. He hugged her close and pressed his face against her hair.

Tenderly, he said, "I can't make you not go, but I'm asking you not to." He removed her arms from around his waist. "I have to get going. Matt and I are having a meeting with the sales staff before the gallery opens."

Lauren clasped her hands, twisting her fingers. "Honey, I feel awful about the timing, but I want to accept the invitation, please understand . . . please?"

He picked up his briefcase and went to place his cup in the sink. "I'm sorry you feel awful, but so do I, and I seem to have no choice in the matter."

She slumped her shoulders helplessly and summoned her best martyr's voice. "Well, I'll just call Nicolas and tell him I can't be there."

"Thank you, sweetheart, I appreciate it." He blew her a kiss on his way out the door.

"Jackson!"

Lauren plopped into the nearest chair. Now what? She wanted to be at that show. It was one of the highlights of the social season. And it was a high honor to be the featured artist, and it didn't happen often. It had been seven years since the last time her name even came up. Her work was so much better now—she'd worked so hard—she deserved it!

She was going to Italy.

Making a beeline upstairs to the studio, she quickly flipped the calendar open and studied the dates—she would leave early on Thursday, September 29th. The exhibit would open the following day, Friday the 30th. She could spend Saturday night at Clair's villa, and fly out early on Monday, the third, arriving home late Wednesday. The only other commitment on her calendar was the meeting at church to help plan the children's new class schedules, which was on the 3rd. But, no problem, Ally would be happy to fill in for her.

How could Jackson object? She'd only be gone four days—maybe five?

Her head began to throb, and the phone's sudden ringing didn't help any. She glanced at caller ID. It was Clair. "Hello."

"I'm in town, what time do you want to get together?"

"Oh, Clair, I'd forgotten. I'm not dressed yet, how's lunch at The Cat In Paris?"

"Sounds good. I'll swing by and get you. Is 11:20 okay? We'll beat the lunch crowd."

"Yes, I'll be ready."

Lauren rubbed her temples and went to find Aunt Willa. Maybe she could help persuade Jackson that he was being unfair. After checking everywhere in the house with no luck, she headed outdoors—of course that's where she'd be in the cool of the morning, cutting flowers. Aunt Willa glanced up with a smile and continued snipping the colorful, long stemmed zinnias that Claude grew for that purpose. The blooms would last for a whole week in the house when kept in cool water. What a blessing to have a yardman like Claude, with a green thumb and a love of flowers.

"I figured I'd find you here." They chatted about the garden and once more heaped praise on Claude. Lauren glanced at the rose bushes and pinched off one of the lush Old Blush roses as she sauntered along beside Aunt Willa, working up the courage to enlist her help in persuading Jackson about the trip.

"I suppose you heard part of the conversation this morning, you . . . you know, about the show in Italy. It's an honor to be selected as the featured artist for that particular exhibit. It would mean a huge boost to my career." She inhaled the sweet fragrance of the rose.

"I suppose it would." Aunt Willa gave her a smile and continued cutting.

"As you might guess, Jackson objects to me going. I really don't understand his worry about the baby. Dr. Stinson says I'm disgustingly healthy and so is the baby."

"Italy is a long way from home." Aunt Willa straightened. "I think I've cut enough for now." She meandered the long way around the cutting garden, checking out the white daisies and cutting a few of them to soften the bright colors of the zinnias.

Lauren fidgeted with the pink rose. "I would greatly appreciate your help in convincing Jackson to see how important this is to me. He listens to you."

Aunt Willa came to a stop and gazed at Lauren. "Sometimes he does." She smiled. "I've been around since he was a small boy." She glanced down at the basket of flowers on her arm. "I may not be a help though. After Jenna died and Jackson had a two-year old to raise, he became sensitive and over protective." Aunt Willa sighed. "He'd gotten better the last few years, but I see him treating you like an invalid." She smiled at Lauren "Try to be patient. I personally would rather you didn't go either."

Lauren stared, astonished. "But why?"

Aunt Willa laughed and touched Lauren's arm. "For purely selfish reasons." She strolled on. "It could change things from the way they've been the last few years."

"But how? And what could it hurt? Change is natural." This was a stretch coming from a girl who basically disliked change. "I've been flying back and forth to Italy since I was ten!"

A deep sigh preceded Aunt Willa's reply. "But this is the first time you've been married or pregnant, my dear—and Jackson's used to you being here." She cast a wary side-glance at Lauren. "He's concerned about Brooke, too. He counts on you for the girl-on-girl talks that Brooke needs, she loves you."

Lauren spoke softly. "I realize that and I'm glad, but it's only four days . . . or five, and it could mean so much for me." Lauren moved along with Aunt Willa as she headed in the direction of the house. "Am I really being selfish in taking the opportunity that I've worked and waited for?" They'd picked up speed in their steps.

Aunt Willa marched into the spacious airy mudroom with Lauren on her heels. She placed the basket of flowers next to the sink. "Of course you're not a selfish person. But that's not the point. But no matter what anyone else thinks or wants, you have to decide for yourself what you have to do. Opportunity doesn't always knock at an opportune time." Aunt Willa ran cold water into a large crystal vase. "And it's unfortunate—"

"Unfortunate—really! It could be another ten years before this opportunity knocks again." Lauren turned and leaned her backside against the counter where Aunt Willa busied herself with the flowers.

"As I said, you have to work this out for yourself, dear. I can't help you, but I trust that it will work out to the best for all concerned." She reached for another vase.

Lauren stood with her head down, slowly twirling the pink rose between her thumb and forefinger. They were both quiet for a long time.

"Well, I've always worked things out for myself, so this is no different." She gazed at Aunt Willa who didn't comment or return her look. "I just know I can't afford to miss this opportunity." She tossed the rose on the counter and headed for the door, where she hesitated, exasperation controlling her voice volume. "It's *only* four and a half days—not weeks or a month!"

# CHAPTER FIVE

# The Struggle

Jackson frowned at the dark brew that streamed from the glass pot; it was as black as his thoughts. Sonya must have gotten to work first. She was a good employee, but she didn't drink coffee and she never made it the same way twice. But, she followed the rule of whoever got there first, made the coffee.

He stood looking at his cup, debating on pouring it all out and starting over when he heard Matt enter the office from the showroom. He set the pot back on the warmer and dumped the stuff in his cup down the drain. Thick black coffee was one small irritation that Matt would make go away in a hurry. How nice if Matt could do the same with Nicolas and his show, and Brooke's growing pains . . . .

Matt entered the break room and reached for a mug and the pot at the same time. He held the glass pot up, shook his head and poured it down the drain.

"I think Sonya does it on purpose to make a point." He grinned at Jackson. "What's wrong? Lost your best friend?" Matt flashed a lopsided grin.

Jackson ran his hand through his hair. "Actually, it feels that way." He pulled a chair out and sat at the table. "Lauren's unhappy with me—and she has a right to be."

"Yep, that does create the feeling you've lost your best friend." Matt pushed the brew button on the coffee maker and sat at the table. "Would it help to talk about it?"

Jackson raked his hair several times before speaking. "Nicolas Conti called early this morning—from Lauren's gallery in Florence. She's been chosen the featured artist for the grand exhibit this fall—in four weeks." He eyed Matt and blew out a long breath.

Matt whistled. "That exhibit is a big deal. Four weeks! That's pretty short notice for an event of that magnitude."

"Not really. They've already got the paintings over there. Thirty-two rather large pieces and a dozen small ones."

Matt stood and poured the fresh coffee. "Makes me think they've known for some time she was the one they were planning to ask. I knew she'd been working a lot. Ally commented once that she'd not seen as much of Lauren this summer as usual."

Jackson took the cup Matt offered. "I hadn't thought about it, but I bet that's the reason for the intensity of her focus lately." He took a sip and set the cup on the table. "Nicolas probably gave her a thumbs up early on to expect the invitation." He shook his head. "She could have told me."

Matt raised his brows. "True, she could have. She probably didn't want to get her hopes up. It's an honor indeed, and it will mean a great boost in her career. I'm proud for her." Matt gazed across the table. "So, what's the problem?"

"I don't want her to go. Don't ask me why, because I don't have a good reason, just that the baby is due in four months." He turned away from Matt's puzzled expression.

"Well, sometimes feelings are hard to explain, but four months is not *that* close." Matt offered lamely.

"In my heart and my head, my reasons loom huge and perfectly reasonable, they're just not logical when put into words."

Matt grinned and said, "Nebulous, I believe is the word."

Jackson grimaced. "Very. How do you argue a cause that its main point sounds foolish and worse, selfish?"

"Give me the spill, and I'll punch holes in its weakest area, then we can figure out how to close those holes." Matt stood and refilled their cups.

Jackson laughed for the first time since waking that morning. "It has already helped just talking about it." He gazed at Matt for a second while he sorted his thoughts. "I just don't want Lauren to fly to Europe and be gone five or six days."

Matt raised his brows, but made no comment.

"I know—I know! Selfish and unfair, but she should have told me what she was working on through the summer. It came as a surprise."

Matt frowned. "But we don't know for sure that Lauren knew anything. Besides, even if she suspected it might happen, that wouldn't take away from her effort and accomplishment—do you think?"

"Of course not. I *said* I didn't have a good reason for my feelings." Jackson stood and rinsed his cup.

"Name some of the reasons. You know, those in here. . . ." Matt tapped his chest before he stepped to the sink, rinsed his own cup and followed Jackson toward the office.

With both hands jammed in his pockets, Jackson ambled ahead. "And open myself to a lecture on selfishness?"

Matt laughed and clapped Jackson on the back. "I'll be fair."

"Yeah, sure. Do I ever stand a chance over Lauren? It's always rigged in her favor."

They were chuckling amidst Matt's denial of Jackson's accusation as they entered the office. Maggie ambled in from her office.

"Here's the photo album of my engagement party, if you guys want to look. I promised Ally and Lauren I'd bring it by as soon as Mom finished showing it to all the relatives." Maggie placed the elegant, leather-bound book on Matt's desk. "Everything was beautiful, just perfect. Jackson, you could rent your yard and gardens out for special events, you know. Everyone's wanting to know the location of the gorgeous place where the party was held."

Jackson laughed. "Let's keep it our secret. How are the wedding plans progressing?"

"The moms are in charge—busy as little beavers. Levi and I could care less—we tease that this wedding is mainly for them." She smiled and traipsed back to her office.

They turned to each other at the same time and Matt said, "Could two people be any better suited?"

Jackson shook his head and cast a guilty look, "I keep forgetting, when is the wedding?"

Matt flipped the pages of his planner. "June 25, 2017. New York City. Write it down."

"Good idea." Jackson opened his planner, jotted a memo and powered on his computer.

Matt did the same, but after several moments, he turned to Jackson. "Seriously, if you need to talk, I'm here."

Jackson nodded and without turning, mumbled, "Thanks, guy."

***

The back entry bell jangled softly, and seconds later Jackson was surprised to see Brooke scoot into the office. She was supposed to have lunch at school. He glanced up at the large clock. Lunch should be over.

"Hi, Dad! I'm getting my bike—

*"Why* are you getting your bike? I'm picking you up after school." He frowned.

"I was going to see if I could ride my bike home with Mandy—just for a little while, I'd be back before you close."

His face must have looked stern—it *felt* stern. He was still concerned that Mandy was becoming a troublesome friend. He didn't like the idea of her and Brooke out on their bikes after school. Just because they said they'd go to Mandy's house, didn't necessarily mean they would go there. Brooke had never deliberately lied to him, but still . . .

"Dad?"

He shook himself, surprised at his thoughts. "Brooke, I'd rather pick you up as usual. Why do you want to ride your bike to Mandy's, anyway?"

Brooke's wide eyes reflected wonder at the stern tone of his voice. He'd never been stern with her. To soften the refusal, he spoke more casually while throwing in a legitimate caution. "That's a lot of biking for one afternoon. You'd be too tired to do homework later."

"But, Dad—"

"Brooke!"

"Yes, sir."

"You'd better hurry to make it back to school before the bell—or, do you want me to take you?"

"No, sir. Bye." She hurried from the office.

Seconds later it struck Jackson that Brooke had taken her leave without a hug for him and Matt. That was a first. He glanced sidelong at Matt—whose mouth was not hanging open, but from his expression, it might as well have been.

"I don't believe I've ever heard you speak to Brooke in that tone."

Jackson wanted to confide in Matt on one hand, but on the other, he didn't want to talk about what had happened with the girls. Instead, out of the blue, he tried to imagine how Jenna would have handled the situation.

Matt stood. "It's lunch time. Let's sample that chicken salad Aunt Willa sent this morning—Jackson?"

"Yeah, sounds good." He shoved his chair back just as his cell phone rang. He pulled it from his shirt pocket and glanced at Matt.

"Hello." He listened for a moment. "Thanks, Lauren. That would be nice if you could pick Brooke up. I appreciate it. Yeah, bye."

Matt set the salad and crackers on the table and got them both an iced tea.

Jackson avoided Matt's frequent glances across the table. Sooner or later he would have to confide in Matt, just not now. So, he'd better get a grip and stop thinking about Brooke, and the Italian exhibit, or Mandy's potential for trouble and even Lauren's cousin from Colorado. Something about the way Lauren behaved after reading her cousin's letter made him wonder. She would normally pass news like that on to him and insist he read it too. But she had slid the letter into her pocket as if she didn't want him to read it. The scene had stuck in his mind, another file for his worry basket.

He gave a ragged sigh. Nearly forty. Did age affect thought patterns and emotions?

"Jackson, wake up. Do you want this salad or not?" Matt held the bowl half way across the table.

"Yes, please."

"I'm sorry that you're troubled about something, but if you won't talk it out with me, what about Lauren or your aunt?"

"Oh, I can't talk it out with Lauren—she's the something—and that exhibit. She wants to accept the invitation, but I've asked her not to, and of course she won't accept just to please me. And I feel really bad that she'll miss it. But there'll be another time, after the baby comes. She's calling Nicolas this morning to decline."

Matt was quiet, his gaze intense. "I'm surprised at you Jackson. That invitation amounts to being touted as artist of the year. It's a big deal; you know how big it is. It may not come along again, anyway not for a long time. Her sales would double."

"Of course it'll come around again. She's good and Nicolas likes her, he'll understand about the baby. And I'm certainly not worried about her sales doubling." He glared. "That could mean she'd be gone a lot." The fleeting expression of disbelief in Matt's eyes stabbed Jackson. Matt averted his gaze.

Jackson groaned and poked at the chicken salad and finally pushed it away. "You don't have to say it, I'm being unreasonable." He pushed his hand through his hair. "But, Matt, I'm also scared. I find myself wishing Lauren was a just a mediocre painter who was happy puttering in her studio. "He glared at Matt. "You don't have the threat of danger with Ally flying back and forth across the world, and you haven't already lost one wife."

Matt said, "No, I haven't. But Jenna didn't fly back and forth, and she died with cancer right here in Valley Ridge."

Jackson suddenly got to his feet and left the break room, making his way to the client office at the back of the gallery. He sat in the large quiet office for over an hour.

This was where he went to pray and find peace. But his prayers seemed to go no higher than the ceiling and peace eluded him. Maybe he'd not found peace, but he'd made a resolve. He would make it up to Lauren for her sacrifice—for giving up something she'd wanted so very much just to please him.

# CHAPTER SIX

# Humbled

Lauren's meeting with Clair cleared her thoughts about how to handle the talk with Brooke after Mandy worked out the problem to be Mrs. Flowers's fault that the girls got in trouble, not theirs. Clair agreed with Lauren that the girls had to understand that they were in the wrong.

Clair was as dismayed as Lauren had been that Brooke seemed to think Mandy's explanation made sense. Lauren was still in shock. She hadn't been able to tell Jackson.

Hopefully she wouldn't have to.

Nicholas couldn't have called about the exhibit at a worse time. As exciting as it had been to learn she'd been chosen for the honor, concern for Brooke and Mandy, too, had overshadowed the news. She liked Mandy and she liked Mandy's parents. Lauren wanted both girls to understand that behavior like that could not be tolerated. She planned to call Mandy's mother after she'd had her talk with Brooke.

Discussing the exhibit with Jackson would come last. The thought of telling Jackson that she'd accepted the invitation produced a dread that gripped her like a vise. She hadn't mentioned the exhibit to Clair when they met to talk over lunch. It had to be cleared with Jackson first.

The pick-up lane just had three cars in line. Good, she wouldn't have to wait long. When Brooke and Mandy wandered through the wide school doors, Lauren sensed something was wrong. They both clutched their books to their chests, heads down. Mandy was talking and Brooke glanced at her then shook her head.

Suddenly the new girl walked past them and bumped into Mandy hard enough to cause Mandy to drop several books. The girl looked neither left nor right, but kept on walking as if she hadn't done it on purpose. Brooke stooped to retrieve the books.

They glanced after the girl and spoke for a moment before Mandy headed for the bike rack and Brooke trudged toward the Ranger Rover and climbed in, quiet and subdued.

She and Mandy hadn't seen that Lauren witnessed the incident.

Lauren swallowed several times before speaking. "How was your day? Did David Holt amuse the class with his clown act again?" She smiled, hoping her voice sounded normal and friendly.

"No. But he got in trouble for talking again." Brooke busily settled her things on the floorboard.

"You don't seem your happy self—anything wrong?" Lauren regretted that something like this happened on the day she'd planned a serious conversation with Brooke.

Glancing up at Lauren with large, serious eyes, Brooke said, "Dad yelled at me today."

Lauren caught the slight tremble of the lower lip. Oh no, what had happened? Had Jackson been grouchy on the way to school that morning? It wasn't like Brooke to remember a slight all day—an hour at most was about her tolerance for grudge festering. What could he have said that had stuck with her all day? Jackson was seldom stern with Brooke. And on top of that, she'd had a bad day at school.

"I'm sorry, sweetie. Your dad may not have gotten enough sleep—sometimes that makes him grumpy in the mornings."

"Not this morning—this afternoon." She turned to look out the window.

"You saw your dad this afternoon? I thought you were having lunch at school?"

"I did have lunch at school. But I went to the gallery to get my bike so I could ride home with Mandy, but Dad wouldn't let me, even though I said I'd be back before closing time and he wouldn't have to wait on me."

She crossed her arms across her chest, the hurt fully remembered.

"I'm sure your dad thought it best for you not to be out on your bike." Lauren puzzled on what could have happened. "What reason did he give you for not allowing you to go with Mandy?"

"He said it was too much bike riding, and I'd be too tired to do homework later—"

"Well, you see, of course he was thinking about you." Lauren gave her a bright smile.

Indignation raised the pitch of her voice. "He didn't even give me a chance to remind him it was Friday, and I don't have homework."

"Oh, yes, of course. Well, he just forgot. You probably caught him at a busy time when his mind was on work."

"He didn't look busy." She sighed heavily.

"Did anything happen at school today?"

"Nuh-uh." She turned to look out the window.

"Did I see a girl bump into Mandy?"

Brooke glanced quickly at Lauren. "It was an accident."

"Really? But why didn't she stop and apologize to Mandy?"

Brooke shrugged and mumbled, "Maybe she didn't know she bumped Mandy."

"Oh, maybe so." Lauren glanced across the console. "I have an idea. When we get home, let's make Coke floats and carry them up to the studio where we can slurp all we want to. We need a private visit—how does that sound—just girl talk. How about it?"

Brooke giggled, and for the first time since she'd climbed into the Range Rover, her eyes brightened and she perked up. Lauren hoped the talk would go well and that Brooke didn't hate her when it was over. If it didn't go well, she could end the day with Brooke and Jackson both angry with her. She breathed another prayer for strength, wisdom, and guidance. It seemed that lately she'd been taking up more than her fair share of the Lord's time.

And the problem at school was far from settled. It looked like there was more to it than they'd been made aware of. That girl had intentionally bullied Mandy.

Lauren had some investigating to do.

When they arrived home, Aunt Willa was in the kitchen making a meatloaf for dinner. She greeted them and told Brooke there were fresh cookies in the big jar in the pantry. The housekeeper had gone by the bakery that morning and picked them up.

She shook her head. "No cookies for me and Lauren, we're having Coke floats upstairs in the studio— just us. It's our private time." She ran to get the ice cream and a Coke from the fridge.

"Lauren and I," Aunt Willa corrected. "That sounds like fun. You girls should do that more often." Aunt Willa smiled at Brooke and then cast a quick glance at Lauren.

She raised her brows at Aunt Willa. "Well, we can have all the private time we want, but Dr. Stinson might have something to say about too many Coke floats." She patted the baby bump and joined in the laughter.

\*\*\*

Winslow and Winnie padded along upstairs as if they'd been invited. Lauren glanced back at the two, wondering if it was wise to allow their presence— distraction was their special talent. But, a touch of comic relief might come in handy if things became strained, the dogs *might* save the day—or Lauren's mission.

In the studio, Lauren dragged the low table closer to the large chintz covered chairs where she and

Brooke were going to lounge. The dogs plopped at their feet, and Winnie looked up at Brooke then to Lauren as if wondering what this party was all about.

Brooke quickly settled into a girl-party mood. She drew her feet into the soft cushions and tucked her toes under the flared skirt of her school uniform.

Lauren guided the conversation along the line of school events and the ever-entertaining, David Holt, but she didn't mention the other incident again.

Brooke giggled and opened up to share the hours of the days she spent out of the company of those who loved her dearly. Lauren began to realize the magnitude of the influence of those hours away from a loving, nurturing environment. Suddenly she felt small and scared. She was not wise enough to know how to help Brooke—she could barely help herself.

Brooke's direct gaze halted her wandering thoughts. Lauren hadn't heard the question she saw in Brooke's eyes.

"I'm sorry, honey. I must have been too deep into this float. What were you saying?"

Brooke giggled. "Don't you love floats? I love them—I could eat two floats!"

Lauren lifted a spoonful of the cold froth to her mouth. "Mmmm, good! I might be able to eat two floats, but then I'd have to explain the extra pounds to Dr. Stinson." She saw an opportunity to make a point. "We often don't do the fun things we'd like to do, because it might not be the responsible thing we should do. Don't you agree?"

Brooke shrugged and took another bite. She eyed Lauren over her spoon, a question in her eyes. "How could two floats hurt anything?"

"If I ate too many floats it could make me un-healthy, and in turn the baby would suffer. Everything I eat or do affects the baby." Lauren took a deep breath. "Just like everything you do affects you in some way."

Brooke giggled and squirmed in the chair. "*Everything* I do?"

"Of course. Absolutely everything." Lauren tilted her head and narrowed her eyes at Brooke. "Name something, and I'll tell you how it could affect you."

Brooke smirked and put a spoonful of ice cream in her mouth, she let her gaze roam the contents of the studio for several moments.

"If I spilled paint on the rug—how would that affect me."

"Hmm, did you spill the paint on purpose, or was it an accident?"

Brooke shrugged again. "Either."

"No, you have say which it was. A thing done with purpose has a different affect than if it's done accidentally." Lauren pursed her lips and waited.

Brooke's eyes narrowed in challenge. "Okay . . . if I spilled it on purpose."

Lauren took her time in answering. "Spilling paint on the rug on purpose would be called vandal-ism—a word meaning a deliberate, mean, destructive act. If you did that, it would make you a vandal, and in some cases you could go to jail." Lauren spoke casu-ally, noting the widening of Brooke's eyes.

"What if on accident?" she said quietly, her eyes on Lauren's.

"If you spilled paint on the rug accidentally—it means you didn't plan it. It wouldn't have much affect on you. You'd clean up the mess and be more careful with the paint next time—a good affect. An accident is unfortunate, but not mean. Sometimes accidents happen when you're hurrying—or not paying attention."

Brooke sat her glass on the table and patted for Winslow to join her in the chair.

Lauren placed her glass on the table, too. "Name something else."

Brooke shook her head. "I don't want to play anymore."

"Okay, then let's talk." Lauren resisted the urge to twist her hands as she remembered doing when her own mother used to lecture her. She had to be careful to speak to Brooke, not lecture—this was a child, with a child's understanding.

"Brooke, do you truly believe it was Mrs. Flowers's fault you got into trouble at school?"

Surprise flashed in the wide amber eyes. "Mandy said—"

Lauren shook her head. "No, I want to know what you think in your heart."

"We were just trying to prove—"

"Yes, I know what you were doing. But do you really believe what Mandy said, that the teacher was at fault?"

She ducked her head. "No, ma'am."

"Can you see how searching the teacher's private desk has affected you?" Lauren spoke softly and reached for Brooke's hand.

The slim brown fingers returned Lauren's gentle squeeze, and she nodded. "I feel bad about it. Is that why Dad's grouchy with me." She looked up at Lauren.

"I won't lie to you. Your dad was very hurt and disappointed. What you did not only had an affect on you, but on those who love you, also." Lauren sighed. "You and Mandy both have to win back your dad's trust."

"Mandy feels bad too. She said when she told her mother that she thought Mrs. Flowers was wrong to be mad at us, her mother cried and told her father that she didn't know what they were going to do with her."

Lauren's hand went to her mouth, hiding a smile. She had guessed that Mandy's parents were at the end of their rope with their lively daughter. Struggling to look serious, Lauren said, "I'm sure Mandy does feel bad. She's a smart girl, just like you are." Lauren touched her fingers to Brooke's chin and lifted her face. "You girls need something worthwhile and fun to use your energy on. Let's put our heads together soon and think of something."

"It wasn't really Mandy's fault—"

"Brooke, it's not good to blame others. It's over, and we trust it won't happen again."

"We won't ever do that again." Brooke's seriousness was touching.

"Good. I think I heard your dad." She glanced at her watch. "It's time he was getting home. Let's go say hi."

Both dogs had jumped up and headed for the door. They knew when Jackson came into the house.

Brooke paused as they neared the hall and put her arms around Lauren. "How can you win back trust?"

Lauren returned the hug. "It's not always easy. You think about a thing before you take action—always considering what the affect will be—on you, and everyone around you. It takes effort and thought, but soon your dad will see that you choose to be a responsible person." Lauren smiled at her. "It's worth all the effort."

As they continued down the stairs together, Brooke slowed her step and tugged Lauren to slow down. "Mandy's scared what her parents will decide to do with her—she's afraid they'll let someone adopt her. Do you think they will?"

Lauren bit her lip and kept a serious face. "I'm sure they'd never do that—they love her too much, and they're very proud of her—no, they'd never let Mandy live anywhere but with them."

Brooke squeezed Lauren's hand. "Is it okay if I tell her what you said?"

"Absolutely, you may tell her."

As they walked into the kitchen where Jackson sat at the island bar visiting with his aunt, he reached out an arm to pull Brooke into a bear hug, making her giggle and squirm. "I forgot this was Friday and you didn't have homework tonight."

"It's okay. Lauren picked me up and we had Coke floats in the studio—just us."

"I'm jealous. Lauren won't have a Coke float with me."

"Dad, it's because Dr. Stinson gripes her out about extra pounds."

"I know. She has to watch those pounds and take care of our baby." Above Brooke's blond head, he cast a tender glance at Lauren.

Oh, yes, she groaned; she still had to tell him she was taking their baby to Italy in four weeks.

# CHAPTER SEVEN

# Determined

The aroma of Aunt Willa's meatloaf and the sight of Lauren and Brooke coming down the stairs laughing and chatting lifted Jackson's mood one hundred percent. After dinner, when he and Lauren could be alone, he planned to tell her how much he appreciated her giving in to his selfish wishes.

And later he'd ask Aunt Willa if she could help him plan something really nice to please Lauren and to let her know how much he appreciated her.

They enjoyed the first relaxed dinner with pleasant conversation in several days. Aunt Willa was clearly relieved that the air had been cleared, and Jackson was glad. He hated to worry his aunt.

Halfway through dinner, she had announced that she and Thelma Wade were planning a couple of days in New York for a bout of serious shopping. They were leaving the next morning.

"Hey, that's great! You girls should do that more often." Jackson was pleased when his aunt and her friend Thelma planned outings together.

Aunt Willa nodded. "I think we should too. But I have a request. Thelma and I discussed it, and we would like for Brooke to accompany us—that is if she'd like to."

Jackson and Lauren immediately turned to Brooke, whose eyes had widened.

"Yes! Yes! I want to go!" She jumped up and ran to her great aunt and threw her arms around her neck. "Thank you, Aunt Willa!"

"You're welcome, dear."

Later, when his aunt and Lauren were straightening the kitchen and Brooke was upstairs, the phone rang. Jackson glanced at Lauren and rose from his chair. "I'll get it." He strolled to the desk in the morning room.

"Hello?" He glanced toward the kitchen where he could hear the girls talking as they finished in the kitchen.

"Lauren is busy at the moment, may I take a message?" He prepared to write on the notepad. "What? Repeat that please. Yes, I've got the information. Thank you." He tore the note off the pad and stuck it in his pocket.

He stepped around the double columns that separated the morning room from the kitchen. "I'm heading upstairs for a shower. Aunt Willa, will I see you girls in the morning before you leave?"

"Oh, yes. We won't leave until about nine o'clock. And we plan to drive home Monday morning, since school is out that day—we'll miss the weekend traffic."

"Good plan."

He glanced at Lauren before heading toward the stairs.

A long hot shower might take the edge off the shock that the phone call had delivered. The caller was the coordinator of the exhibit. She wanted to know if Lauren would be staying at the hotel they provided, and if so, how many days should they reserve a suite for her?

Lauren was going to Italy—against his wishes.

She had sat through dinner, enjoying herself and not caring that he had asked her not to go. And if anything happened to his son—their son, grudgingly he backed up—he'd, do what?

He grabbed his faded jeans and a clean white t-shirt, expelling a noisy sigh. Why was he acting like a jerk? And why couldn't he stop acting like one? He didn't hear Lauren when she opened the door to their room.

"Who was on the phone?"

He jerked around to face her. Now was his moment of truth. Was he a selfish jerk or not? Hadn't he promised before they were married that he didn't want her to change? Funny, he seemed to be the one doing the changing.

"Jackson, who was on the phone?"

"Were you expecting a call?"

She shook her head. "Not especially. Who was it?"

"The coordinator in charge of the Italian exhibit. She wanted to know—well, you should call her back." He handed her the slip of paper he'd written the number on.

Lauren walked to the windows. "I was going to talk with you this evening after we were alone." She crossed her arms on her chest as if she was cold and stood quietly. "I knew the call was from Italy when I saw your face. I'm sorry to disappoint you. I hate that this worldly event is so important to me, but it seems to be."

Jackson slid the t-shirt over his head and went to her. He released a weary breath. "You have nothing to be sorry for. I'm sorry to have the audacity to ask you not to go. I'm aware of how hard you've worked for this."

Lauren rushed into his arms. "If you're worried about the baby, you shouldn't be. Dr. Stinson said I was the picture of health. I won't stay in Italy an hour longer than needed—"

He shushed her. "I don't know what's been the matter with me. Seeing Brooke growing up is harder than I expected, I don't want to let go . . . and speaking of Brooke, she seemed more her old self this evening than she has since the fiasco at school. Did you talk with her?"

Lauren wrapped her arms around him. "We talked. I believe she's going to be able to hold her own with Mandy from now on."

He lifted his brows.

"Uh-huh. Mandy's had a scare. She's afraid her parents may be going to adopt her out."

Jackson laughed. "What?" Not really—Mandy knows better than that!"

"Well, maybe not, she's a smart little girl, but not very worldly. One of her aunts who was childless, adopted a little girl—one day there was no child, the next time Mandy saw her aunt, she had a little girl.

Mandy doesn't grasp the concept of adoption. It must appear to her that adoption means that children can float from parents to parents."

Their voices joined in laughter, and he liked the sound. "Why don't we have a word with Brooke," Jackson said, "and then turn in early?"

"Sounds wonderful to me. I may sleep late in the morning." She went to her closet for a robe, coming back into the room, she went to Jackson. "We do need to talk about the exhibit, I have an idea I want to discuss with you."

He sat on the edge of the bed. "Let's discuss it now," he said.

She folded the robe over her arm and sat next to him.

"What's the idea?"

Lauren fidgeted. "I'd like to take Brooke to Florence with me—"

"Absolutely not!" He rose abruptly. "I'm resigned to *you* going, but not Brooke. You'll be preoccupied with your show and—well, anything could happen."

"Jackson, you surprise me. What do you mean, 'Anything could happen'? Brooke is not a baby! You know Maria, Clair's maid; she lives in the villa full-time now and would be happy to entertain Brooke while I was busy at the exhibit hall. They got on beautifully the time I was there and you and Brooke came over. "

"No. Discussion over." He couldn't believe she would ask to take Brooke with her to Italy. "I'm going to say goodnight to Pumpkin." He stormed from the room before he said more that he might regret later.

"Jackson!"

He closed the door firmly on her wail. He couldn't believe she would even ask!

Knocking softly on Brooke's door, he called, "Pumpkin?" and opened the door a foot. "May I come in for a minute?"

"Uh-huh, Dad." She sprawled in the middle of her bed on her stomach, barefoot. A spiral-back sketchbook lay open. A tray of colored pencils snuggled at her side. Her bag was already packed and by the door. She glanced up from her drawing, her small feet waving leisurely in the air.

Jackson pulled the chair from her desk and placed it next to her bed and took a seat. "What are you working on?"

She angled the sketchbook around a bit and to give him a better view. "It's Winnie with her the pink bow."

Jackson shook his head in true admiration. "You really are very good, Pumpkin. That's a great likeness of Winnie."

"Lauren is a good teacher. She showed me how to do shading." She glanced up and tapped an area on the page. "That's what this part is—shading."

Jackson studied her drawing. "Well, I'm impressed with both student and teacher, very impressed indeed."

"Thank you, Daddy." She continued drawing.

Jackson stood and replaced the chair at the desk. "I just wanted to say goodnight, sweetheart. I understand you and Lauren had a nice visit this afternoon?"

She giggled. "Uh-huh, I liked the Coke floats, too. Lauren said she couldn't have floats very often— Dr. Stinson would get mad at her."

Jackson had to smile along with her. She seemed her happy self once again. He knew whom to thank for that, to his chagrin.

"Well, goodnight and don't stay up too late; you have a big day tomorrow."

He made his way back to the bedroom. Lauren was already in bed, propped up with a book in her hand. She laid it across her lap as he came inside and closed the door.

"Is Brooke still excited?"

"Yes. Did you help her pack?"

Lauren nodded. "It took all of ten minutes. She has a definite sense of her own style."

Jackson grinned. "She's doing a drawing of Winnie. It's very accurate, a good likeness." He hesitated briefly. "You are doing a good job with her instruction."

Lauren smiled. "Thank you. She's a good student. She wants to learn. I'm glad Aunt Willa invited her to go to the city with them."

"Yeah, that was nice of her and Thelma."

"Jackson, I don't mean to pester or aggravate you, but it would be nice to hear a good reason why Brooke shouldn't go with me."

Jackson kept his back to her as he dug in his bureau for clean pajamas. "My reason might not fit your idea of a good reason." He slipped out of the faded jeans and pulled on the pajama bottoms, then jerked the t-shirt over his head and threw it in a chair.

"I'd like to know your thoughts on it anyway."

"You've heard my thoughts on it." He wandered across the room to the antique, floor-to-ceiling bookshelves, browsed momentarily, pulled out a volume and strolled toward the bed.

Lauren made an impatient sound and raised her book.

Not mindful of thoughtfulness to the reader beside him, he flopped onto the wide bed and leisurely settled in. Another impatient sound from Lauren warned him he was pushing it.

The words on the pages blurred as his eyes followed the lines one after another, while his thoughts took him years back and miles away. How could he explain his actions to Lauren without coming off as one very selfish man? *Was* he that selfish? Maybe Jenna's death had made him selfish of those dear to his heart.

Lauren suddenly closed her book, turned her light off and scooted down in the bed—her back to him. He gazed across the mile-wide gulf of bed between them. From the back she looked the same as ever, not at all as if she carried his child.

She was angry. Well, he couldn't help that; he didn't feel so hot himself. He relaxed the book on his lap and wearily hung his head and scrubbed his face. It felt good to close his eyes—he wished he could close his mind as easily. He dozed until suddenly the bed shook like an earthquake had hit it. He jerked his head up.

"Jackson, I'm tired and angry—and I can't sleep with this tension between us." She had sat upright in the bed with her legs doubled under her as she sat on her heels, her back stiff. "Did you hear me? We have to settle this—now."

Jackson stared. "I hear you. How could I not?" A long silence followed. "Do you realize we've never really had a marital fight?"

She softened an inch. "Now is as good a time as any to take care of that."

"That's not fair. You know I'd never win a word fight with you." He tilted his head and grinned at her.

Lauren's body relaxed. "I have a win-win idea. We could makeup now, for the fight we're going to have in the morning—it'll save time."

"Finally! Something we can agree on."

Jackson breathed a great relief as Lauren quickly crossed the gulf of white linen between them. He'd been miserable for days, maybe weeks, but he hadn't realized just how miserable. He reached for the light switch.

CHAPTER EIGHT

# Call from Max

Lauren woke late the next morning to find Jackson's side of the bed empty. The clock on the night table read 9:47 a.m. She felt wonderfully rested as she treated her body to a leisurely stretch.

The house was unusually quiet; she remembered the reason for the quietness. Aunt Willa, who usually had music playing, or the TV on, was on her way to New York with Brooke in tow. Lauren tossed the covers back. She had a full day ahead.

She planned to write out a formal, business-like proposal on why Brooke should be allowed to travel to Italy with her. At lunch she would present it to Jackson—and cross her fingers he'd see the logic in her request. For Jackson to agree to Brooke's traveling with her wasn't enough. Lauren wanted him to realize what a wonderful learning experience it would be for their budding artist.

As she was stepping out of the shower, she strained at a sound. As she'd guessed; the phone was ringing. Alone in the house, she ran from the shower into the bedroom in time to answer it. "Hello." She wrapped the ample towel around her body. "Max?" Lauren instantly felt the bubble of laughter rising. "I can't believe how hard you are to catch!"

She was laughing as she put the phone on speaker and bent forward attempting to twist her hair up with one hand, while hanging onto the towel at the same time. Successful with the hair twist, she clasped the phone between her shoulder and neck and hobbled to the bathroom for a hair clip. With the clip in place she strolled back and sat on the bed.

They played catch-up for forty minutes before ending the call.

A smile lingered as she continued sitting on the side of the unmade bed for a moment longer. Conversation had flowed easily, as if they talked regularly. She didn't know whether to be anxious or excited. It was exciting that Max was flying to New York in three days, but she felt a twinge of anxiousness about Jackson. How would he see this strange, sun-tanned, wild-haired ranching person? Lauren shook her head, smiling at the image of her cousin that flashed across her vision.

Max had touched briefly on her reason for coming to the city and it concerned the sale of the small bronzes she'd written about. She had spoken lightly, her voice nonchalant, but Lauren heard something else, something she couldn't put her finger on.

The sudden realization that she'd forgotten to share the news of her pregnancy with Max jolted Lauren off the bed. She glanced at the clock again. "Ah, Jackson—love! Why did you let me sleep late!"

She wouldn't have time to write out her proposal. Lauren smiled, remembering what he'd said about a word fight with her—she was about to find out if she could beat him in a word fight or not.

Lauren met the housekeeper at the back door as she was coming in from the garden. "Good morning, Carrie! You've got the house to yourself." Lauren grabbed an apple. "Aunt Willa and Brooke are gone for a couple of days."

"Yes, your aunt left me a note with instructions."

They spoke about the pleasant weather for a moment, before Lauren continued on to the garage. The crisp morning air charged her senses and announced that fall lurked just around the corner. Lauren lifted her face and slowed her step to catch the first teasing smell of her favorite season. The invigorating air made it difficult to stay within the speed limit as she drove into town.

Seeing Ally's vehicle in the gallery parking lot was a peasant surprise. Lauren always enjoyed seeing the baby. She climbed out of the Range Rover and glanced down at the clingy front of her too-tight-knit top and quickly gave it several hard forward pulls. She sighed, wishing now she'd chosen one of the big tops—but she disliked wearing them. It was quiet as she stepped inside the gallery, except for the murmur of voices. Lauren followed the sounds, which led her to the back of the showroom.

She entered the office to find everyone gathered around a large painting. Lauren joined the gathering. "Ohh! Nice!" She moved closer, checking the signature. "James Hawk?" Is his style changing?" She questioned Matt who stood next to her.

Matt nodded. "He sent this back from Arizona. He's just finished an intensive three-month workshop." Matt grinned and crossed his arms. "It's made a huge difference in his color palette, too."

"It's the quality of the air out there. I used to attend those long workshops—in my carefree days. They were fun!" She cast a sidelong glance at Jackson. The comment wasn't lost on him. He began to sidle in her direction.

He draped an arm around her shoulder and said in a low voice, "I haven't forgotten we have a fight to finish, but let's not do it here in front of all these innocent people—okay? He took the liberty of stealing a quick kiss.

Lauren smiled and touched his arm. "I agree, later. So excuse me for now, I want to speak with Ally. I see she didn't bring my baby with her this morning!" She started toward Ally and Maggie. Ally said something to Maggie and they came to meet Lauren.

"Congratulations on the exhibit!" Ally gave her a quick hug. Maggie smiled and hugged her too, adding her congratulations before headed back to her own office.

"I was stunned when Matt said you hadn't accepted." Ally moved closer and lowered her voice. "I can't imagine Jenna would ever have given up something like that just because Jackson asked her to." Ally sipped from a china tea mug and eyed Lauren.

Lauren felt foolish. Ally still thought she wasn't going because of Jackson. An appropriate comment didn't rush to mind—nothing anyway that would make sense to Ally.

"I'm . . . well, it hasn't been settled entirely; we plan to talk." Lauren glanced at where Jackson and Matt were the only two left discussing the new painting. She groaned. "Oh, Ally, we have talked, and though I'm still on thin ice with Jackson, I'm going to Italy."

"Good for you! But Matt said Jackson asked you not to go and you agreed not to." A half smile hovered on her lips.

"No, I didn't exactly agree. What's amusing?"

Ally said, "I was just wondering, was that the first time you've said no to Jackson?"

Lauren rolled her eyes. "Problem was I hadn't said no, just insinuated it, but I couldn't bring myself to lose such an opportunity. Jackson accidentally found out that I'd accepted the invitation." Lauren lowered her voice as the guys were walking toward them. "He was very unhappy with me." She turned her face slightly. "We had our first spat last night."

The guys stopped in front of them, and looked from one to the other. Matt glanced at Jackson. "Girl talk."

Jackson's wary gaze rested briefly on Lauren. His expression told her he'd guessed they'd been talking about him. She fought the tiny head of steam gathering behind her eyeballs. As a gallery owner, Jackson of all people knew what an opportunity like this could mean to an artist, yet he'd asked her not to accept the honor, and he just assumed she wouldn't. She continued smiling, and nodding, but she didn't hear a word of what the others were saying.

As they made their way back to the front office, Ally moved closer to Lauren.

"I'm looking forward to our get-together next week."

Lauren stopped dead still. She had forgotten their coffee plans. Max was due in New York the same day. The guys slowed and looked back, Matt waved for them to come on.

"You girls don't have to show great eagerness at having lunch with us, but a *little* interest would be nice."

As they laughed and hurried to the guys, Lauren grasped Ally's arm. "I need to speak with you, will you be home this afternoon?"

Ally nodded, her eyes widening. "Yes, of course."

"We'll talk then!" Lauren became aware that her near frantic actions were either making Ally nervous or building excitement. Her eyes shown brighter than Lauren had seen them in a long time. Come to think of it, She'd never really seen Ally excited. Lauren took a closer look into the sky-blue eyes. "I'm aware that I'm acting like a wild person, but I can't seem to help myself, there's so much happening. Am I making any sense?"

Ally's eyes grew bigger, and she did a tiny jerk-shake of her head. "Of course you are!"

Jackson jangled his keys. "We can all ride in the Range Rover." He turned back to the showroom door and stuck his head in Maggie's office, and called out, "Off to lunch, be back soon."

\*\*\*

The club wasn't crowded, due to their arriving later than usual. No one bothered looking at a menu. Orders for the Caesar steak salad and iced tea went around the table. Matt teased the waiter that soon the staff would just nod at their table and turn in the usual salad and tea order. The waiter laughed and said that would work for him.

While waiting to be served, Lauren brought up Maggie's wedding plans. "Has Maggie shared any exciting design details of her gown?" She directed the inquiry at Ally.

Ally assumed an amused expression. "Oddly enough, she's been rather quiet about the whole thing. Of course it's still a year away."

Lauren trailed a pattern on the tablecloth. "Maggie's keeping secrets?"

"Oh, I don't think so. She's just not concerned about the details. Her mother and Levi's mom are doing everything."

Matt spoke up. "Actually that doesn't surprise me. Maggie's different than a lot of young women. She's a no-nonsense girl."

"Yes, but her wedding . . ." Lauren glanced at Jackson when he made a motion to speak.

"You were the same way, Lauren," he said. "Aunt Willa prodded and reminded you to take time for some of the things she thought you'd wish you'd done later."

"Really? I don't remember that." She had been in a daze during that time. Counseling with Dr. Brickman, struggling to convince herself she was making the right decision. And even now, remembering the fear of losing her independence quickened her breath and sent a reflex glance at Jackson. He'd promised he didn't want her to change, that he didn't expect her to change—but had he meant it?

The waiter politely held a plate just above her water glass, waiting for Lauren to move her hands off the table so that he could serve her salad.

"Oh, excuse me," she said and quickly dropped her hands to her lap.

She sneaked a sidelong glance at Ally, whose blue eyes flickered a question. Lauren ducked her head and kept her eyes on the food.

Jackson glanced around the table. "The salad is exceptional today."

Ally laughed and leaned closer to Matt. "Does he say that every time he has lunch here?"

"I believe he does." Matt was quiet for a minute. "Lauren, congratulations on being selected top dog at the Italian exhibit."

"Thank you, Matt."

"I can't believe you're turning it down," he said.

Before she could open her mouth to reply, Matt turned on Jackson. "And I still can't believe you asked her to."

Lauren froze with a load of salad on her fork.

Jackson turned to give her a long scrutinizing look. "I can't believe I did that either, but the request has been withdrawn. She is going." His eyes never left hers. "And if she'd like an escort, I'd be pleased to go too."

Lauren placed the loaded fork on her plate. "Oh, Jackson—thank you!" She smiled. "What about Brooke?"

Jackson's brows rose. "We'd never hear the end of it if we didn't take her with us."

Lauren reached for his hand. "This is Christmas, birthday, and anniversary all in one beautiful package." She looked across the table where Ally had leaned against Matt and blinked to keep tears from her eyes.

Matt grinned at Jackson. "I'm glad you came to your senses."

Jackson nodded his head toward Lauren. "I had some help."

Forty minutes later, Ally folded her napkin and tossed it on the table. "I hate to break up the fun, but I have a tiny person at home who may be missing me."

Lauren felt as if the world's troubles had been lifted from her shoulders. "And I missed Eli, tell him hi for me."

As they stood and made their way toward the door, Ally reached for Lauren's hand, to give it a little squeeze. "Do you still need to talk?" She had as close to a smirk on her face as Lauren had ever seen.

She still needed to ask Ally to take her place at the church meeting, and a peep at Eli always made her day brighter. "Yes, I'd still like to come by if you have the time?"

"Absolutely, come on."

Lauren was happy enough to cry, except she didn't feel like crying—and she was sure Ally would take her place at the Bible study meeting. Lauren had one more hurdle; explaining her cousin Max, to Jackson.

But, tomorrow was another day.

#

# CHAPTER NINE

Lauren raced home after they left the club. She had things to do at home before it was time to run to Ally's house. The chance that Clair would see the notice about the exhibit wasn't likely, unless Nicolas decided to call her, since they were friends.

Lauren wanted to be the one to break the news, and she could happily do so now that Jackson and Brooke were going also.

Claude wasn't working in the yard today, and the housekeeper had already gone. The house seemed different without people in it.

Hurrying up the stairs, past a kitchen without the good aroma of Aunt Willa's cooking, Lauren planned how she would break the news to Clair. Casually and matter-of-fact, she'd mention that Nicolas had called. She was smiling as she pressed Clair's number.

Clair sounded as if she had just awakened from a nap.

"You'll never guess!"

"Probably not—"

"Nicolas called—I've been chosen as the featured artist for the Italian Exhibit!" So much for playing it cool.

"Really! Are you serious? It's a done deal?"

"Positively! The secretary of the committee has already called with the arrangements for my accommodations, but I'd rather stay at the villa."

"Why the villa? The hotel near the exhibit hall would be more convenient, less walking for you."

"Oh, Clair, I'm overcome with excitement. Of course, I'll stay at the hotel. Jackson and Brooke are going with me."

She explained about wanting to take Brooke. And that's why she'd planned to stay at the villa, so Maria could watch her while Lauren was busy during the day. "But since Jackson is going, he'll be with Brooke." Lauren sighed. "I still can't believe it."

Clair laughed. "You deserve the honor. I had hoped you'd get it last year, but this is good. I suppose Jackson is bursting his buttons? How did you ever talk him into going?"

"He wasn't at first. We had a spat over it." Lauren laughed. "But I'll tell you everything this weekend." They planned Sunday lunch together and ended the call.

Placing the phone on the table beside her, Lauren pulled her feet into the chair as she was suddenly tired and wished now she'd not promised to run by Ally's later. But on second thought, she and Jackson could go on to dinner after he closed the gallery. She glanced at her watch, she could spare another few minutes. She put her head back and closed her eyes. What had changed Jackson's mind? She recalled at lunch when Matt brought up the exhibit. She'd held her breath, wondering what was about to happen. What if Jackson had confided to Matt that even though he was unhappy about it, she was going on to Italy? In the end, she wouldn't have gone against his wishes. But it would have altered her belief in him.

She opened her eyes and gazed around the room that had been Jackson's first wife's studio. "I love Jackson so much." There was still wonder at the depth of her feelings for him. Who was she speaking to, her own heart? Jenna Perhaps?

*** 

The next day Drew made it from New York in time for him and Clair to attend church services together. Lauren hadn't expected to see them until they met at the small restaurant near the edge of town, one that Matt favored.

But Ally cornered the group after services and begged them to come to their house and help finish off a huge roast that Polly had made two days before.

Matt chimed in, "I'd consider it a favor if you'd come help us. Polly won't stand for waste in her kitchen." He motioned to get the show on the road. "A roast beef sandwich on the patio should hit the spot."

Lauren hugged herself. "That'll be fun! And we can enjoy this perfect fall-like weather."

Ally said, "Polly will help prepare the sandwiches."

Lauren gazed around the group of friends gathered on the patio and thought how wonderful it was when they were all together. Would Max like her friends? And what would they think of Max. Thinking of Max reminded her to speak to Ally about their coffee date; it was the same day Max arrived.

With the thought still on her mind, she heard Ally say to Clair, "How long will you be in town, Clair?"

"I think Drew plans to stay most of the week—maybe longer." She lowered her voice and shifted in her lounge chair. "I don't know why we don't just move all our clothes here and quit pretending we live in New York."

Drew slowly turned his head toward her. "I heard that." He smiled his lazy, infectious smile, which made Clair, Lauren, and Ally all smile in his direction.

Clair sipped her tea and set the tall colorful patio glass on the table. "It's my fault we haven't moved out permanently." She cast a tender glance at Drew. "Dad likes us being close, and I enjoy seeing him often, and we're all he's got."

Drew pointed a finger in their direction. "You girls should gang up on Charlie and find him a wife. You're all good at stirring things up and getting things done."

Matt heard the comment. "AKA minding other peoples business."

All three girls glared momentarily at Matt, then burst into laughter.

Suddenly, Lauren nearly jumped off her chair. "I've got it!"

Her excitement caught Matt's, Jackson's, and Drew's interest and startled Clair and Ally. Expectation threw a hushed silence on the group.

Matt spoke first. "Well, what do you have?"

"A plan. I love Charlie as if he were my own father. He practically was while I was growing up." She smiled in Clair's direction. "Clair always shared her dad. I for one would be thrilled to see him happily married—to the right person."

Clair recovered slowly from surprise at the turn the conversation had taken. "Dad has lady friends, but he's never shown an interest in anyone in particular."

Drew said, "Maybe that's because he's concerned you wouldn't approve—"

"Well, why would he think that? I've never—"

Ally held her hand in the air. "Wait, guys, just a minute." She turned to Lauren. "You said you had a plan?"

Lauren smiled smugly. "Uh-huh, just waiting for the storm to pass."

Jackson groaned. "What's the plan?"

Five pairs of eyes focused on her.

She smiled. "Caroline Brickman." Another interminable stretch of silence followed. Lauren turned her palms up. "Well? Caroline is perfect. Charlie would love her." She turned to the stunned Clair. "Why haven't we put those two together before now?"

Ally said, "Dr. Brickman?"

"Yes." Lauren nodded. "I grew to love Dr. Brickman—Caroline, when she counseled with me before Jackson and I were married. I think Charlie would like her too."

"I . . . I never thought about Dad and Caroline." Clair continued gazing at Lauren "He's much older than her. Caroline is just eight years older than me."

Lauren saw the wheels turning. Clair might not be capable of picturing her good friend, involved with her dad. But Drew had perked up.

"When I think about it, they'd be perfect for each other." He glanced hopefully at Clair.

"But, Caroline's seeing someone, well, sort of." Doubt troubled her face. "I just don't know about their age differences. . . ."

Ally had been relatively quiet, but now she glanced at Clair. "I don't know your dad or Dr. Brickman as well as you guys do, but, the little I do know, it seems they might have a lot in common."

Clair twirled a strand of hair and shifted uncomfortably. "It's just the age thing. . . ."

Ally surprised everyone by saying, "Pooh! I've only just met your father. And speaking from the side of the fence of a happily married woman, I could have been attracted to him."

"You could have?" Disbelief tinged Clair's voice.

"Very much so." Ally laughed at Matt's scowl.

Lauren clapped her hands. "Okay, we need an outing where Caroline needs an escort. Only they'll both have to think each is just doing Clair a favor." She thought for a moment. "Maybe a dinner party here. . . ?"

"Why the charade? They're both adults." Clair said.

Lauren smiled. "Yes, but doing you a favor would be hard for either of those two to refuse, and . . . if they happen to be interested at the end of the evening, they could call later for a real date. If there was no interest on either part, no harm done." She looked around the group of faces. "Right?"

Drew looked to Clair for the cue, and the others followed suit.

Clair's expression didn't give a clue. "Let me think on it." She glanced at Drew. "We should be going."

The party began to break up. The guys all stood, and standing extra straight—too much of Polly's delicious roast sandwiches and apple pie topped with ice cream, left no room for slumping.

Ally motioned to Clair and Lauren. "Clair, I never got to finish after asking how long you'd be here; could you join Lauren and me for coffee on Tuesday?"

"I'd love to, especially since I didn't get to see much of Eli after church."

"Oh, good! I know, Eli went to sleep in church and slept until we tucked him into his bed." She glanced at her watch.

Lauren needed to speak up. She glanced to see Jackson and Drew involved in a deep conversation near the door—good, she wanted to tell him about Max's arrival later, in private. "Ally, you may shoot me, but something's come up that I can't make coffee."

"Oh? We could postpone to the following day—Wednesday the seventh."

Lauren frowned. "I thought we were doing coffee on the fifth? Tomorrow—Monday."

"No, it's the sixth, Tuesday."

Lauren gave a huge sigh. "Wonderful! I'd gotten confused on the days. I'll be here, and I may have a surprise with me."

They shared a relieved laugh, and Clair's firm fingers clasped onto Lauren's arm. "You don't leave until you tell us the surprise."

Lauren recognized the glare—Clair wouldn't let her go until she told them! She laughed. "My cousin is flying into New York—tomorrow morning at 10:40."

"How delightful," Ally said."

Clair turned her head sidelong and cut her eyes to Lauren. "I thought Max was coming in November for Thanksgiving?"

"She is. This is a quick business trip, but I hope to persuade her to come to the house for a day or two." Lauren's eyes met Jackson's across the terrace, and he waved for her.

"I've got to run. We'll talk on Tuesday—I'm so glad I was just confused on the date!" She grabbed Ally's hand. "Thanks for a lovely impromptu lunch."

Clair echoed her thanks for lunch, and the troupe headed to their vehicles.

***

As soon as they pulled out of the driveway, Lauren reached for Jackson's hand. They entwined their fingers and smiled across the console.

"What were you girls huddled about? It looked serious," he said.

Lauren took the plunge. "I was telling them some news that I haven't had a chance to share with you. My cousin is flying in tomorrow morning." She glanced at Jackson's profile and rushed on. "I only learned of it yesterday. I'm driving to New York to meet her flight."

"Oh, she's coming before Thanksgiving?"

"Yes, but she's still coming for the holidays. This is just a quick business trip." She held her breath; afraid he would worry about her driving back and forth to New York.

He nodded and freed his hand. "Would you like me to go with you?"

Her shoulders relaxed. "You're a dear to offer, but it's not necessary. Max has a business meeting. I offered to meet her for lunch."

Jackson had lowered his window halfway, and because of the noise, he inclined his head nearer to her. "How long will she be staying?"

"She said just overnight. I hope she'll come home with me. But she may prefer a hotel."

He raked his hair several times.

Lauren waited patiently to hear what was on his mind.

"Lauren, I don't mean to be a worrywart, but you probably don't need to be driving to New York by yourself much longer. You don't rest as you should." He glanced at her when she laughed. "I know you think you're indestructible, but you're not—and neither is the baby. I wish you'd slow down a bit."

She reached for his hand again. "I promise I'll slow to a lazy crawl once we get back from Florence." She widened her eyes at his doubting scowl. "No, really, I've been thinking about it. I've even asked Ally and Clair to help me with the finishing touches to the nursery." Lauren smiled at Jackson.

He squeezed her hand lightly. "That's great—and it relieves my mind."

Lauren's mind had been relieved too. Now she was free to consider finding a project that would con-

structively involve the girls. Her first thought was vol-
unteer work at the animal shelter, until the memory of
the experience she and Brooke went through that time
sent a shudder up her spine. No, the shelter was not the
place to send two emotional adolescent girls. "Honey,
help me come up with a constructive project to involve
the girls in. Something fun, but challenging."

"The girls?" he said.

"Brooke and Mandy. They both have sharp
minds. Minds that need to be engaged ninety-nine percent of the time."

"Funny you should bring it up. Steven Ryder
dropped by the gallery a couple of days ago, enquiring
about an equine artist. He wants to commission a por-
trait of his favorite Stallion." He smiled in her direction. "I was thinking about taking Brooke over to his
stables for a look around and see what she thought
about riding lessons." He nodded. "She needs to be
occupied with something fun and physical."

"That's a wonderful idea, and I agree one-
hundred percent. I'd like to go too."

Jackson patted her knee and said, "Of course, I
want you to go."

He'd ignored her mention of Mandy. "I wish
you'd invite Mandy to come along."

He inhaled deeply and let it go. "I'm still not sure
about Mandy . . . she may be growing up faster than
Brooke, and that might not be good."

Lauren was tempted to tell him about the incident
with Mandy that she had witnessed on the schoolyard.
She held her tongue, better to have the facts first.

Jackson wouldn't stand for another student bullying his daughter or her best friend.

CHAPTER TEN

# Adventure

Sunday afternoon passed swiftly once they left Matt and Ally's house. Lauren had a couple of hours before time for evening services, just time enough for a short nap before starting to work on her to-do list for the coming week.

She was excited about the conversation with Jackson. The riding stables were a stroke of genius.

Brooke had never mentioned anything about horses, but what little girl didn't love a horse? She hated to press him about Mandy, but if necessary, she would. Mandy was at a crucial age, she could use some guided intervention.

Lauren sighed and focused again on the list she'd started. Jackson would make the call to Steven Ryder, she was going to call Mrs. Flowers and schedule a visit with her, and she had to get back with Nicolas about details of the exhibit—In the midst of all the planning, her cell phone rang. She peered at the screen; Clair. "Hello."

"Well," Clair said. "It must be fate."

"What must be fate?" Lauren asked.

"You won't guess what just happened."

Clair's tone of disbelief told Lauren it was big news. She didn't get a chance to guess.

"Caroline called and asked if Drew could act as her escort on the tenth of the month, a Saturday evening event that she must attend." Clair paused. "I still can't believe it."

Lauren burst into laughter. "Fate indeed! It's meant to be!"

Clair was laughing too. "I nearly choked on the words when I suggested that Dad would be delighted to escort her—I almost didn't mention it! I figured she'd hedge and make an excuse why it would be better if Drew could do the favor. Drew's acted as her escort before when she was desperate. But I told her that Dad would be happy to help her out."

Lauren said, "Well, what did she say?"

Clair sounded surprised. "She seemed genuinely pleased that Dad would be her escort. Now I have to call Dad and line him up."

"You haven't asked Charlie if he's free?"

"It's an evening thing. He stays home most evenings, and I won't take no for an answer."

Clair's reservations about the age difference seemed to have vanished. They visited a while longer then ended the call with Clair reminding Lauren to let the others know that the plan was underway—sooner and smoother than she would have ever guessed.

That turn of events was too exciting for Lauren to return to her to-do list. She had to share the news with

Jackson. She found him in the office on the far side of the large study. He sat at the desk with the latest Art Talk News spread open, reclined in his chair, head back, snoozing. She stopped just inside the door of the office. The thick carpet had absorbed the sound of her footsteps. He looked so relaxed; she didn't have the heart to wake him. She turned.

"Lauren, I'm awake, what's up?" He sat up and ran his fingers through his hair, then dry washed his face. "I didn't realize I was so sleepy." He reached for her as she came close.

Lauren sat on his lap. "Uh-huh, too much of Polly's good food?"

He hugged her and nodded. "I'm afraid so. I sure miss that Pumpkin."

She snuggled against him. "Speaking of, when will you call Mr. Ryder about Brooke visiting the stables?"

He buried his face in her neck and mumbled, "I already have. Steven said we should drive out this next Saturday and look around. He suggested Brooke might like to observe one of the private classes in progress."

Lauren gave him a tender kiss. then stood and strolled to the front of the big desk. "What about Mandy? Brooke would be more inclined to take lessons if her best friend did too."

"If it means that much, fine, invite Mandy."

From across the desk she smiled. "Thank you, dear. I'll go call right now."

Jackson nodded and reached for the Art Talk News as Lauren headed to make the call.

***

After the evening church service was over and they were back home, Jackson opted for a glass of cold milk and crackers for dinner while Lauren consumed a plain yogurt and a rather large clump of purple seedless grapes. She then meandered upstairs to shower and slip into cool cotton pajamas. After her shower, while sitting in the middle of the bed rubbing lotion on her hands, she suddenly remembered she hadn't told Jackson about Charlie and Caroline! Not believing she'd forgotten that news, she bounded from the bed and ran toward the door and was skimming down the stairs when Jackson started upstairs.

"Lauren! What's wrong?"

She halted, wide-eyed. "Nothing's wrong, why do you ask?"

"You're running on the stairs! Good heavens, girl, why are you running on the stairs?"

"Oh, I'm sorry. I just forgot, I have something exciting—"

"You'd really be sorry if you fell and hurt yourself or the baby and ended up in the hospital!"

"Jackson, I'm sorry. You're totally right. It was a foolish thing—"

"Promise me you won't ever do that again."

He gripped her shoulder until she pulled away.

"I promise, I'll try not to do it again." She headed back up the stairs with him following.

"What does that mean—you'll *try*?"

"Just that. I'll try not to do it again. I didn't run down the stairs thinking what fun it would be to fall," she said testily. "Just because I'm pregnant doesn't mean I'm used to thinking about my every movement."

When they reached their bedroom he gathered her into his arms. "I didn't mean to bark at you. But what would I do if something happened to you?"

Lauren lamely patted his arm. "I know. I'm sorry I scared you."

She waited. Was he not the least bit curious about what exciting thing had caused her to dash madly down the stairs? No, apparently not. Charlie and Caroline were no big deal to him—men! She climbed into bed and reached for the book that lay on the bedside table. Her cell phone lay beside the book. Lauren shifted her gaze to the clock, it wasn't late, Ally would still be up. She got comfortable, reached for her phone and pressed Ally's number.

"Hi, Ally. I couldn't wait to tell somebody—Clair called earlier—she's already got an evening planned for Charlie and Caroline!" From her peripheral vision, Lauren saw Jackson run his hand through his hair, groan and drop his book onto his lap.

She felt immensely better.

She and Ally giggled, trying to imagine the outcome of the event between the two people they both loved. The conversation lasted twenty minutes or so before Lauren said goodnight and ended the call. She laid the phone down and reached for her book.

Jackson propped on his elbow and leaned toward her. "I'm sorry, honey. I got so anxious about you that I forgot you were coming down the stairs with a purpose—I cut you off. I'm sorry, honey. I do want to hear what Clair had to say about her dad and Caroline. Tell me everything, how did the outing come about so soon?"

Easily mollified, Lauren quickly forgave. "It's strange that the very evening after we'd talked about getting them together, Caroline called Clair and confided that she needed an escort for a formal event that she had to attend." Lauren beamed at Jackson. "Well, don't you think it's strange?"

"Yes, I do, strange indeed. Whoever said the stars never align perfectly to sprinkle miracles on us mortals?"

She laughed, pushing him away. "Stop making fun! Wait and see. This will work out."

He tossed his book on the table and flopped on his back. "I hope so, they're nice people."

"Uh-huh, they are."

"Clair said Caroline seemed pleased for Charlie to escort her." Lauren moved across the bed to lie on her side and snuggle close to Jackson. 'Who knows, Caroline may have had a crush on Charlie all this time."

"Oh, I doubt that. . . ."

"Maybe not, but it's still strange."

They settled into a pleasant quietness, enjoying the closeness.

Jackson suddenly squeezed her. "But enough about other people, let's talk about us." His arm tightened around her. "I was thinking that since we'll be in Florence anyway, why not take an extra couple of days and show Brooke the galleries?"

"Oh, Jackson! That's a wonderful idea. Brooke will soak it up like a sponge."

For Brooke to go to Florence and attend the grand art exhibit was something her mother would have approved of. Jackson had once shared that when Brooke was a toddler, Jenna used to show her pictures of the old masters and tell her that someday she'd take her to see them for real.

Lauren stretched her body full-length beside him and pressed closer. "You're the best dad ever, and Brooke is a lucky little girl."

Jackson jerked back. "What was that? Did you feel it?

"Umm, your son just kicked you."

"Wow, that bump really is a baby? And I thought it was just chips and cookies."

Lauren grabbed a pillow and threw it over his face. "Dr. Stinson says my bump is a baby, and he should know!" She laughed and clambered to sit on his stomach while struggling to keep the pillow over his head.

Jackson pushed it aside, "Yeah, but does Doc know how many chips you go through?" He suddenly flung the pillow to the end of the bed and wrestled Lauren onto her back.

"If it's a boy, just promise you won't name him Chip."

"That's one promise I won't have any trouble keeping." She laughed. "But what do you mean, *if* it's a boy?" She lightly traced her finger over his mouth. "You know it's a boy."

"I don't think I'll really believe it until I see him and hold him."

"But, Jackson—"

He cut her words off with a kiss—his favorite way to end a conversation.

# CHAPTER ELEVEN

# Homecoming

Waking to the sound of Jackson in the shower, Lauren grabbed her robe and slipped downstairs to start the coffee. The kitchen felt strange without Brooke's chatter and Aunt Willa laughing and answering her questions.

When Jackson came down the stairs with a quick, light step, Lauren's heart swelled to see him happy and looking rested.

"Ready for coffee?" she asked.

"Uh-huh, smells wonderful. Why didn't you sleep in? The house is quiet—your last chance." He grinned, gave her a kiss and took the cup of steaming coffee she offered. "Aunt Willa said they'd be home around one o'clock."

"I won't see them until later this evening. Too much on my agenda today to sleep late."

Jackson gave a quizzical glance. "That busy?" He sipped the hot coffee and lowered the cup. "What all do you have to do?"

Lauren sat in the chair opposite him. "Remember, I'm driving into the city to meet my cousin's flight." She glanced at the grandfather clock. "And I don't have time to linger."

Jackson sighed. "I'd forgotten that. Please be careful, Lauren."

She leaned forward and returned his gaze. "Jackson, this baby is important to me, too, I'll be careful. Don't you believe me?"

"Of course I believe you. It's just that your idea of careful is not the same as mine." He barely took time to finish his coffee and glance at the paper. He carried his empty cup toward the kitchen.

Lauren followed.

He gave her an extra long hug and a goodbye kiss. "I'm going on to work so you won't have an excuse for being late and end up driving too fast."

She smiled and nodded. "I won't start late and drive too fast. I promise."

Driving too fast was not a concern; she had control over that. But the excitement of seeing Max was building and it proved almost uncontrollable.

***

At the airport Lauren pulled into the busy covered parking area. She had left home in plenty of time so that she was a few minutes early and could stroll through the airport without haste. She had refreshed her memory of Max from a photo of her as a young teen. She probably hadn't changed much. The photo showed a tall, tanned girl in faded jeans and a wide-brim Aussie hat. The curly dark hair was big and windblown. A smile lit her face and crinkled the corners of wide, gray-blue eyes. Those eyes. Lauren had been envious as a child. But Max had always insisted she'd trade for Lauren's violet-blue ones in a heartbeat.

A smile lingered from the memory as Lauren took a seat in the terminal where Max's plane should arrive. A while later she was startled when a smartly dressed, beautiful young woman with a mane of dark, sleek, shoulder length hair, sat close enough to Lauren to be considered rude. Lauren smiled and turned slightly away; a polite signal to the woman that she was intruding. The woman in the seat leaned toward Lauren. An elusive whiff of expensive perfume kept Lauren from moving even farther away. Nice fragrance. But when the woman brushed her shoulder against Lauren's it was too much.

"Excuse me." Lauren smiled stiffly and swallowed her rising irritation, she moved out of the person's range.

"Oh, don't be a snob." The woman drawled in a butter smooth voice.

Lauren froze, that voice? She whirled. "Max?"

"What—do I look like a mugger or something?" Max teased.

They jumped up at the same time and Lauren threw her arms around her cousin. "I didn't recognize you! You're early."

Max was amused at Lauren's shock. "Well, after all it's been a while, and yes we arrived ahead of schedule." Her gaze traveled over Lauren's stomach. She patted it. "What's this?"

"Just what it looks like." Lauren grinned.

"Why didn't you tell me you were expecting?"

"I didn't think about it when we spoke, but now you can see for yourself."

Max quickly pulled Lauren into another tight hug. She released her and said, "Come on, let's find a sandwich shop where we can talk. It's good to see you, Lauren. We have a lot of catching up to do."

Max flashed the smile Lauren remembered, and though she looked like a model from Vogue, it was still Max. Lauren shook her head. "It's wonderful to see you too, but where's the cowgirl I remember? Everyone's going to believe I was making up stories!"

"The cowgirl is still here." Max touched her heart and gazed at Lauren, then glanced away, saying, "I'm in disguise."

"Tell me what's going on—"

"I will, but while we have a sandwich."

Lauren helped her collect one small bag before they headed to the Range Rover.

The bistro that Lauren and Clair used to go to a lot was not far from the airport. As she pulled into the parking area of the noisy eatery, Max wrinkled her nose. "Let's find a place where old folks hang out—they're usually much quieter." She laughed. "I'm going to make a great old person."

"Somehow, I can see that," Lauren muttered. "I'll take you to a place my friend Charlie Weston likes. You'll approve." Lauren guided the Range Rover back into the traffic and just minutes later she expertly maneuvered into a tight parallel parking slot. "We'll have to walk a block, but it's worth it."

"That's fine. I always liked walking in New York."

After a block and a half they turned into a courtyard. "This is it." Lauren pushed on a large carved door with the word MARTINS above it, and seconds later they were ushered to a table. The room was quiet and airy, the tables sat far apart to afford privacy. The room was comfortable in the old New York style, but not stuffy or pretentious.

Max nodded in approval. "Yeah, my style—I bet they even serve Coke."

"Uh-huh, they do." Lauren grinned.

They ordered vegetable soup with soda crackers, a Coke for Max and tea for Lauren. As soon as the food was served Max got straight to the story.

"In the first place, Lauren, if I had known you were expecting, I wouldn't have asked you to meet me."

"Why do people think pregnancy numbs a woman's brain and renders her less capable?" Lauren shook her head. "I can still drive and feed myself!" She placed her napkin in her lap. "Are you in some kind of trouble? Is danger involved in what you're doing?"

Max raised her brows and shrugged. "That's just it—I don't *know* what I'm doing. But I do know something is going on. My bronze horned toads at thirty bucks apiece are nothing, yet this guy is buying them in volume. It doesn't make sense." She swallowed a spoonful of soup and munched a cracker. "Whitney flew up to meet with one of her clients a couple of weeks ago and while she was here, decided to look around, you know, check the man out.

There was not one bronze toad in his gallery." Max blotted her lips with the white cloth napkin. "She inquired of a salesgirl about them and the girl looked puzzled. Later the girl told Whitney they didn't have any left and she didn't know when they'd be getting anymore in." Max looked smug. "But the order went out last week for another shipment of twelve."

Lauren frowned. "That is strange, but what can you do? And why do you care how many toads he buys? What do you suspect he's doing?"

Max lowered her voice. "I believe the guy may be using the bronze toads to smuggle something." She sipped her Coke. "And if he is, I don't like it."

Lauren widened her eyes in disbelief. "You don't really believe they're being used for smuggling?"

Max nodded. "Uh-huh, could be."

"But they're so small."

"And cheap, an ideal carrier for, say, gems?"

Lauren began to laugh and Max gazed at her like she'd lost her mind. "I'm not laughing at you, it's just looking at you and listening to you is like being with two different people."

Max smiled and shrugged. "I do occasionally clean up and pretend to be a lady." She grimaced. "But these heels wear me out!"

"Why didn't you wear comfortable clothing?"

Max again lowered her already soft voice, "This guy doesn't know me, but he knows that the bronze artist who sculpts the toads lives on a ranch in Colorado. I tried to look as opposite to a ranch hand as I could." She turned her palms up. "In case I should run into him."

"You plan on going to the gallery hoping to see this guy?" Lauren bit her lip and pushed her hair behind her ear. This could get serious. "Max, won't you consider staying over at least a couple of days and come back to Valley Ridge with me? I'd love for you to meet Jackson and Brooke and Jackson's aunt." Lauren held her breath. If she could get Max to the house, maybe they'd have an opportunity to talk this through more.

"Well, actually, I thought about it during the flight, and since you've kindly invited me, I'll stay a day longer. But for now, let's locate the gallery and take a look. I can do my sleuthing later."

Sleuthing—Lauren shivered. She liked the sound of the word. "Wonderful!" Let's finish lunch, locate the place, and head home." Lauren eyed her cousin. "But could we sleuth the day after tomorrow? I want you to meet my friends tomorrow."

Max grinned. "You could always talk me into anything."

Lauren hoped she could talk her into forgetting about smugglers and sleuthing—as exciting as it sounded, it was also a bit scary.

After they finished the light lunch, Max insisted on renting a car so that Lauren wouldn't have to make the drive back to the city later, but Lauren wouldn't hear of it. "Don't be difficult, Max. I'm coming back with you no matter what. Besides, I don't mind the drive. I like the countryside from Valley Ridge to New York." She glanced sideways and grinned. "The pretty drive between the two places is the reason I house-hunted in Valley Ridge in the first place."

"Is the pretty countryside what kept you there?" Max smirked.

Lauren smiled sweetly. "Among other things."

Max nodded. "Uh-huh." She began to scramble around in a small purse. Finally she dumped its contents into her lap. "I wrote that address on a scrap of paper, it must have gotten stuck in something—ah—there it is!" Max quickly chucked everything back into the soft leather clutch. She passed the paper across the console to Lauren.

Lauren whipped the Range Rover to the curb at the first opportunity, and with her foot on the brake she studied the paper. "I know this place. It's very high end."

Max grinned. "I know. Not a shabby neighborhood. Let's go."

"Right." Lauren checked the traffic and merged into the flow. "It'll only take a few minutes or so to get there."

Max took a lipstick out of her bag and applied fresh color without looking in a mirror.

"How do you do that without looking?"

Max grinned. "Sometimes a little goes astray, no big deal." She pressed her lips together to set the color and cleaned up the corners of her mouth with a thumb and forefinger.

They rode in silence for several moments.

"So, Max, what if you should learn that your toad customer is smuggling jewels?"

Without hesitation, she said, "I'll turn him in to the proper authorities."

"Couldn't that get dangerous? Jewels could involve large amounts of money. . . ."

Lauren felt Max's steady gaze focused on her. She glanced briefly at her cousin.

Max spoke softly. "You mean like, enough money to kill for?"

Lauren shook her head. "No, that's *not* what I meant—don't even say that!"

Max breathed a deep sigh. "I don't know, perhaps it could get dangerous, but I have to know what's going on."

"You haven't changed." Lauren slowed the Range Rover and slid to a stop at the curb.

"Well, there it is. Gallery Rusko. It's a beautiful old structure." Lauren pressed her back against the seat to give Max a better view of the building that sat across the street.

Max leaned forward onto the console and stared past Lauren and through the driver's window. "It brings to mind the sepulchers in the Bible. Whitened, clean and beautiful on the outside, but full of dead men's bones on the inside."

"Max, really! You don't know that the building is not clean and beautiful on the inside as well." Lauren suddenly felt shaken. As kids, her cousin had been dramatic, but never given to morbid imaginations.

Max laughed softly and touched Lauren's shoulder. "I was just teasing. You're absolutely right, I don't know. Shall we go inside?"

Lauren hesitated before saying, "I'd rather not today. Let's go home."

Max studied Lauren's face with an intense gaze, as if she wanted to say something, instead she turned her attention back to the building for several moments before she spoke again. "Yes, of course, let's go. Besides, I'm anxious to meet the man who clipped your wings." Max smiled and relaxed.

Lauren guessed that Max was maybe a little nervous in finding out what was going on, even though she wouldn't drop it. She confided that Whitney had suggested they walk away from something that really wasn't their concern. Lauren agreed with Whitney. After all, the man didn't steal the toads—they were his.

Max settled into the leather seat as they pulled away from the curb. Lauren gave the elegant, white stucco building with its lovely arched display windows a final glance. What mysteries *did* it hold?

# CHAPTER TWELVE

# Intrigue

The farther they left New York behind, the more Max began to sound like her old self. She commented on the beauty of the countryside and asked many questions about Brooke and Jackson.

"Since you're staying longer than you planned, you can borrow anything of mine that you need. Lauren glanced sideways at Max.

"Thanks, but I shouldn't need anything. My bag may look small, but it's full." She laughed. "I have all I need, boots, jeans, several shirts, and my toothbrush."

"What about pajamas?" Lauren asked.

Max shrugged and grinned. "I can make do without those for several nights."

"Uh-huh, but not at my house."

Max rested her head on the back of the seat and laughed. "You're right. I'm not used to a man or a child in the house. I'll borrow your pajamas."

Lauren grinned. "You can have the plaid flannel ones."

Max laughed again. "Fine with me. How much farther are we?"

Lauren glanced at her watch. "About twenty minutes." Thinking she should let Jackson know, she pressed his number. The speaker was on.

"Hello."

"Hi, sweetheart! I'm about twenty minutes from Valley Ridge. Do you know if Brooke and Aunt Willa have made it back or not?"

"Yes. They're home. Aunt Willa called around one-twenty. I thought you were going to be late getting back?"

She glanced at Max and they grinned. "I didn't know what time it would be; I said late just in case."

"What happened to the cowgirl—she head home after seeing the traffic in New York?"

They smothered their giggles.

"She's not afraid of traffic, besides, I have Max with me. I twisted her arm to come meet you and the others."

"Good! I'm anxious to meet her. If she's half as pretty as you, she can stay."

Lauren and Max exchanged glances and mouthed, "Aww."

Lauren said, "I think you'll approve of this cowgirl. Should we plan to have dinner at the club since Aunt Willa may be tired?"

"Oh no, she's already informed me she'd had enough restaurant food for a while and she couldn't wait to have dinner at home. I think she mentioned smothered pork chops."

"Yum! Sounds wonderful!" Lauren glanced at Max. They raised their brows and nodded.

"We'll see you at the house."

"Tell your cousin I'm looking forward to meeting her."

"Will do . . . bye, honey."

Lauren was relieved that Max looked and acted like a normal person. She didn't have to worry about Jackson getting a bad impression. They were approaching the private drive to the house. When Lauren turned onto the drive, Max sat straighter and let out a whistle—a soft whistle, but one that Max could do in a volume that could turn a herd of cattle.

"I'd forgotten how you do that." Lauren shook her head. "You have to show Brooke."

Never taking her eyes off the lake, Max said, "The ranch foreman taught me how to whistle when I was about ten. I used to help him with the cattle."

"Mother referred to you as a wild Indian and forbid you to whistle." They both laughed.

"Aunt Elizabeth was right. I was a wild one."

Lauren mused, "How did two sisters grow up to be so different as our mothers did?"

"The same way Whitney and I did, I suppose." Max was taking in everything. "This is so beautiful. I love the mountains of Colorado, and I never plan to live anywhere else, but I see how people get attached to this part of the country."

"Mention that to Jackson, and he'll tell everyone what an intelligent woman you are."

Lauren parked the Range Rover in the garage and Max grabbed her bag from the backseat. They crossed the slate tile garage floor toward the back door, still discussing the differences in the terrain of the country as Lauren opened the door into the kitchen and moved toward the island counter. She glanced over her shoulder to see that Max had stopped just inside the door.

She turned fully toward her. "Max, what's wrong?"

"Absolutely nothing! That wonderful smell takes me back to the ranch when mom and our cook created smells like that in the kitchen."

Lauren relaxed. "Oh, the smell. Give credit to Jackson's Aunt Willa. She's the cook."

They both turned when Aunt Willa came from the direction of her rooms.

She patted her hair in place, a smile on her face. "Did I hear my name?"

Lauren went forward and hugged her, saying, "Did you girls have fun in New York?"

Aunt Willa's smile broadened, and she nodded, her eyes on Max as she spoke. "We had the time of our lives. I see you have company."

Max smiled, slipped out of the four-inch heels and strode barefoot across the kitchen. She held out her hand as Lauren made the introductions. "It's good to meet you, Willa. Lauren's been filling me in about everyone."

Aunt Willa glanced at Lauren. "Oh?"

"I know nothing but good stuff to tell about you." Lauren grinned at Jackson's aunt.

Max gazed around the room. "What a lovely home you have. I feel comfortable already. Where's the young Brooke that I've heard so much about?" Max smiled at Aunt Willa.

"She's upstairs. I'll go tell her you're here—"

Max put her finger to her lips. "Let me go to my room first and change clothes." Lauren had explained to her that Brooke was expecting to meet a real cowgirl at Thanksgiving. "I'd like to change clothes before we meet."

Lauren motioned for Max to hurry and follow her upstairs. "Maybe we can sneak you in the guest room before Brooke knows you're here."

They rushed toward the stairs and lowered their voices as they crept up and out of sight.

Lauren settled Max into her room and she went to her own room to change into comfortable leggings and a long, comfy, white shirt. She couldn't resist sinking into the big chair and laying her head back.

She awoke an hour later and stretched her body long and hard and rose to her feet. She brushed aside the thought that she was being a bad hostess. She knew Max would understand.

Upon entering the den, she was pleased that Aunt Willa, Brooke, and Max had settled into pleasant conversation. No one seeing them would have guessed from the tone of the conversation that they'd met barely an hour before.

Brooke jumped to her feet when Lauren strolled into the room. "Why didn't you tell me Max was coming before Thanksgiving!"

Lauren returned her hug. "I didn't find out until after you had left for New York. It was a surprise to me too."

Lauren stopped and stared at the transformation. Max's hair looked more relaxed than before. She had pulled it into a ponytail that was reverting to its natural curl; held by a silver clip that was circled with turquoise and coral. Soft Indian moccasins of rich worn leather had replaced the four-inch heels. A white linen shirt, soft from age, and creased lightly from being packed was loosely tucked into pale-blue, threadbare jeans that fit her slender body, but not tight. A belt the color of her moccasins, set with a buckle of silver and turquoise completed her outfit.

Lauren blinked. She had worried needlessly about what Jackson would think of Max. She could guess what he would think. Max looked like one of the models often seen on the cover of Southwest Art magazine.

Lauren experienced a twinge of envy, a short-lived twinge; but one that packed a wallop. Envy was a new experience—she'd never envied anyone that she could remember.

Brooke ran to Lauren, chattering away.

Lauren pulled her gaze from Max. "Sorry, dear, what were you saying?"

"I love Max's turquoise! I've never seen any like hers before."

Lauren squeezed the slim shoulders. "That's because Max has antique, handcrafted turquoise. A lot of her jewelry is museum quality, dating as far back as the 17th century. Max's mother collected turquoise, as did our grandmother.

"Wow!" Brooke's voice hushed in awe. "Did your mom collect it too?" she whispered.

"No. Unfortunately my mother didn't like turquoise at all. The pieces she inherited from our grandmother, she passed on to Aunt Jane."

"Aww, I wish you'd gotten some." She turned a wistful eye to Max's belt buckle.

Lauren sympathized. "I know, but different people like different things."

Brooke skipped over to where Max sat on the plush leather sofa with her feet propped on a table sized matching footstool. Sitting close to Max's side, Brooke studied the half-inch disks of hammered silver earrings that Max wore.

Clearly, Brooke was taken with Max and her jewelry.

"Someday I'm going to pierce my ears." Brooke pinched her earlobes between her thumb and forefinger. "Did it hurt when you got yours done?"

"Nah, not much. It was worth it." Max pushed the hair back from Brooke's ear and said, "You have nice ears. Earrings will look good on you."

Lauren placed Winnie in her lap. "Her dad doesn't want her to have pierced ears for a few more years. Maybe when she's thirteen."

Brooke rolled her eyes. "My best friend has hers pierced, and she's only twelve."

Max shrugged and smiled at Brooke. "Thirteen will be here before you know it." She glanced at Lauren and back to Brooke. "Our grandmother had a wonderful collection of diamonds as well as the turquoise. Lauren's mom got those." She gazed at Lauren. "Has Brooke not seen them?"

Lauren shook her head and looked down at Winnie snoozing in her lap. "I haven't looked at them in years." She sighed. "Mother didn't like diamonds either."

Max laughed. "Isn't it funny that Grandmother got it right. I'm a turquoise person all the way and you're diamonds. She couldn't have known that, but we each got what suited us, didn't we?" She smiled at Lauren.

Lauren sat Winnie on the floor. "I'm really not a diamonds type. I never wear Grandmother's jewels." Lauren looked at Max. "She'd be pleased that you wear yours."

"Mother wore Grandmother's turquoise all the time. But it's more suited to everyday wear than diamonds. Did Aunt Elizabeth wear Grandmother's diamonds?"

"No. Never." Lauren stood. "I think I heard Jackson. I'll let him know where we are."

Jackson laid his briefcase on the end of the bar as Lauren greeted him. "We're all in the library." She wrapped her arms around his neck as he pulled her close.

He said, "I'm glad you're home safe from the trip. Are you girls enjoying a good visit?"

"Hmm, of course I'm safe, and we're having a wonderful visit. It's good to have the whole family, plus one, in the house." She took his hand. "Come meet my cousin."

As they entered the room, Max stood from the sofa and flashed her wide smile at Jackson. Lauren sensed his surprise. He paused the briefest of seconds before stepping forward, his hand offered in greeting.

"Max, it's so good to meet you!"

"And you, Jackson! I feel as if I already know you. Lauren's told me so much." Her voice held genuine warmth. She stepped around the footstool and clasped his hand.

"Well then, you have the advantage. Lauren's told me very little about you. Welcome to our home." He smiled and glanced at Lauren hovering at his side. "I'm glad your business brought you our way. Did you get it taken care of?"

"Uh, not quite. I'll finish up tomorrow." Max beamed at Lauren and back to Jackson. A sound from Lauren made Max glance once more toward her. "Oh, I forgot, not tomorrow! Lauren invited me to stay over an extra day to attend a coffee social and meet her friends tomorrow." She stuck her hands in her jean pockets. "I'll finish my business day after tomorrow and fly home." She directed a smile at Brooke, which encouraged Brooke to change the subject to Max's jewelry.

"Look Daddy, Max has lots of turquoise jewelry. It belonged to her grandmother, who gave it to Max." Brooke played with the silver bracelet on Max's arm and counted the rows of coral mountings across the top half of it.

Jackson leaned closed and examined the bracelet. "I see. It's an antique design. Very rare these days to see a piece like that."

Max lit up with pleasure. "It is a rare old design." She gazed at Jackson for a moment. "I have a really good collection. You'll have to see it. I love showing it to people who appreciate the early handcrafted pieces."

"Thank you! I'd love to see it someday."

Brooke tugged her dad's arm. "Lauren has a collection too. Her grandmother gave her lots of old diamonds."

Brooke glanced up from one face to the other as silence greeted her announcement. "Well, that's what Max said." Uncertainty clouded the wide amber eyes.

Max pushed her hands deeper into her pockets and laughed. "I did say that Brooke, and it's true. Lauren inherited Grandmother Collins's diamonds.

"Did you know that, Daddy?"

"No, sweetheart. I didn't know that." Jackson turned as Aunt Willa strolled into the library to announce that dinner was ready. Jackson motioned for Brooke and Max to go ahead of him to the dinning room. He offered Lauren his arm and gave her a searching glance. An expression flashed in his gray-green eyes; one she'd seen before, and regret flowed all the way to her feet.

# CHAPTER THIRTEEN

# Cousin Max

Lauren slipped her arm through Jackson's and smiled up at him as the party made its way into the dining room. She had all but forgotten about her grandmother's diamonds.

It had never occurred to her to discuss them with Jackson or anybody else. And Max was wrong. The diamonds didn't suit her. She had always preferred the beautiful and varied colors of turquoise, coral, and the other semi precious stones set in gleaming silver. Lauren sat deep in thought, her hands folded in her lap. She did wear her grandmother's diamond studs. Instinct drove her to caress the stud in her right ear before she thought.

Jackson lightly tapped the table for her attention. He smiled and offered his hand. Lauren returned his private smile and put her hand in his as everyone around glanced at her. They had all linked hands for the prayer.

To cover her apparent absentmindedness, she gave the table a swift glance. "I was admiring the table. The flowers are beautiful, Aunt Willa."

Everyone nodded and murmured agreement before bowing their heads.

After the prayer was offered, Max also commented on how pretty the table looked. The setting was casual but elegant with the creamy white stoneware they used for most evening meals. The flowers came from their own garden. Aunt Willa had outdone herself with smothered pork-chops, steamed asparagus and a green salad, along with home-baked rolls.

Jackson sat at one end of the table with Lauren at his right side and Brooke on the other. Aunt Willa sat at the other end of the table with Max sitting between her and Brooke.

"This is wonderful. May I call you Aunt Willa too?" Max inquired of Jackson's aunt.

"Of course, my dear. I'd be honored." Aunt Willa smiled and offered Max the napkin-covered basket of rolls.

"Thank you, they smell delicious, and I'm inspired by this lovely table; when I get home, no more TV trays in the den. I shall dine at the table even if it is by myself."

Suddenly Brooke said, "You could come live with us, and you wouldn't have to sit at the table by yourself."

"You're a kind person, Brooke. Thank you for the invitation. But I'd have to leave the ranch, and I have my work there." She smiled at Brooke. "Besides, my uncle and aunt and my sister are there quite often."

"How did your meeting go in New York?" Jackson glanced at Max.

"Well, actually—"

"Dad, Max is an artist, only she doesn't paint. She makes things."

"You interrupted our guest. And yes, I know Max is a bronze artist."

Brooke had her mouth full. "Uh-huh." She swallowed. "It's like iron or something."

"Brooke," He raised his brows. "Please mind your manners."

"Yes, sir." She turned to Max with a big smile. "I'm sorry."

"It's okay, you're forgiven, and when I get home," Max touched a napkin lightly to her mouth, "I'll send you a bronze bunny I made. It's very cute. I think you'll like it."

"Oh, thank you! I have something for you!"

"Really? But you didn't know I was coming." Max smiled at Brooke's secretive grin.

"I already had it made. I want you to have it."

Lauren glanced between the two of them. She liked that Brooke had taken to Max, and it looked like Max reciprocated the friendship.

"As I was saying, did you get your business taken care of?"

Lauren tensed the moment Jackson brought up the subject of Max's business again. Would she tell him the whole story? Lauren hadn't told her that Jackson didn't know what was going on.

"Just gallery business. I'll finish up before I go home." She smiled, glancing at Lauren.

"Well, I hope it goes well. And by the way, we could use another good bronze artist in the gallery. If you ever find yourself looking for another gallery, keep us in mind."

"Thank you, and I may take you up on that."

Lauren relaxed. Max had smoothed over the reason for her trip. Glad on one hand that she hadn't gone into detail with Jackson about her suspicions, but also uneasy about not telling him everything. The expression in his eyes earlier in the evening flashed across her vision. It had bothered him about her grandmother's diamonds, just as it had bothered him that she hadn't told him about her cousins. She tried to think if there was anything else—

Jackson placed his hand on her arm. "Since you girls are getting together tomorrow, come by the gallery and show Max around."

"Hmm, good idea. We couldn't have her come to Valley Ridge and not see the gallery."

Later in the evening, after their guest had said goodnight and gone to her room, Brooke settled into her homework. She had protested to her dad about having to do homework while company was in the house.

Back in their room, Jackson scratched his head. "What does company have to do with her homework?"

Lauren hugged him and explained the workings of an eleven-year old, female mind. "It's been an exciting day. Your daughter returned from a shopping trip to find an exotic visitor who lives on a ranch, rides horses, and wears beautiful turquoise jewelry, right here in her own home—how is she supposed to concentrate on schoolwork?"

Jackson returned her embrace. "Put that way, I can almost understand." He plopped on the bed. "I'm beat. I need my shower before I can talk."

"Get yours first. I can wait." This day had been an exciting one, and a tiring one. Jackson didn't know the half of it. He would probably give her another one of those looks, if he found out what was going on—or worse.

***

Propped in bed, seconds from dropping off to sleep, Lauren's book slipped from her hand. She glanced to see Jackson propped against his pillows, still reading.

"I have to give it up. I can't stay awake another minute." She placed her book on the bedside table.

"Honey, can we talk?" He placed a marker at his page and laid the book on his lap.

"Uh-huh, if I can stay awake." She rested her head back on the pillow and studied Jackson's face. "What about?"

"Why did I get the feeling that Max evaded my question about her business meeting? Is there a problem? Maybe I could help if she's having difficulty with her gallery."

"I don't think there's a problem." Lauren kicked herself. Why didn't she just tell him about the man and the bronze toads? Maybe he could help. Maybe Jackson had a right to be unhappy with her about not telling him things, but for the life of her, she didn't understand why some of it mattered. She told herself she didn't want to worry him and that was true about the deal with Max. But the diamonds, and the fact that she had cousins in Colorado just never occurred to her;

*what did it really matter?* She loved him more than her own life, and she was happy to share anything she thought really mattered—he probably had a lot in his life he hadn't thought to share with her.

"Are you asleep?" Jackson leaned toward her.

"No. I was thinking." She reached to caress his face. "You're a good person. I think Max likes you."

He caught her hand and kissed her palm. "I'm glad you think I'm good. And I'm glad Max likes me." He kissed her hand again. "I wish I understood you better. Sometimes I feel like I don't really know you at all."

Lauren couldn't stand the lost tone of his voice and the look on his face. She scooted over to nestle her head on his chest and wrap her arm across him. "Oh, please don't say that. It's just that there's not much to know. Really, I'm an open book."

Jackson settled back on his pillow. He tightened his arm around her and pulled her closer. "An open book maybe, a book of twenty chapters, and I can't get past chapter three."

*** 

Lauren woke early to the sound of rain. She slipped quietly off the bed and went to stand at the wide double windows. The gardens took on richer colors when they were washed with a rain shower.

She studied the wet scene from the window and mentally mixed color combinations to re-create the subdued colors of pink blooms in the pale-gray light of dawn. Totally absorbed, she didn't hear Jackson stirring until he stood next to her and pulled her into his arms.

"Good morning."

"Mmm, good morning to you too." His body was still warm from the bed. She ran her hand along his forearms, enjoying the warmth.

Jackson rested his chin on the top of her head as they looked down on the gardens below. "A nice slow rain. Just what we needed."

"Yes, but I wish it had waited until later."

Turning her around, Jackson grinned, saying, "Max won't melt, and the lake needs the water." He hugged her. "What time are you girls all meeting?"

Lauren sighed against his chest. "Thankfully, not until two-thirty."

"Why thankfully?"

"I'm tired, and I want to have a leisurely morning at home and a visit with just Max. We have a lot of catching up to do."

"Could you come by the gallery before you have coffee? I'm anxious for Matt to meet your cousin."

Lauren drew back from Jackson's embrace and tilted her head and eyed him. "You offered her a place in the gallery, but what if you don't like her work?"

"But I do like her work. Right after you told me she was a bronze artist, I did some research. Talent must run in your family—she's very good."

Lauren smiled. "And she's easy on the eyes."

"I'll say she is! I was surprised after the way you described her. I expected a wild-eyed, gun-totin' cowgirl dressed like Annie Oakley or something."

Lauren threw her head back and laughed delightedly. "That's pretty much the way she used to be when we were kids."

Lauren ran her hand down his arm and moved away from the windows. "I watched your face when you met her. I was curious about the impression she'd make." She smiled across the room at him. "But don't feel bad, I almost didn't recognize her at the airport."

Jackson crossed the room to take Lauren's hands in his. "I'm glad to see that Max has apparently grown up to be as pleasant and sensible as you did." He hesitated briefly. "Speaking of sensible, I'm sure it's not necessary to ask you to please be careful and take care of yourself and our child—but I'm asking anyway. And I do want you to have fun with your cousin."

Lauren squeezed his hands. "I know you do, and Jackson, I love this child. I would never put myself or our baby at risk." She resolved in that instant to have a talk with Max, and put an end to any *serious* sleuthing when they went back to the city tomorrow. "And Max and I always have fun together."

He relaxed, and let go of her hands. "I'd better get dressed, or I won't have time for my one cup of coffee before leaving for the gallery." He gave her a quick kiss on the forehead and headed for the bathroom.

Lauren wandered back to the windows to see that the rain had slowed to a drizzle. She trailed a finger along the back of the chair she'd leaned against and hoped the hollow feeling in her stomach was hunger and not misgivings about Max.

Her cousin looked like a Fifth Avenue model that could charm a cougar out of a tree, but Lauren wondered if under the makeup, the clothes, and pleasant manners, still lurked the same old Max.

# CHAPTER FOURTEEN

# The Guest

Passing the open door to Brooke's bedroom, Lauren paused, surprised to see that the room was empty. Brooke usually straggled down just in time to inhale a bowl of cereal and catch an early ride to school with her dad.

As Lauren neared the bottom of the stairs, she heard murmurs of conversation. She passed between the entry columns from the dining room into the morning room. Brooke sat as close to Max as was possible and not be in her lap. They were engrossed in fastening a bracelet onto Brooke's arm.

As soon as Brooke spotted Lauren she dashed from the floral overstuffed sofa, and held her wrist inches from Lauren's face.

"Look what Max gave me!"

Lauren took hold of the slim wrist and lowered it a bit. "Ohh, how very pretty! I may have to borrow it sometime." She admired the gift appropriately before glancing at Max. "How long have you been up? I didn't hear you."

Brooke had hurried back to Max's side. And now admiring her new bracelet, she volunteered the answer to Lauren's question before Max could answer.

"We've been up for an hour. Max likes to watch it rain—I do too, but I didn't know it before."

Max laughed softly and patted the sofa for Lauren to have a seat with them. "I'm an early riser. At home I go to bed early, and I get up early." She glanced toward the windows. "Watching it rain is one of my very favorite things to do." She looked at Brooke. "And camping in the mountains in the cabin while it rains, is the very best." She patted Brooke's knee. "You'll have to come try it sometime."

"I will! If Dad will let me."

Lauren sat next to Max on the sofa and traced a hole in Max's jeans, just above the knee. "Now this is more like the cousin I used to know." She laughed and continued her scrutiny of Max's appearance. The sleek hairdo of the evening before had reverted back to its natural curl and volume. Caught back in a loose ponytail, the warm highlights in her dark hair shone more in its natural relaxed state. "We're still the same size." Lauren glanced down and passed a hand over her stomach. "Except for this, so you may borrow anything of mine you'd like."

"Thanks, but if you're not afraid I'll offend your friends, I'll just be me." She grinned. "I even brought my old hat for shock affect."

Brooke danced to the bar and carefully set the worn, camel-colored felt hat on her head. The hat sported a leather and silver hatband. She swaggered toward Lauren and Max, but turned when Jackson entered the room and raced to his side.

"Dad, look what Max gave me!" She thrust her arm with the bracelet into the air inches from his face. "And this is her hat!"

"My goodness, what a nice gift—you look like a real cowgirl."

Brooke dashed to the bar and grabbed Lauren's cell phone. "Take a picture of me! I have to show Mandy."

Jackson took the phone. "Just say when."

Brooke held her hand close to her face, showing the bracelet and did a fake smile. While holding the smile, she mouthed, "When."

Jackson lowered the phone. "Are you sure that's your smile . . . ?"

"Da-a-d! Now!"

He took several pictures then cast a wary glance at Lauren before handing the phone back to Brooke and picking up his coffee cup. He strolled over to sit in a chair across from Lauren and Max. He glanced toward the bar where Brooke was carefully replacing the hat. "Where did she learn to pose?"

Lauren sighed. "She goes to school with several dozen other little girls who are all ten and twelve going on sixteen—they watch television. Besides, she feels grown up wearing the bracelet and an authentic cowgirl hat."

"Well, can you edit the photos and bring her smile back?"

Max and Lauren shared a laugh and Lauren said, "I'm not *that* good in Photoshop."

He settled into the chair and balanced his cup. "A belated good morning, Max! Did you sleep well?" He sipped his coffee.

"Yes, thank you. I slept like a log until I heard the storm roll in, and I had to get up and watch it."

Lauren nodded and smiled. "I thought you might like that room. You watched the storm from the balcony?"

"Yes. Thank you. You were thoughtful to remember that I like storms."

Lauren smiled at her cousin. "You're welcome. I remember a lot of things about you.

Jackson perked up. "Share some of the things you remember. Since I know nothing about Max, it'll help me get to know her better." He glanced from one to the other as Brooke rejoined them and sat on the arm of her dad's chair, her arm around his neck.

Lauren wished she hadn't said anything. But now she had to follow through since Jackson wanted to be included in their reminiscing. He waited, smiling along with Max.

"I remember you could whistle loud and long enough to break my eardrums and make the cows run to the barn."

Max laughed and nodded. "I could."

Brooke bounced off the chair arm and landed at Max's side once more. "Can you still do it?" She gazed wide-eyed at Max.

"Yeah, it's like riding a horse, you never forget once you learn."

Brooke inched closer. "Will you show me?"

Max gazed at Brooke as if considering a demonstration. "I can show you, but at low volume. Aunt

Will left earlier I believe to make phone calls, we don't want to disturb her. Will that work?"

Brooke nodded, her eyes wide.

Max locked the fingers on her hands a certain way and placed them to her lips. A lonely wail started as if it came from a distance and rose to a low pitch that seemed to go on and on until she dropped her hands to her lap. Every one was quiet. Max glanced at Brooke. "That's how you do it."

Jackson ran his hand through his hair and down the back of his neck. "That sound made my hair stand up."

Max laughed and Brooke continued to stare wide-eyed. She reached for Max's hands and studied them. "But what made the sound? It didn't come from you."

"Sure, it came from me." She held both hands up, fingers spread. "See, no whistle. Sounds were the way the Indians communicated in the old days."

"Did an Indian teach you how to do it?" Brooke asked.

"Yes, actually. He was an Indian and a cowboy. He was our ranch foreman when I was growing up, still is." Max smiled at Lauren and grew thoughtful. "I took every step he did. He taught me to ride and he let me help gather cattle on branding day."

Lauren bit her lip to keep from laughing at the expressions on Jackson and Brooke's faces. They were struck speechless.

Max gazed at Brooke. "You should come spend a summer on the ranch and learn to ride. We have a young mare that would be perfect for you."

The wide amber eyes flashed at Jackson the moment Max finished speaking.

"Could I, Dad?"

Jackson darted a glance at Lauren. "I don't know, Brooke, we can talk about it later. You've never mentioned riding or anything to do with horses—do you think you'd like to learn to ride horseback?"

Her wide gaze never wavered. "I would, Dad."

"Why haven't you ever said anything about taking lessons?"

Brooke spread her fingers, palms up. "How could I? I didn't have a horse!" She glanced at Max. "I barely got a dog!"

Lauren cast a glance at Jackson—sure enough his stricken eyes met hers. He'd felt bad about not allowing Brooke to have a dog for so long. Lauren smiled, giving him a, 'we've got a secret look' and he quickly recovered.

"As a matter of fact, Lauren and I wondered if you'd like to take riding lessons."

"Yes, yes I would, please!" She jumped from the sofa and ran threw her arms around her dad's neck. "When can I, and where would we get a horse? Where would we keep my horse—"

"Hold on, one thing at a time. I've already contacted a riding stable and we have an appointment to go out and look around. We don't have to worry about a horse right now."

Brooke could hardly speak. "When do we go?"

"This coming Saturday."

Brooke counted the days on her fingers. "That's just four days!"

Lauren said, "Jackson, tell her the rest of the surprise."

He gazed at Lauren. "I wasn't sure that part had been worked out yet—"

Lauren nodded. "It has been."

Jackson hugged Brooke. "I'll let Lauren tell you the rest of it—it was her idea."

Lauren said, "It's something you can't tell right away—can you keep a secret for another day or two?"

Brooke nodded. "I can keep secrets."

There was a look in her eyes that let Lauren know that Brooke had a particular secret in mind. Lauren had suspected there was a secret to do with school, now she was sure.

"I spoke with Mandy's mom and about Mandy coming with us to the stables and she said yes. She may take lessons also. But her mother wants to talk with her father first, so don't say anything until Mandy mentions it."

"I won't!" Brooke danced around the room clapping her hands and hugging everyone.

Jackson stood. "Enough celebrating for now, it's time you and I were going." He nodded to Brooke. "Run and get your things."

"Yes, sir!" She ran to hug Lauren bye first, then shyly went to hug Max. "I think you're a good luck person, and I wish you lived with us, too!"

Max blinked and glanced at Lauren. "Miss Brooke, you're one of the sweetest persons I've ever met, and I think you may be the good luck one." Max gave her a squeeze. "I'll see you this evening."

\*\*\*

After Jackson and Brooke had gone, Lauren refreshed their coffee and raised the cover from a serving dish to find a fresh batch of Aunt Willa's apple strudel.

"Yum! You have to try this strudel. It's scrumptious."

"I know. I've already had some." Max joined her. "This is a lovely antique sideboard."

Lauren glanced at it. "Yes, it is, and we do it a disservice by calling it the serving bar."

The coffee maker, along with the strudel, boiled eggs, and toast set on the piece of antique furniture. Aunt Willa had put the food out earlier. Lauren glanced toward the kitchen. "I can't believe Aunt Willa wasn't here to say bye to Jackson and Brooke. That isn't like her. I hope she's feeling all right."

Max carried a plate and her coffee back to the seating area. "She seemed fine. All she said was that she had to make several phone calls."

Lauren sat her strudel and coffee on the table next to her chair. "I think I'll check just to be sure." But just as she reached the kitchen door, Aunt Willa met her.

"Good morning, dear. Did you find the fresh strudel?"

"Yes we did, it looks wonderful. I was worried about you when you weren't here to say bye to Jackson. . . ." Lauren watched Jackson's aunt as she moved to the sideboard and began pouring a cup of coffee.

"Yes, I'm sorry I didn't get off the phone in time. But I missed a call from an old friend yesterday, and I needed to return it." She smiled at Lauren. "Sadly, she's not doing well. Thank you, dear, for worrying about me."

"Of course I would worry about you—when you break your routine."

"Thank you, dear. This is a lovely rain," she said.

Max stood and went to stand at the windows. "Yes, it is. Gardens are even more beautiful in the rain." She turned to Lauren. "What time are we seeing the gallery?"

"Anytime. I thought we might have a long visit here before we head out."

"Oh, we can visit tomorrow morning as we drive into the city. Show me the town—and let's run by the gallery. I may be showing there someday, if Jackson was serious."

Lauren laughed. "You may rest assured Jackson wouldn't have mentioned it if he didn't want your work. So, we'll see the town." Lauren carried her plate and cup toward the kitchen. "We should probably go ahead and dress, that way we won't have to run back before lunch and coffee with the girls." She glanced at Max.

Max stood and spread her fingers, palms up. "I am dressed." She looked down. "See, I have on clothes.

Aunt Willa chuckled behind her cup.

Lauren rolled her eyes and continued to the kitchen. Matthew and the girls would be in for a surprise—or a treat.

# CHAPTER FIFTEEN

# Bronze Art

Jackson guided the Range Rover into the school lane and followed the procession of other parents dropping their children off. Brooke's chatter hadn't slowed down from the moment they left the driveway at home.

He would be glad to deliver her to school. After the same question was asked the third time, Brooke said, "Dad, you're not listening."

"Sorry, sweetheart, I'm not tracking very well this morning, am I?"

"You didn't answer my question. What will I do about a horse?"

"Oh, well, the stables keep what they call school horses, they're just for lessons. We'll have to see how it goes before we consider buying a horse. Owning a horse is a big responsibility—" He glanced at her excited face and remembered the times she'd asked for a dog. He would handle this better. "Let's take one step at a time. First make sure you like horses and whether or not you enjoy riding. Okay?" He came to a stop at the sidewalk.

"Okay, Dad, but I know I will." She opened the door, flashed a big smile and gathered her backpack before sliding out of the seat. "And I want a hat just like Max's."

She banged the door shut and raced up the walk toward the wide double doors of the school. Jackson sighed, the slamming of the door echoing in his head. The first inkling of concern raised its worrisome head, a hat, just like Max's? Would she want riding lessons only because Max rode?

Jackson entered the gallery at the back entry to the smell of Matt's fresh coffee. He barely remembered the cup he'd had at home. Suddenly he heard again the low lonely sound Max had made with nothing but her hands and her breath. How did she do that? He'd been as fascinated as Brooke had been. He couldn't wait to talk to Matt about the possibility of having another bronze artist in the gallery.

"I thought I heard you come in. The coffee's ready."

"Yeah, I smell it." He headed to the break room and Matt followed. "I may have found another bronze artist for the gallery."

"Great. Where did you find him?" Matt reached for the mugs. "Someone we know?"

"He's a her. Remember I told you Lauren had a cousin—in Colorado?" Jackson gazed at Matt. "I went online and looked at her work. She's really pretty good." Jackson stirred a healthy dollop of rich cream into his coffee and grinned sideways at Matt. "Max Quinn's her name. She's very personable and pretty, like Lauren—only in a different way. And she'd certainly liven up an art show in Valley Ridge."

"So, she has more assets than just her bronze works?" Matt had a funny expression on his face. "I get the feeling there's a *but* coming—what's the catch? A prima donna?"

Jackson shook his head. "No! Anything but."

Matt shrugged. "Well, what's the catch? She can't be talked into showing with a small town gallery?"

"Matt—there's no catch. I think she will show with us. She'd be pleasant to work with."

Matt stood and headed for the office. He paused and looked at Jackson. "Great. We've been considering another bronze artist for years. We only have Scott Houser, and he's rumored to be slowing down production."

Jackson topped off his cup and followed Matt toward the office. "I get the feeling you're hesitant for some reason."

"Oh no, I just keep waiting for the other shoe to drop."

Jackson slouched into his chair. "There's no other shoe and no buts . . . it's just that, well Max is different and Brooke fell completely under her spell."

"I don't understand?" Matt swiveled his chair to face Jackson.

"Max is not your average woman, she's really different." Jackson heard censure in his voice. He didn't like it, but neither could he help it. "She was raised on a ranch and still works as a cowhand in a pinch."

Matt chuckled. "It's honest work I suppose. Why do you care what she does as long as she's a good bronze artist?"

Jackson leaned forward, his forearms on his knees, hands clasped. "She's Lauren's cousin—a working relationship with her could expose Brooke to a way of life that's . . . that's different." He could understand that Matt wouldn't realize the impact an association with someone like Max could have on Brooke as she was growing up. He hadn't told Matt about the trouble at school.

Matt laughed and turned back to his computer. "I think you're looking for trouble."

Jackson plowed his hand through his hair. Yeah, Matt's child wasn't even a year old. He could afford to laugh now. "Maybe so, but I wouldn't have thought about Brooke reacting to Max as strongly as she has. I still want Max in the gallery, but we have to be careful. I may consider sending Brooke to boarding school."

Matt glanced at him and shook his head.

"I know, I know, but just wait until you meet Max. She and Lauren are coming by before they meet at your house for coffee with the girls—you'll see."

"Good. I'll try not to let my mouth hang open when I meet her."

Jackson laughed. "It's not that bad, but I have an impressionable daughter at home. And I don't want her to grow up and move off to live on a ranch in Colorado."

They looked at one another with raised brows when the conversation coming from the gallery showroom grew loud with laughter.

Jackson eased out of his chair and stepped to the door. One of the gallery artists, Maria Dawes had come in and found Maggie with a client, which happened to be one of Maria's biggest fans. The incident prompted the rowdy greeting.

Matt rose from his chair and he and Jackson strolled into the gallery showroom and greeted Maria. Maria's work was among their best sellers. Her lively, colorful ocean scenes had proven to be very popular.

Matt suggested that Maggie take her client and Maria to lunch at the club.

Sonya would be there in case the guys were lucky enough to talk Lauren and Max into having lunch with them. After lunch plans were settled, Jackson trailed Matt back to their office.

"That was a happy accident," Matt said. "For Maria to run into a fan here."

"Yes, it was." He glanced at his watch. It was close to eleven o'clock. He wondered what time Lauren and Max would stop by. He'd barely gotten to work on a spreadsheet when the bell jangled softly. Expecting it to be Brooke, Jackson didn't glance up until Matt stood and spoke to Lauren and Max.

"Hi, Lauren. And you must be Max. Pleased to meet you." Matt held out his hand.

Max clasped Matt's hand. Jackson observed that the smile on her face was enough to make a man believe she'd been waiting all her life just to meet him.

"I'm glad to meet you too, Matt. Lauren's told me that you and Ally are two of her closest friends." She stepped back and pushed her hands into the pockets of her faded jeans, worn threadbare at the knees.

Jackson had stepped around to Lauren and stood with his arm draped casually around her shoulders.

"Did you girls get enough visiting this morning? And do you have time for a quick lunch at the club?"

Lauren glanced at Max. "Yes, we had a long visit. And we do have time for lunch."

Jackson motioned for Max to follow him into the showroom as he continued talking. "But first I want you to see the work of the other bronze artist we handle." Jackson led her to a dark oak pedestal with a statue of a woman holding a small child, the wind blowing her skirt and hair as she gazed into the distance. "Scott Houser. His work sells very well."

Max studied the bronze statue. "Yes, I know Scott—this is very typical of his work—his careful attention to detail."

"You know Scott personally?" Jackson regretted the surprise in his voice.

Max nodded. "I met him years ago at a workshop. We did some fly fishing together."

Matt's ears perked up. "Fly fishing, hmm." Matt grinned at Jackson "We've heard he may start slowing down his production pace?"

"I wouldn't doubt it. He's building a cabin in the wilds somewhere and needs a break from work to finish it. He's been threatening to cut back for years."

Max and Jackson wandered on to another piece of Scott's work. Max ran her hands over the cool metal.

"He's very good. I see why he sells so well." She crossed her arms and walked slowly around the pedestal. "I have three of his pieces from when he was only doing animals."

"Animals? Really? All we've ever had are figurative." Jackson was amazed to learn that Scott had at one time only done animals.

Matt and Lauren approached them.

"If we plan to have lunch, we really should head to the club before it gets crowded." Matt suggested.

After letting the other sales girl Sonya, know they were going to lunch everyone climbed into Jackson's vehicle and continued visiting on the drive to the club. Once inside, the waiter ushered them to their usual tablet. Jackson waved away the menu. "I'll have my usual."

The waiter nodded.

Matt studied his menu briefly and ordered the same salad he always ordered as well.

Lauren glanced at her menu and laid it aside. "I'll have my usual." She leaned toward Max. "The Caesar salad is—"

"I'm too hungry for just a salad." Max scanned the menu. "I'll have the small rib eye and a plain Caesar with iced tea." She smiled at the waiter. "And a couple of rolls, please."

Matt cast a furtive glance at Jackson and grinned.

Lauren reached for her menu. "On second thought, a change sounds good. I'll have the same as Max."

Jackson had worried about Max's influence on Brooke. It looked like Lauren wasn't immune to her either. Lauren thought a change sounded good? He suddenly had a hollow feeling in his stomach.

# CHAPTER SIXTEEN

# Back to Normal

Lauren sneaked a glance at her wrist and groaned. Soon it would be time to meet at Ally's for coffee and she was stuffed from too much lunch. There wasn't room for a cup of coffee.

Why had she changed her order? Keeping up with Max had been a childhood thing. She didn't have to do that now, so *why* had she changed her order? To compound her misery, the expression on Jackson's face told her he knew what she was doing. In defiance of his silent disapproval, she ate everything on her plate.

Now she was paying the price, and there wasn't enough elastic in her maternity slacks to ease the discomfort. To make matters worse, Max picked up the dessert menu and looked at Lauren.

"What do you think?" Max raised her brows. "We could share."

From her peripheral vision Lauren saw Jackson glance quickly at her. "Not for me," she said. "Besides, we're due shortly at Ally's for coffee, and she'll have a pie or something."

"Oh yes, I forgot." Max tossed the small dessert menu back to the middle of the table.

Matt laughed, shaking his head. "How do you stay so slim with such a hearty appetite?"

Max widened her eyes and laughed along with Matt. "I don't eat this way everyday. I'm on holiday." She sipped her water and said, "Sometimes I get busy and go for days hardly eating at all."

Jackson joined in. "I'm relieved to hear that! It might have created a problem for Lauren." He glanced from one to the other. "I mean keeping up. . . ."

Lauren returned his look. "You need not worry about me, Jackson. I have room to splurge on special occasions." Though she smiled, her tone let Jackson know she didn't appreciate his comment. She gathered her bag and sweater and glanced at Max. "We probably should be going. I have to make a stop on the way to Ally's."

Max grabbed her oversized leather bag. "Sure. I'm ready."

Matt stood, and Jackson slowly unfolded from his chair. He motioned to their waiter, who nodded, and the group moved toward the door. Jackson put the tab on his account, the same one he'd had at the club since his teens.

Outside in the crisp cool air, Lauren pulled on her sweater and turned to Jackson. "We'll be home before you. Shall I pick Brooke up from school?"

Jackson pulled her into his arms. "I'm sure Brooke would love that." He gave her a hug before they joined Matt and Max for the drive back to the gallery.

\*\*\*

After the guys let them out at Lauren's SUV and they were headed for Ally's house, Max turned her gaze on Lauren. "I like Jackson. I see why you fell for the countryside around Valley Ridge."

Lauren laughed. "I told you it wasn't entirely the countryside that made me stay in Valley Ridge." She took her eyes off the road to peer at Max. "I'm glad you like Jackson. He's a good person to confide in— why don't you tell him everything you've told me and let him and Matt look into your toad client's background?"

"No, I want to do this myself. If it looks like the situation might get sticky, I'll reconsider."

Lauren nodded. "I understand, but I don't want you to take any risks." She looked at Max again when she burst into laughter. "What's so funny?"

"You are." Max sobered. "I never told you that I almost got my investigator's license. I know not to take risks."

"The point is—you may not *know* it is a risk until it's too late. What do you mean, *you almost got your license?*"

Max looked out of her window for several seconds before turning back to Lauren. "On a whim and for fun, I went through training for an investigators license."

"Then why didn't you get the license?"

Max sighed. "I don't really know. Whitney, I suppose. She was terrified something would happen to me and she'd be alone."

"Ohhh, I see." They drove in silence for a good stretch. "Max, we must never lose touch again. We're family, we need to stay close."

Max leaned her head back on the headrest, her face toward Lauren. "Yes, I'm glad you feel that way, we must stay close. I'll see if I can persuade Whitney to break away for a few days at Thanksgiving and come with me."

"That would be great if you could!" Lauren's spirit suddenly lifted. "Simply great!" Ally's drive was up ahead. "Well, here we are!"

Clair's white Lexus sat in the drive. Lauren smiled to herself. Clair and Ally couldn't wait to meet Max.

Max smiled. "Hmm, nice townhouse."

"Uh-huh and it's gorgeous inside. Ally's done a fantastic job of decorating."

Before they could knock, Polly, the housekeeper opened the door for them. "Hello, girls, the others are waiting." With a big smile she directed them to the sun room."

Lauren took Max's arm. "Clair, Ally, this is my cousin—Max Quinn." Lauren glanced from one to the other. "Max knows you guys—I've told her everything about you both."

Clair took Max by the arm and ushered her to the sofa. "And you were still willing to have coffee with us?"

Max glanced at Ally and said, "Not only willing, but anxious—Lauren speaks of you both as paragons of everything good."

Clair raised her brows and smirked at Lauren as she settled onto the sofa next to Max.

Almost shyly, Ally sat on the other side, sandwiching Max between her and Clair.

Moments of light banter helped break the ice.

Two hours, a pot of coffee, and a plate of scones later, Lauren pushed her sleeve back and looked at her watch then glanced at Max. "We need to be going. I told Jackson I'd pick Brooke up from school."

Max nodded and moved to the edge of the sofa. Looking first to Ally, and then to Clair, she said, "This has been fun, girls. Lauren is lucky to have you two in her corner."

Clair caught Max's hand in a light squeeze. "We are the lucky ones! If not for Lauren, Ally and I would never have met."

"Lots of things wouldn't have happened if not for Lauren." Ally nodded. "Yes, we have a lot to thank Lauren for."

Lauren stood, and the others did the same. "Max, we'd better leave before their *thanking me* turns into *blaming me!*"

They laughed and chatted as they ambled toward the door.

Later as Lauren and Max buckled their seatbelts, Lauren still smiled over the parting remarks, but her thoughts were already moving ahead to the next day in New York. What would they encounter? As the time drew nearer, her apprehension grew, and she wished she'd insisted that Max include Jackson in their plan.

In *Max's* plan.

They were quiet on the drive to school. As Lauren pulled into the pick-up lane she immediately spotted

Brooke and Mandy with the girl who'd intentionally knocked the books from Mandy's arms only days before. They appeared to be talking. As the girl spoke, Brooke moved closer to Mandy.

Max followed Lauren's gaze. "What's going on with the girls?"

Lauren shook her head. "I'm not sure, but I don't think it's good."

Max already had her hand on the door handle. "Let's find out." She had bailed to the sidewalk and was strolling toward the girls as Lauren hurried around the Range Rover and caught up with her.

The girls hadn't noticed them approaching.

"Hey, Brooke, what's up?" Lauren smiled brightly, looking from one to the other. The other girl glanced at Lauren and quickly hurried away. "Is that a new friend?"

Brooke darted a look at Mandy. "Um, yes, she's new."

Mandy was staring up at Max. With wide eyes, she turned to Brooke. "She *really* is a cowgirl!"

"I told you so!" Brooke giggled and grabbed Lauren's sleeve. "Please, please can Mandy spend the night—she wants to hear Max whistle!"

Max was laughing and looking to Lauren. "That would be fun, don't you think, Lauren?"

"What about your mother—will she care?"

"We've already called her and she said yes if it was okay with you."

Lauren glanced at Mandy. "Well, call your mom back and let her know." She turned to Max, "We'll load Mandy's bike in the back." Then to Mandy she said, "Run get your bike." Lauren opened the back of the Range Rover as both girls ran toward the bike rack.

Max edged closer to Lauren. "I got the feeling that something was going on with those three. Mandy seemed angry, but Brooke looked apprehensive—I'm sure of it."

Lauren watched the girls wheeling the bike toward the Range Rover. "Uh-huh, me too."

The new girl was definitely up to something. Lauren had also seen apprehension in Brooke's face. The sooner she found out what was going on, the better.

But tomorrow she had to go with Max to New York. Lauren wondered if there was anyway she'd get Max on a plane bound for home, without getting herself in hot water with Jackson. The bike was loaded and the girls settled in the back seat as Lauren gripped the steering wheel tighter and tried to relax.

She'd have to figure it all later. She squared her shoulders and headed for home.

# CHAPTER SEVENTEEN

# Apprehension

Lauren smiled and strained to hold her eyes open. Would the evening never end? Brooke and Mandy's energy was draining. After dinner Max had told them stories about the ranch and had done the cattle whistle over and over as they were sure if they could hear it just one more time, they'd figure out how she was doing it.

Aunt Willa dozed off and on in her chair until Jackson came to the rescue. He tapped his wrist and said, "Bedtime, girls."

Brooke was sitting on the floor close to Max. She scrambled to her knees and lurched toward Jackson's chair. "Dad, could we just—?

Jackson was shaking his head as she knee-walked toward him. "No, ma'am. It's bedtime. School tomorrow."

"Shoot!"

"Mind your manners, Miss."

Grinning, and casting a glance at Max, Brooke said, "Yes, sir." She jumped to her feet and gave her dad a hug. "Good night, Dad. Can Lauren and Max take us to school in the morning?"

He glanced to Lauren. "I'm not sure what time they're leaving for the city. . . ?"

Max said, "My flight's not until the afternoon." She glanced at Lauren. "We could leave early and drop the girls by school. If that's okay with you, Lauren?"

"Oh . . . sure. Fine with me." She glanced at Jackson. He seemed to want to say something, but decided not to. She was relieved he didn't start questing them.

After the girls had told everyone goodnight and gone upstairs, Jackson laughed and pushed a hand through his hair. "Thanks for your patience, Max, but I admit I enjoyed hearing about life on a cattle ranch myself."

Max moved to the sofa and stretched her legs onto the ottoman. "I'm glad you did. Talking about the ranch reminds me of why I love it so much, and I've enjoyed the girls."

Lauren sighed. "They have way too much energy at this time of the evening."

After chatting for a while, Max got up. "Speaking of energy, mine's all gone. I think I'll get a shower and turn in. So, goodnight, everyone."

Aunt Willa said, "Goodnight, dear. We'll you see in the morning."

Max smiled. "Yes, bright and early." She turned to Lauren. "What time do you take the girls to school?"

Lauren thought for a moment. "Eight-thirty."

"Good." At the door she turned and said, "Today was great, thanks."

Aunt Willa smiled "What a charming girl! I'm headed for bed too. Goodnight."

Jackson and Lauren chorused "Goodnight, Aunt Willa."

They sat for a while without speaking, enjoying the peace and quiet for the first time that day. Lauren broke the silence. "I'd like to be upstairs in our room, but I'm too lazy to climb the stairs."

Jackson raised his head from where it rested on the chair. "I could try to carry you up, but we might not make it—there've been too many chips and cookies under the bridge—"

Lauren laughed and threw a pillow at him. "I've cut way back. Dr. Stinson is pleased with my weight."

Jackson quickly stood and crossed the room to take her hand. "Come on. I'll go first and pull you up."

"I'll take that." She allowed him to help her up.

As they reached the top of the stairs, Max opened her door. She had a towel around her head and was wearing one of Lauren's robes. She laughed at the sight of Jackson huffing and pretending to push Lauren toward their door.

"Lauren, could I see you for a moment before you go to bed?"

"Uh-huh." She kissed Jackson. "Thanks for the help, sweetie. I'll be right back."

"You girls don't start talking and stay up all night. You have a long day tomorrow." He raised his brows at Lauren before he entered their bedroom and closed the door.

Lauren sighed, Jackson's raised brows were a meaningful signal—like, you are carrying our son, be careful! If he only knew what Max was up to tomorrow, he'd send her off to New York by herself. But Lauren couldn't back out now and leave Max on her own.

Max stood waiting by the door. "You look very thoughtful to have been giggling like a schoolgirl moments ago."

"Yes, I am thoughtful. I'm worried about tomorrow—what if something awful happens?"

Max took her hand. "Come sit down. That's what I wanted to speak with you about." She settled on the chintz loveseat next to Lauren. "Nothing awful is going to happen. But you don't need to go with me. I can handle this with my client—"

"I'm going with you and that's that!"

"Just listen to me. I didn't realize you were expecting a child when I wrote you about this, and like Whitney said, it's not really a problem. I'm just curious, as you know, but I can back off at any time." She gave Lauren a raised brow gaze much like Jackson had, then continued. "Why don't I take a cab into the city and you stay here and rest tomorrow?"

Lauren studied Max's face for a long moment. "I *know* you and you are going to find out what's going on—no matter what happens. I'm going with you."

Max stood and repositioned the towel around her head. "You're not being fair. Had I known you were expecting, I'd never have mentioned all this you."

"And how would I feel reading about you in the—"

"Oh good grief, Lauren! Nothing bad is going to happen." She sat back down on the loveseat.

"Good! If you're sure nothing is going to happen, then I can go without worrying." She stood. "I'd better get back to Jackson, or he'll think we've decide to talk all night." Lauren headed toward the door and paused to look back. "If something does happen, if we get into trouble, you know Jackson will never forgive either one of us."

"Come back here—!" Max hissed as Lauren closed the door behind her.

Hurrying to her room, afraid Max might try to catch her; Lauren sailed into the bedroom and quickly closed the door.

Jackson glanced at her and dropped the book he was reading into his lap. "Something wrong?"

"Nothing's wrong." She moved away from the door. "Just a long day and I'm tired."

Uh-oh, that was the wrong thing to say. Jackson put his book on the bed, scooted over, and motioned for her to come. She ambled over and sat on the bed.

"You don't really need to drive Max back to New York. She wouldn't mind taking a cab, or I'll drive her. You stay home and rest, okay?"

"Thank you, Jackson. You're sweet to offer to drive Max to the city, but I want to go with her and it shouldn't be too tiring." She gazed at him, wanting to tell him about Max's suspicions of a possible smuggling ring.

He huffed. "I'm not trying to be sweet for Max's sake, I'm worried about you."

Lauren didn't want him to get started on her lack of rest. He still worried about the trip to Italy. He'd even called Dr. Stinson behind her back. The doctor gave him away at her last visit. She tried to look rested by widening her eyes and giving him a bright smile.

"That's your phony smile, " he said dryly.

She rose quickly from the bed, went to her closet and grabbed a robe and started to the bathroom. At the door she leaned against it. "I promise to rest all weekend."

"You can't rest all weekend. Saturday we're taking Brooke and Mandy to the riding stables and Sunday is church." He stared back at her. "And then we'll be getting ready to go to Italy."

Lauren rubbed her forehead. "Okay! I'll rest all day, the day after tomorrow—I'll even stay in bed all day if you want me to!" She turned and escaped into the shower. She was glad Jackson loved their child so much, but she was tired of being worried over. He seemed to think she should act like an invalid.

But deep inside a voice nagged, how would she ever explain or expect Jackson to understand if something happened while she was helping Max. She turned the water on full blast and closed her mind to that possibility.

*\*\**

There had been no need to set an alarm since she always woke early, but to her surprise, Jackson was not in bed and no sounds were coming from the bathroom. When she peeked inside there were damp towels and water spots; proof he'd already been there.

Lauren dressed quickly, keeping a watch on the time because she wanted to have breakfast with the others before everyone scattered in their different directions.

When she entered the morning room, Aunt Willa, Max, and both girls were chatting like old friends. Aunt Willa had made breakfast scones and fruit salad.

"And I thought I was early. How long has everyone been up?"

Max laughed. "You have to be downstairs earlier than seven-thirty to beat us."

Brooke chimed in. "Mandy and me got up when Max did. We waited for her to come out of her room."

"Hmm, I see. You're all such a bunch of early birds." She glanced around. "Where's Jackson?"

Aunt Willa said, "There was a business meeting at the gallery this morning. He just left."

Lauren choked back a sting of regret. She hadn't given Jackson a chance to tell her he'd be leaving early—or had he decided to leave early after her rude offer to stay in bed all day?

Max came to sit beside her on the sofa. "How long do you plan to stir that coffee?"

"Oh, my mind was on something."

"You don't have to drive me back to the city."

"Please, not again." Lauren sipped the hot coffee.

Max patted her knee. "Well then, we'll head to the city as soon as we drop the girls off." She rose to refresh her coffee and loaded a plate with fruit and a scone before wandering over to join Aunt Willa.

Lauren watched Brooke and Mandy giggling and trying on Max's hat. She'd taken a big gulp of hot coffee and scorched her tongue. She wanted to call Jackson and apologize for last night. But she wouldn't because in a pang of guilt, she might blurt out everything else.

A little later Brooke ran and plopped on the sofa beside her. "Could we leave early?" She moved closer and almost whispered, "Mandy and I have to make sure the chalkboards are clean every morning." She put her mouth close to Lauren's ear. "It's our punishment, remember?"

"Yes, I remember—whenever you're ready."

"Um, I think we're ready."

"Gather your things." She carried the half-full cup of coffee to the kitchen. "Max, I think the girls want to leave a little early if you're ready."

Max and Aunt Willa rose from their chairs and shared a hug before Max joined the girls. "I'm ready. My things are by the door."

Lauren seldom hugged Aunt Willa before leaving for the day, but she needed the comfort of Aunt Willa's arms. She went and put her arms around her. "Aunt Willa, if I decide to stay overnight, I'll call."

"Do you think you may spend the night?"

"Probably not, but you never know." Lauren glanced at Max.

She was giving herself an excuse in case she *needed* to stay overnight.

# CHAPTER EIGHTEEN

# The Client

On the drive to school Lauren recalled the incident on the schoolyard the day before. She hadn't told Jackson about it, which was probably as well. Better to do fact checking before jumping in.

So many things crowded her thoughts—the mystery at school, possible riding lessons, Max, the art exhibit . . . how would she work it all in and rest enough to keep Jackson from worrying?

"It's your turn," Max said.

"My turn—?"

Max waved a hand. "The drop off, people are waiting."

"Oh, sorry people." Lauren quickly guided the Range Rover into position. "Kisses and hugs, girls!" After many promises to write and send pictures to Max, they were on the sidewalk with Mandy's bike— that Max unloaded, in her four-inch heels. The girls hurried to put the bike in the stand and gave one last wave as they ran toward the large entry doors.

Max slid into the passenger seat and followed Lauren's gaze. "What are we looking for?"

She moved out of other parents' way and continued searching the playgrounds. "The young girl we saw Brooke and Mandy with the other day." Lauren scanned the groups of children. "I don't see her."

"Do you think she's bullying the girls?"

Lauren sighed. "I think Mandy more than Brooke. The times I've witnessed, it seems directed at Mandy."

"Mandy's so sweet and friendly, what would cause another child to dislike her?"

"Who knows what makes children do what they do." Lauren's gaze swept the schoolyard one more time. "Maybe the girl is absent today. I'll have a talk with the girls' teacher tomorrow." No, she had to rest tomorrow; she'd promised Jackson—unless she could somehow work it in.

Gathering speed as they left the city limits, Lauren decided the butterflies in her stomach might be from excitement to what lay ahead—not fear. It had been a long time since she and Max had been grounded. She turned to Max. "How long has it been since you and I got in trouble together?"

Max pursed her lips and her brows rose. "Lets see—way *too* long?" They giggled and tried to remember the very last time, as girls, they'd been grounded.

"Remember that Saturday when your mother took us to the park? We were not to play with the stray dog that was hanging about?"

Lauren smiled. "And we slipped around and gave him our lunch and used my best sweater to make a bed for him."

Max laughed. "Then later we helped your mother search and search for that sweater." She sighed. "That poor old dog needed that sweater a lot more than you did."

Lauren nodded. "Yes, he did, and I gladly sacrificed it." She'd forgotten about that dog. He'd haunted her dreams for days after seeing him in the park so thin and hungry.

"But it doesn't count if we didn't get caught—does it?"

Lauren thought for a moment. "I guess not if we're remembering the last time we actually got in trouble."

Max said, "Your mother was the only person we ever got in trouble with. Mom and Dad were probably too easy on me."

"Yeah, I was envious." Suddenly Lauren didn't want to remember those days. She'd rather think of the possible trouble they were headed for now. She glanced over at Max, once again looking like a fashion model.

"So, what's the plan when we reach the city?"

"Let's go straight to the gallery." She returned Lauren's gaze. "We might as well start there. I hope the owner is in."

Lauren mumbled, "I hope he's not. Anyway, if he is, what are you going to do, or say?" She slowed her speed as they approached the city.

Applying fresh lipstick, Max spoke through stiff lips. "I'll go in first, you wait twenty to thirty minutes then stroll in."

"Wait thirty minutes then go in?"

Max dropped the lipstick into her tiny bag. "Yes. We'll pretend not to notice one another at first. But if I think I need you, I'll suddenly recognize you."

"And if you don't need me?"

"I'll simply walk out the door and shortly after you can join me down the street, or back at the Range Rover."

Lauren maneuvered the city traffic on the busy streets until she was within blocks of their destination. "We're two blocks away, do you want to get closer than that?"

"I have on four-inch heels—yes, I want to get closer! Can you hide us half a block away?"

"Oh, sure . . . I didn't think you'd want to take a chance."

Finding a parking place in New York was never easy, but Lauren always seemed to get lucky. She parked. "We're one block from GALLERY RUSKO, good enough?"

"You did good! Wish me luck, I'll see you in thirty minutes unless the owner is not there and in that case, I'll come right back."

Lauren checked her watch as Max headed down the sidewalk.

The weather was perfect and it felt good to just sit in the warm quiet of her vehicle, watching New Yorkers going about their business. Across the street was a small park and she could hear the muted voices of children shouting and playing.

Lauren checked her watch—ten minutes had passed. Max had barely gotten there. Her thoughts turning to Jackson, Lauren hoped she never had to tell him about this caper with Max. She checked her watch again. Sighing Lauren could hear Aunt Willa saying a watched pot never boils. She put her head back and closed her eyes.

With a start she saw that it was twenty-seven minutes since Max left. Lauren scrambled to the sidewalk and walked as fast as she dared without running. Poor Max! Some help she was! Lauren would only be a couple of minutes late. Good thing she'd worn comfy loafers.

With the white stucco building in sight, Lauren tried breathing calmly; she didn't want to rush through the door totally out of breath.

She slowed her steps and opened the gallery door. Max was across the other side of a large showroom, in conversation with a tall dark-haired man. A smart looking woman walked toward Lauren.

"Good morning! May I help you?"

"Thank you, I'm just looking." Lauren smiled at the salesgirl and glanced over her shoulder at Max, who was in an animated conversation with the tall gentleman—they were both smiling.

The sales person hovered. "I'm Karen, if I can help you, please let me know."

"Thank you, Karen, I will." The woman smiled and went to a large desk sitting at the end of the room. Lauren took advantage of the time to browse while waiting to see what Max would do. The gallery had some really good modern art. Not Lauren's favorite genre, but very good.

She perused everything, even becoming absorbed in the jewelry, where she found a turquoise bangle she thought Brooke would like.

How long did Max need to determine her next move. Lauren pushed her sweater sleeve back from her watch and did a double take—forty-seven minutes! Max and the man were still talking—and still smiling. She turned away; should she amble closer?

"Did you find something?" The happy salesgirl stood at her side.

"Yes, thank you. I'll take this." She handed the turquoise bracelet to the girl. "Who is the tall, dark-haired man over there?" She indicated with a glance.

"Oh, that's Simon Lankford."

"Um, is the owner in today?"

The salesgirl looked blank for a moment. "Mr. Lankford *is* the owner."

"Oh. Thank you," Lauren mumbled and followed the girl to the desk to pay for the bracelet. With her purchase in hand, she wandered closer to where Max and Mr. Lankford were obviously not having a conflict. Lauren moved closer to get Max's attention. It worked.

"Lauren Ashby! What are you doing here? How good to see you!"

"Max! It's good to see you too!" Max should have been an actress. Lauren smiled to herself and went along with the act.

Max motioned to the man and said, "This is Simon Lankford."

Lauren smiled at Simon Lankford and he immediately stuck his hand out.

"Hello, Lauren, nice to meet you."

"Nice to meet you, too."

Max smiled at Lauren. "Simon is the *owner*. He buys a lot of my small works and donates the pieces to a monthly charity auction. "

Max's tone of voice and wide eyes were sending a message, but Lauren wasn't sure what the message was. "How wonderful! You have a lovely gallery, Mr. Lankford"

"Thank you, glad you like it. Do you live here in the city?"

"No, actually I'm—"

"Oh, Lauren—I'm so sorry!"

Max turned to Simon Lankford. "I'd forgotten that Lauren was married recently. She's Lauren Montgomery now."

"Really? I don't suppose you know Jackson Montgomery?" he said.

Lauren heard what he said, but it didn't sink in at first. "You . . . you know Jackson?"

"Yes. We were in college together. I majored in Art History. I knew Jenna, too." He glanced from one to the other. "I see Jackson's gallery in Art Talk news now and then."

"It *is* a small world." Lauren murmured. "I'm Jackson's wife."

It was his turn to look stunned. "I didn't realize Jackson had remarried—when?" He looked puzzled as he studied Lauren with renewed interest.

She returned his gaze. "Going on three years now."

"That's good. I'm glad to hear it."

Lauren thought he looked genuinely pleased. If he was a crook, he certainly didn't look the part. "Thank you. I'll tell Jackson I ran into you today."

"Please do! We need to get together for dinner one evening soon."

Max began to search her small bag. "Simon, here's my card. I'd like to talk more about your idea for your charity work. I may be able to help."

He took the card and studied it for a moment. "Are you free this evening? We could discuss it over dinner."

Max smiled, and with no hesitation or pretense that she might be busy, she said, "That sounds great! I'm free, and I'd love to have dinner—what time?"

Lauren's curiosity ran rampant trying to guess how this all came about in less than an hour. They settled the details of their dinner plans without her hearing much of it. She heard her name mentioned as Max linked her arm through Lauren's.

"And now I'm taking my friend to lunch," Max said. "And I'm looking forward to the evening."

"Yes, me too." Simon toyed with the card she'd given him.

***

When they stepped outside, a cool breeze had picked up so they hurried back to Lauren's vehicle. By the time they got back, Max's hair had begun reverting to its natural curls. They climbed into the Range Rover and as soon as Lauren closed her door, she took a deep breath and waited for Max to get settled. "Max, tell me if I get this right."

"Okay. . . ." Max looked uncertain.

"You walked up to the man that looked like he *might* be the owner, and asked if he was a diamond smuggler—he said no, he was just your average nice guy. You said, fine that's all I wanted to know and started a conversation with him about charity work—am I right?"

Max put her head back on the headrest and laughed. "Almost, but not quite."

Lauren laughed, too, and said, "I'm eaten up with curiosity, what *did* happen?"

"I had just walked in and was getting up the nerve to speak to this guy when I noticed that he kept glancing at me." She laughed again. "I'd about decided to go speak to the lady at the desk, when all of a sudden the man was hurrying toward me."

Lauren drew in a breath. "What did you do?"

"Well, at first I glanced around to see if there was another person behind me—but I was alone." She flipped the mirror down, looked at herself in the small glass, then pushed it back up and gazed at Lauren.

"Well? Then what!"

"He came right up to me and said, 'I know who you are—you're Max Quinn!'" Max reached up and undid the clasp that was holding her sleek, low-placed ponytail. She shook her head and let her hair fly.

"How did he recognize you?"

She smiled. "I have photos of myself on my website. He looked me up when he started buying my bronze pieces."

"Oh, of course. Well, did you find out what he does with the toads?" Lauren said.

"Yes. It's a long story, and I'll explain at lunch, but right now I want to check into Clair's husband's hotel—the Bel something or other. We can lunch there."

"The Belmont. But, Max if you don't mind I'm not up to lunch, can we skip it?"

"Of course, if you'd rather." She peered at Lauren. "Are you okay?"

"I'm fine, just not hungry. You've decided to spend the night? Should I stay with you? You don't know this guy—"

"Lauren! He went to college with Jackson, and he's a reputable businessman. There's no reason to worry about me."

"I don't mind staying."

Max shook her head. "Absolutely not. As soon as you drop me at the hotel, I want you to head home. You'll get back in time to have dinner with your family, and I'll catch a taxi to meet Simon at the restaurant. I'll fly home tomorrow."

Lauren secretly breathed relief. She wanted to be home. She was going to tell Jackson everything, and they'd have a quiet, restful evening. "Are you sure?"

Max nodded, her curls getting tighter, "Positive. And I'll call you later tonight and fill you in on everything."

Lauren eyed her across the console. "About what he's doing with the toads?"

"Yes." Max laughed. "You won't believe it."

They arrived at the hotel and Lauren parked the Range Rover in the portico of the Belmont. She had her hand on the door handle, but Max quickly stopped her. "Since we're not having lunch, there's no need for you to even get out." She reached across to hug Lauren, then jumped out and grabbed her bag from the back seat and waved goodbye.

Lauren watched until Max was inside the hotel. She headed home, with a thankful, grateful heart for the way things had turned out.

# CHAPTER NINETEEN

# A Heads Up

Headed home, on the open road, Lauren relaxed and smiled to herself about the sleuthing she and Max had thought they'd do. It had been exciting to think of solving a mystery, but it turned out rather nice in the end.

Jackson would be pleased they ran into an old friend of his and that she was home early. She would rest tomorrow to make him happy.

But even the thought of resting brought all the things she needed to do crowding in. The vision of the girl on the schoolyard bumping into Mandy, pushed to the forefront of her thoughts. She had to talk with Brooke's teacher.

Her phone rang, she glanced at the screen; it was Jackson. "Hello."

"Where are you?" He asked.

"You'll be glad to know I'm headed home. Max took care of her business early, and I got away sooner than expected. I have a lot to tell you." She laughed happily.

"Well, that's good news. A quiet early evening sounds good to me. The gallery has been dead today."

They finished their conversation and ended the call. Speaking with Jackson reminded Lauren of the expression that briefly touched his face when Brooke mentioned her grandmother's diamonds. She really didn't understand why something like that should bother him. But at that moment she promised herself that she would never keep anything from him again, except the thing with Max and now she could even share that.

She made good time, the traffic was light and in no time she was turning onto the drive to the house. She glanced at her watch; there should be time for a short nap before Jackson got home. Aunt Willa's car was in the garage and as soon as Lauren approached the back door, tantalizing smells reminded her she'd talked Max out of taking time for lunch. Her tummy hadn't felt up to it, but now she was starving.

Just as she reached for the doorknob, Aunt Willa opened the door and gasped. "Goodness! You surprised me." She slipped her purse on her arm.

"I'm sorry." Lauren laughed. "I got back earlier than I expected. Where are you off to?"

"Jackson just called. Something came up at the gallery last minute and he asked me to pick Brooke up from school."

"I'll run get Brooke. My car is already warmed up."

"Are you sure, dear? I certainly don't mind."

"I'll run get her. You've been working—I smelled something good when I pulled into the garage."

Aunt Willa smiled. "I baked today. Okay, if you're sure, I'll stay and finish dinner." She went back inside. It was a little early, but Jackson's aunt always got to school early, as she wanted to be first in line for pickup.

Lauren entertained the thought that if Mrs. Flowers wasn't busy, she might manage a talk with her today about what was happening on the schoolyard.

When she arrived at school she parked away from the pickup lane and strolled to the wide entry doors and down the hall to Brooke's room.

She peeked in through the long narrow window in the classroom door and scanned the faces for the new girl. She sat two seats behind Mandy. Brooke's desk was closer to the front, four desks ahead of the girl on the third row.

The bell rang. Lauren stepped away from the door and to the other side of the hall. Soon the students began to file out. Most of the boys struck out running the minute they were away from the door, loud and happy. She tried to imagine having one of those little creatures in her own home.

Brooke and Mandy didn't see Lauren standing across the hall by the wall. They came out together walking shoulder to shoulder laughing and chattering. Suddenly the new girl came up from behind and shoved hard between them, almost tripping Brooke. She never looked back. Lauren put her hand to her mouth to keep from calling out. She hurried to the girls. "Brooke, can you wait for me in the car, just a few minutes? I want to speak to Mrs. Flowers, okay?"

Brooke nodded. "Uh-huh." She darted a look at Mandy. "I'll wait."

"Good, I'll not be long." Lauren didn't let on that she knew what had happened. She stepped into the classroom. "Hello, Mrs. Flowers. Do you have a moment?"

"Oh, hello, of course I do." She glanced at a young boy across the room. He was taking long swipes at the chalkboard. "How may I help you?" She motioned to a chair. "Have a seat."

Lauren smiled and sat in the chair the teacher had indicated. "I'm concerned that one of the students dislikes Mandy and Brooke and may be acting it out on the girls." Lauren paused. "I wondered if you've noticed anything during class?"

Mrs. Flowers sighed. "Nothing to call the girl on, but I've suspected a time or two. Mandy nor Brooke have come to me about anything." She rolled a pencil between her fingers. "Have you actually seen something happening?"

"I have. More than once, on the schoolyard, and just now in the hall."

The teacher's lips pursed. "What happened in the hall?"

"The girl, the one with the long blond braid, came up behind them and shoved between the girls nearly causing Brooke to fall. She did it on purpose, and I've seen other incidents."

"Mrs. Flowers shook her head. "I'm sorry, and I appreciate you coming to me. Give me a few days to look into this. I will get to the bottom of it."

Lauren rose. "I'd rather Brooke didn't know that I've spoken with you, she nor Mandy know that I'm aware of what's going on."

"Of course. And I will keep a closer watch on the situation. Thank you, for telling me."

"You're welcome and thank you." Lauren paused near the door. "If I can ever do anything . . . if you need my help, please call me."

Mrs. Flowers smiled. "Thank you, I will."

Lauren breathed easier knowing the teacher was aware of what was going on. With this new peace of mind, she could fully enjoy a quiet evening with Jackson now.

*** 

Brooke was sitting quietly in the Range Rover when Lauren opened the door and slid into the seat beside her. She was looking at a book about horses. Lauren spoke in an easy, casual manner, "Are you looking forward to the stables on Saturday?"

"Uh-huh. I'm learning about different kinds of horses."

"Breeds. It's different breeds of horses, an interesting subject." She adjusted her seatbelt and started the engine.

"What did you talk to Mrs. Flowers about?" Brooke closed the book, but kept her hand inside, marking her place.

"Well, I wanted your teacher to know if I could ever help with anything in the class, you know, class parties, field trips, things like that, she is to be sure and call me."

Brooke relaxed and smiled. "She already knows that. You helped with the Valentine party and the Christmas one, too."

Lauren nodded. "Yes, and I had fun! I don't want Mrs. Flowers to forget and not call me when it's party time."

Brooke giggled and returned her attention to the library book. Lauren drove without speaking, allowing her little passenger to enjoy the pursuit of knowledge regarding her latest interest. They were almost home when Brooke closed the book.

"I can't wait for Saturday, but I'm scared."

"What are you scared of?" Lauren took her eyes off the road briefly to gaze into the small upturned face.

What if I can't ride? What if I fall off the horse?"

"Oh, honey, that's why you go to a good riding instructor—a good instructor won't allow you to ride alone, not until you're ready."

"Will my instructor hold the rope to my horse?"

Lauren saw doubt in the young eyes. She kept her voice light and casual. "Yes, the instructor will hold a rope, it's called a lead rope, and the instructor will control the horse with that rope, but you'll have the reins in your hands. Your horse will only walk until you're ready for the next step." Lauren searched for an analogy. "Remember when you learned to read?"

"Uh-huh."

"The teacher didn't give you a book with big words until you were ready for big words—and now you can pronounce big words very well."

Brooke nodded. "I can't do some big words yet."

Lauren laughed. "Well, it will be a while before you can jump poles, too!"

Brooke joined in with Lauren's happy laughter for a time and then she sobered. "Will you and Dad stay at the stables when I have a lesson?"

"Of course we will." Lauren hesitated, not sure how to reassure her. "Brooke, it will be fun, I promise. Try not to worry, okay?"

"I won't worry if you and Dad are there."

"Good, we'll be there." They were home, and Lauren guided the Range Rover into the garage.

\*\*\*

Still talking about Saturday, they entered the kitchen just as Aunt Willa answered the phone. "Wait a moment, Brooke just came in." Aunt Willa placed the phone on the bar. "Brooke, Mandy's on the phone."

Brooke skipped to the phone. "Hello." Her eyes lit up and she squealed, beginning to hop about. She lowered the phone. "Guess what! Mandy's mom and dad said yes, and she's going to get riding lessons!"

Lauren and Aunt Willa exchanged looks. "That's good news, dear!" Aunt Willa laughed and covered her ears in a playful gesture.

"May I take the phone upstairs? Mandy and I need to make plans."

Lauren nodded. "Yes, you may, but remember to bring it back." The only phones upstairs were the ones in the master bedroom, and the guest rooms. Those phones never left the rooms they belonged in, and Brooke wasn't allowed a phone in her room yet.

After Brooke flew up the stairs, Aunt Willa put the teapot on. "There's roast beef for sandwiches tonight. Thelma and I are going to the movies; it might be late when we get back.

"Oh, that's nice. You two have fun. We'll manage fine with the roast beef."

Aunt Willa offered Lauren a cup of tea.

She declined, saying she was going upstairs and take a quick shower before Jackson got home. "We may just have sandwiches in our room and watch a movie—"

Brooke burst onto the stairs calling out, "Lauren! Lauren!" She flew down the stairs to the kitchen and wrapped her arms around Lauren's waist. "May I spend the night with Mandy? Please, please! Tomorrow is Friday, and we won't have homework."

Lauren brushed hair back from the small face and glanced at Aunt Willa. "Oh, honey, I don't know. Has Mandy's mom given permission?"

"Yes! It was her idea! She told Mandy to ask me." Brooke was bouncing on her toes.

Lauren glanced at Aunt Willa. "Do you think it would be okay with Jackson?"

Aunt Willa set her cup down. "I can't imagine why it wouldn't be. I can drop her off as I pick Thelma up."

Brooke ran to her great aunt. "Thank you, Aunt Willa!" Brooke hugged her and headed for the stairs, singing, "I'm so happy—I'm so happy!"

Lauren gazed at Aunt Willa. They both sighed and smiled.

Aunt Willa sipped her tea. "Looks like you and Jackson will have a quiet evening alone."

Lauren smiled. "Yes, and I'm looking forward to it. I think I'll go ahead and make sandwiches, then have my shower." She'd have everything ready for a pleasant evening when Jackson got home.

She would tell him all about meeting his friend, Simon and about Clair's bronze horned toads

.

CHAPTER TWENTY

# Differences

A quiet house would be nice for a change. A rush of longing swept over Lauren. She needed to be with Jackson. She couldn't remember the last time they'd had an evening together, just the two of them.

Jackson would be surprised to hear that she'd met an old college buddy of his.

She lingered in the shower enjoying the warmth from the flood of pounding water. Her mind wandered. Max would be having dinner with Simon Lankford about the same time she and Jackson were enjoying their fat roast beef sandwiches.

Lauren turned off the water, reached for the thick towel and wrapped herself in its warm softness and briskly toweled her body. She pulled on a long terry robe and smiled at her short career as a sleuth. And now that it was over, and the whole thing had been nothing but Max's imagination, she couldn't wait to tell Jackson all about it.

Jackson came into their room as Lauren walked out of the bathroom; he stood with his hand on the open door. "Where is everyone?"

Lauren went to him and twined her arms around his waist and snuggled against his chest. "There is no one except us." She raised her face. "Your aunt went to the movies with Thelma, and Brooke is spending the night with Mandy."

Sounds nice. Are you sure about Brooke staying at Mandy's? Is this Friday?"

"No, it's Thursday, but there was no homework and they want to talk about riding."

He returned Lauren's hug. "I guess they'll be safe from mischief in Mandy's room—maybe." They laughed and said in unison, "*Maybe.*"

Lauren led him to the overstuffed chairs near the windows and waited for him to be seated, she sat on his lap. "We're having sandwiches for dinner. Do you want to eat here or downstairs?"

Jackson squeezed her tight. "I don't care—you choose."

"I'll fix a tray while you shower, and we'll eat here." She gave him a long tender kiss. "I have so much to tell you, so be prepared to have your ears talked off." She got to her feet.

Jackson grinned. "I've been talking all day, it'll be nice to just listen for a change." He stood and pushed his hand through his hair and went toward the bathroom.

As Lauren reached the door she paused, looking back. "This is nice. I've missed you the last few days."

He nodded. "Yes, very nice, and I've missed you."

By the time Lauren returned with their dinner tray, Jackson was in sweats and loafers. A white t-shirt lay on his chair, his hair still tousled and damp from the shower. He had pulled the chairs closer together with a small table between them to hold the tray. Lauren placed the tray on the table.

Jackson glanced at the food. "That looks good." After offering thanks for their food, he reached for one of the tall glasses of tea. "I need to relax a few minutes first. Tell me about your day—Max get off okay?"

Lauren drew her feet into the big chair and smiled. "No, Max didn't get off at all. She's staying the night and leaving in the morning."

Jackson frowned. "Trouble with her gallery? I wish she would have let me—"

Lauren laughed. "No, no trouble at all. Let me start from the beginning and you'll understand." She explained about Max's bronze toads and her suspicions about the buyer in New York. "Max and I were going to snoop a little to find out if something illegal was going on. Lauren laughed. "Max just knew the gallery owner was smuggling diamonds or something like that, but when we got to the gallery . . . " Lauren laughed. "You'll never believe who the owner was—"

"Lauren! I don't find that amusing." He hauled himself from the chair. "What *were* you thinking? You promised me you wouldn't do anything foolish or un-safe—and to think that all I was worried about was you driving too fast or overtiring yourself—I don't believe it—I don't believe you!" He stomped back and forth across the bedroom, raking his hands through his hair. Then quickly he grabbed the white t-shirt from the chair and jerked it over his head, pulling it into place over his chest.

"Jackson, nothing happened, nothing would have happened—"

"But you and Max didn't know that when you set out to catch jewel smugglers!" He glared across the room. "You're five months pregnant—what were you thinking?"

Lauren had never seen Jackson that angry. It was like he was shouting, but his voice wasn't raised. The words that came to her mind were *controlled fury*. She wanted to shrink into herself.

Jackson glared at her, his shoulders sagged, he shook his head and muttered, "I'd better take a walk." He jerked the bedroom door open and was gone.

Lauren set her tea glass on the table. She'd been gripping it like a lifeline. She wanted to cry but no tears came. Numbness set in. Finally, she stood on wooden legs and gathered the tray of untouched food and slowly made her way downstairs to the kitchen. She stuck the sandwiches in sandwich bags and put the tray away.

It had grown dark outside. She dragged her body back upstairs and into the studio. Finding her way to the paint-stained chair that had been Jenna's refuge, Lauren curled her shaken body into the wide chair and tucked her robe around her bare feet.

And then the tears came. She pulled the afghan from the back of the chair and scooted deeper into the cushions. What could she say or do to make things right again? Drained of energy, and sick at heart, she recalled the words she'd said to Brooke; trust, once lost was hard to gain back. The difference was, Brooke was a child, she had an excuse for her irresponsible behavior—she was still learning. But Lauren, of all people, had no excuse. It had been a foolish thing she and Max did.

Jackson was right—and he had every reason to be angry. The tears were hot on her cheeks, as they flowed unchecked.

A cramp in her right leg jerked Lauren from a drugged-like sleep. "Ohh, ouch, ouch, that hurts!" She moaned, carefully straightening her cramping leg. The bed felt strange, why was she hanging over the side? She flexed her leg until the cramp let up and the pain eased and she could move a tiny bit. She pushed up, onto her forearm, and immediately recognized the wide arm of the chair, not her bed—and it all rushed back—the look on Jackson's face and his terrible anger.

She pushed into a full sitting position and gasp as every joint in her body ached. She glanced at the studio clock, rubbed her aching forehead and looked again. "But . . . how can that be?" The clock read 5:42 am. Lauren continued to stare at the numbers, but they didn't change.

She remembered curling into the chair after Jackson stormed from the house. The time had been close to seven o'clock in the evening.

She had slept curled in the fetal position almost eleven hours? No wonder her body was locked at each joint. Lauren moved to the edge of the chair, planted her feet on the floor and tested her weight on wobbly legs. By the time she reached the hall, she was steady enough to make it downstairs. But first, she crept to their bedroom door to check on Jackson. She couldn't believe he had left her to sleep in a chair all night.

Quietly Lauren turned the doorknob and peeked in. She pulled the door shut and wiped at the fresh tears that filled her eyes. Their bed hadn't been slept in. He'd probably slept in the den.

Blotting her eyes with the back of her hand, Lauren hurried downstairs as fast as her stiff legs could move. She'd throw herself on Jackson and beg his forgiveness. The smell of coffee met her as she neared the last few steps. Her robe flying, she headed into the morning room and stopped abruptly. The room was empty. She whirled and rushed toward the kitchen and found Aunt Willa, alone.

"Oh—have you seen Jackson?"

Jackson's aunt was taking a ham from the freezer. "No, I haven't. I suppose he's already left for work." She glanced at Lauren. "It's awfully early, problems at the gallery?"

"Oh . . . no problems." She gazed at Aunt Willa. "I . . . I had hoped to see him before he left." She averted her face and hoped she hadn't seen Lauren's tears or her guilt. She didn't want to tell Aunt Willa that Jackson had left the house angry last evening.

Aunt Willa crossed the kitchen and took Lauren's arm, guiding her toward the morning room and the serving buffet. "The coffee is fresh, and you look like you could use a cup, and I haven't had my second cup." Aunt Willa poured their coffee

"Thank you." Lauren took the steaming cup. "I didn't sleep well last night." She walked across the room to stand at the tall windows. The gardens lay peaceful under the silvery dawn just before sunrise.

From behind her Aunt Willa spoke. "My dear, if you want to talk, I'm here."

Lauren turned, and going to one of the big chairs, she sat and crossed her ankles. Holding the hot cup with both hands, she touched the rim to her lips and studied Aunt Willa's face for a long moment. "Thank you, it is a comfort knowing you care."

Aunt Willa nodded. "You're welcome." She sipped her coffee and glanced to the windows. "This is a new day. We get to start fresh again." She smiled at Lauren

Lauren returned the smile. She swallowed the coffee, one sip after another. Just a half-cup more to go and she could casually mention that she better not have seconds, since she was meeting Jackson and he'd want her to have coffee with him. She gulped the last of the coffee and strolled to set her cup on the buffet tray.

"I'm seeing Jackson this morning . . . I'd better not linger. . . ." She made for the stairs and thought of taking them two at a time, but Jackson's face of disapproval flashed across her vision.

She reframed.

# CHAPTER TWENTY-ONE

# Broken Promise

Jackson sat up and glanced sidelong at the sofa he'd spent the night on. It had been in the break room since shortly after Brooke was born. Jenna had ordered it. She'd said it would be handy when she had the baby with her and needed more room than the table and chairs offered. Jackson dry scrubbed his face.

What a miserable night.

He gave the expanse of rich brown leather another glance and stood, wondering what Jenna would think of him spending the night on her sofa. He shook his head, not a good idea to go there.

Scrambling through one of the cabinet drawers, he found a bottle of aspirin. He shook two into his hand and downed them with a gulp of water before heading for the bathroom that served the break room.

He and Matt both kept toothbrushes and toothpaste there. As he brushed his teeth, he eyed Matt's extra set of clean clothes—he glanced down at the t-shirt and sweats he had on, and was convinced Matt would want to share his clothes.

Several hours later Matt unlocked the back door and came into the office. He lifted his brows when Jackson looked up from his computer screen.

"You're early." He laughed. "Or did you spend the night—you were still here when I left last evening."

Jackson scowled.

"Umm, that was a joke." Matt moved closer and flicked Jackson's shirt collar. "Is that my clean shirt?"

Jackson nodded. "Uh-huh, your clean slacks too, thanks for the loan."

"Sure, anytime." Matt eyed Jackson's loafers without socks. "You must have left in a hurry this morning. I'll go make coffee."

Minutes later Matt ambled back into the office, swiveled his chair, and sat facing Jackson's back. "You didn't really spend the night did you?"

"Uh-huh, I did." Jackson turned his chair.

Matt frowned. "You're not worried about the new contract, are you?" When he got no reply, he continued. "TechRom Industries is an old established company. Why would you be concerned about them?"

Jackson shook his head. "I'm not worried about TechRom." He rubbed his hand over his face and continued the motion up through his already unruly hair. "Lauren and I had words last night. I needed to walk, and I just didn't want to go back to the house. So I came here instead and looked over the contract again." He glanced at Matt. "They'll need at least thirty-five to forty large canvases for the whole job."

Matt tilted his head. "Yeah, good for business. Did the contract have anything to do with you guys having words?"

"Uh, no. I haven't had a chance to share the details of it with Lauren or Aunt Willa."

Matt got up, saying, "I smell the coffee, let's go get a cup."

A somber mood followed as they walked to the break room, each deep in thought. They got their favorite mugs and Matt poured the coffee.

Jackson clinked and stirred the half and half until Matt cleared his throat and nodded to Jackson's cup. "Trying to make whipped cream, there?"

"Oh, sorry." He tapped the spoon on the rim of his cup.

They headed back to the office carrying their mugs.

"I did have time to do some thinking last night. TechRom is about finished with their renovations, all except the finishing touches and the wall art we are to install."

"That should be no problem for us, we're ready." Matt gazed at Jackson. "Aren't we?"

Glancing down, Jackson said, "No problem, but I feel like I should be here to help." He looked up briefly. "According to the contract, we agreed to start on our part the week of the twenty-sixth of this month."

"What are you saying?"

"That I need to be here—not in Italy." Jackson heard the edge in his voice.

"You can't do that to Lauren—besides, it isn't necessary." Matt was shaking his head.

"Do you think I can run off and leave the whole thing on you?"

"I'll have Maggie, and I know Clair would come help if we needed her."

"No. All the paintings are very large. Maggie couldn't handle them like we could." Jackson stood and paced the office.

Matt's gaze followed him. "Jackson, I'd planned to hire a couple of guys to do the lifting and hanging the canvases." He gulped a swallow of coffee. "Maggie and I will decide which one goes where and the placement—that's all." He grinned. "We don't need you."

Jackson ran his hand through his hair. "I want to be there."

Matt stood with his cup. "Fine. But wanting to be there and needing to be there is not the same thing. What will Lauren think? You'll be breaking a promise."

Jackson stared into his cup and muttered darkly, "It won't be the first promise broken."

*** 

The day dragged, but Jackson didn't mind since he wasn't looking forward to going home in the evening. Having to face Lauren and Aunt Willa after storming out and staying away all night wasn't something he looked forward to. Thank goodness Brooke had been at Mandy's house. Lauren hadn't called all day.

Speaking of Brooke, he glanced at the wall clock the same instant she came flying into the office. Everything got brighter when she entered the room, and the air that swept in with her carried the fresh smell of the outdoors. He didn't want to let her go when she hugged his neck. "Did you have a good time at Mandy's—did you both do your homework?"

"We didn't have any homework."

"Oh, right. But don't make a habit of asking to stay over on a week night, okay?"

"We won't. Last night was special; we had to talk about the riding lessons and decide what to wear. We can't wait to go see the horses tomorrow! Mandy's mom is going too." She wiggled away from Jackson and ran to give Matt a hug. "How is Eli?"

Matt returned her hug. "Growing like a weed—just like you seem to be doing."

"I know! Lauren said we have to buy new school uniforms before long." She stepped away from Matt. "Look how short!" She pressed the plaid skirt against her thin colt-like legs and laughed happily before turning to pounce on Jackson. "What time are we going to the stable in the morning?"

"Umm, not sure, but Lauren will know."

"Uh-huh—Lauren knows everything." As quickly as she had blown in, she grabbed her books and vanished to the break room.

Jackson called after her, "I didn't think you had homework on a Friday."

"I don't. I'm going to draw a horse."

Jackson frowned. "What did that mean—Lauren knows everything?" He stared at the back of Matt's head until he swiveled his chair to look Jackson in the eyes.

Matt chuckled. "I believe she thinks Lauren knows everything."

Jackson glared. "You know what I mean. What is *everything* to a kid?"

Matt turned to his computer again. "Beats me, Jackson. Maybe I'll know by the time Eli's that age." He glanced over his shoulder at the wall clock. "Why don't you and Brooke take an early evening and go on home. I'll lock up."

Jackson ran his hands over his tired eyes. "Sounds good to me—are you sure?"

"Yep, I left early yesterday while you stayed and worked, today's your turn."

Matt had left early to take Ally out to dinner and a movie. Jackson sighed, if only he had a movie and dinner to look forward.

He dreaded what the evening might bring.

***

Brooke climbed into the passenger seat and dumping her backpack on the floorboard, she waved a sheet of tan construction paper in his face. "This is my very first horse. What do you think?"

A fat, swaybacked, black horse stood in a bright green pasture. A white fence disappeared in the distance. Jackson smiled to himself. "That's a neat horse. Your perspective on the fence is very good."

"Thanks, Dad. Lauren showed me how to do fences and roads like that."

Jackson remembered what she'd said earlier. "Uh-huh, that Lauren knows everything, doesn't she?"

Brooke turned her face up to his, her expression serious. "She does. I'm glad too."

"I'm glad too, sweetheart." The look in her eyes, and the tone of her voice told Jackson that Brooke had a particular thing in mind. When she said she was glad, she was in earnest. Her comments stirred his curiosity.

He turned onto their driveway. Home; their home, and no matter what lay ahead, he'd rather be there than anywhere in the world.

He guided the Range Rover into the garage, and took a deep breath of relief that Lauren's vehicle was in its place in the garage. Brooke chattered on about horses and riding lessons, but Jackson couldn't concentrate.

He opened the door and held it for Brooke to enter first. Good smells of cooking filled the kitchen and suddenly Jackson was ravenous. He hadn't eaten since lunch the day before.

Aunt Willa sat at the bar flipping through a garden magazine while having a cup of tea. "Hello, you two. You're early—how nice!"

Jackson walked to the other side of the bar and hugged his aunt. "Something sure smells good."

"Baked ham." It'll be ready when you are." She turned another page. "Since we're all here, we could have dinner a little early."

"I'd like that. I'm starved," he said, and took a seat at the bar.

Aunt Willa closed her magazine and chatted with Jackson as she put food on the table. She moved back and forth to the informal kitchen table that was set with plain white crockery.

"Brooke, will you please run upstairs and tell Lauren we're eating early since you and your dad are home."

"Yes, ma'am." She skipped toward the stairs.

Aunt Willa always enjoyed a minute alone with Jackson. They discussed the yard for several minutes, then she smiled and said, "Since Lauren got home just a short time before you and Brooke, I was afraid you two might have had a late lunch today and wouldn't be hungry—"

Brooke and Lauren strolled into the kitchen, Brooke hanging onto Lauren until she skipped over to her great aunt. "Aunt Willa—why don't you come with us to the stables in the morning?"

Aunt Willa smiled and put an arm around Brooke's shoulders. "I just might do that."

Jackson gazed at Lauren. She came slowly over to where he sat at the bar. He pulled her into his arms, his face pressed against her chest. "I missed you today."

"I missed you too," she whispered, and cradled his head.

Jackson heard his aunt laughing and chatting with Brooke, and Lauren was in his arms. His world was up right again.

The next moment Brooke had her arms around the two of them. "Come on! I'm starved, the school lunch was awful, and I didn't eat it."

Jackson grabbed her in a hug. "What! I pay for school lunch and you don't eat it!"

"Da-a-d! Your face is scratchy, you have a beard." She pulled away from him and giggling, headed to the table with Aunt Willa.

Jackson stood and clasped hands with Lauren and they, too, moved toward the table.

Giving Lauren's hand a gentle squeeze, he said, "Did you get the impression that Aunt Willa thought we had lunch together today?"

Lauren nodded. "Yes, I . . . I think I gave her that impression, I'll explain after dinner."

CHAPTER TWENTY-TWO

# Discovery

At last they were alone in their bedroom. Lauren's chest tightened at the sound of the door closing. The need to explain his aunt's confusion about lunch, pressed hard upon her.

She wanted no more secrets, no hidden agendas—nothing—ever again. Jackson would know everything from now on—when she bought stamps—to what kind and how many. She took a deep breath when Jackson ambled from the bathroom. "Jackson—"

"Lauren—" Jackson smiled in her direction. "Sorry, you go first." He sat in one of the chairs in the sitting area and motioned for her to join him.

She quickly crossed the room and sat on the edge of the chair facing him. "Before I forget, I want to explain why your aunt thought we lunched together today." She clasped her hands and took a deep breath. "After you left the house last night, I . . . I went to the studio and fell asleep in Jenna's big chair. I . . . I didn't intend to, but I slept there all night. When I woke early this morning, I peeked into our room, to check on you, but our bed hadn't been slept in. I didn't want your aunt to know we'd argued, so I told her we were meeting for coffee."

Jackson reached for her hand. "Why *didn't* you come find me? I would've been glad to see you. It was a miserable night and day."

Lauren sighed. "Yes, it was. I was afraid you wouldn't want to see me."

"Ohh, Lauren." He stood and pulled her into his arms. "I acted like a fool, and I'm sorry for that. But I had good reason to be upset with you—can't you see my point?"

"Yes. I do, and I'll never do anything like that again."

Relieved, she tightened her arms around him, but Jackson relaxed his hold on her and moved away. He paced the floor, running his hand through his hair. Her relief was short lived. His habit of pacing and raking his hair meant something serious was up.

"Jackson . . . you forgive me, don't you?"

"Yes. Of course I forgive you." He halted his step and glanced at her. "But there's something I have to tell you."

Lauren swallowed. "Okay . . . ?"

He paced several more turns to the windows and back.

Lauren's breathing became more difficult with each turn he made. "Jackson, tell me before I scream."

He sighed heavily. "I can't go to Italy with you after all."

Lauren moved toward the bed on wooden legs. She sank to the side of it and the wooden sensation crept up to her face. Her expression must have resembled a lifeless mask. She tried to speak. Jackson looked away. Finally, over the lump in her throat she managed a whisper, "You're punishing me."

"Don't be silly!" Jackson huffed. "I'm not punishing you." He scrubbed his hands across his eyes.

"I did behave irresponsibly," she continued in a hollow voice.

Jackson stood in front of her, glaring down. "Okay, yes, your actions were irresponsible!" His voice was hard; it grated with anger. "It *still* angers me just thinking about—" He stopped speaking and looked toward the closed door; after listening a second, he strode across the room, opened the door and glanced into the hall. "I thought I heard something."

Lauren rose from the side of the bed, went to her closet and returned with a robe across her arm. In the same lifeless voice she said, "If you'll excuse me, I'll take my shower—"

"Lauren, please, let's discuss this . . . it so happens that I need to be here in Valley Ridge the same week your exhibit takes place, it's business. Please try to understand."

Lauren paused at the bathroom door, her back to Jackson. "It's okay. Truly, it doesn't matter." She had no energy left. All she wanted now was to stand under a hot shower and pound away her pain and disappointment.

"Of course it matters—can't you understand the position I'm in? The new contract is a big deal—I need to be here."

She saw his anger turn to desperation and she didn't care.

"I didn't know we were getting that contract with TechRom when I agreed to go with you."

Lauren said, "What about Brooke? Will you still allow her to go?"

He stared as if she had asked him to let Brooke take the car out. Tears trickled down her cheeks. "Oh, yes, I remember. I can't be trusted."

Jackson groaned, slumped onto the side of the bed and sat with his head in his hands.

Quietly closing the door to the bathroom, she undressed and stepped into the shower, turned the water on and adjusted the temperature toward the hot side.

Her tight muscles welcomed the heat and she needed time alone to cry her eyes out. She *couldn't* cancel the trip to Italy at this late date—much as she'd like to right now. How would they break the news to Brooke that she wouldn't be going to the exhibit? She had been so excited about the trip.

Huddled in the shower until her feet and hands threatened to wrinkle, Lauren reluctantly shut the water off. After briskly toweling her body, she slipped into a soft white batiste gown.

Sitting at her dressing table, she gazed into the mirror for a moment, averted her eyes and began twisting her hair into a single fat braid.

Finishing with her hair, she braced herself and entered the bedroom. The room was lit only by Jackson's bedside lamp. He was asleep, sitting half slumped, still clutching a book.

Lauren stood at the side of the bed, undecided— should she wake him? She didn't want to talk anymore, but she hated to leave him in that uncomfortable position. He was worn out and needed his rest. Lauren moved quickly to the bathroom and closed the door with a firm pull on the brass knob. Then she strolled to the bed.

Jackson straightened himself and raised the book, but after several minutes he closed it and got off the bed. "Guess I'd better get a shower."

Lauren slipped into the bed and pulled the cool linens up around her neck. Much later when she heard Jackson come to bed, she pretended to be asleep. He climbed into bed and moved close. She breathed deeply of the fresh dampness of his body, his nearness. Her heart ached—her stubborn heart.

"Lauren. . . ?" he whispered.

She lay still and quiet. Pain and sadness gripped her soul as she bit her lip and held back the tears. Love was not supposed to hurt, but comfort, support and make whole. She didn't answer him. There was nothing more to say.

***

Early the next morning while the room was still dark, Lauren woke to Jackson whispering her name. She rolled onto her back. "What time is it?"

"Early. 6:40," he said.

"Why are you awake at this hour?"

"We need to talk—"

She started to roll back over. "I told you it doesn't matter, you don't have to go."

Jackson pulled her back. "It's not about the exhibit—it's Brooke. Today's her big day at the stable." He sighed. "Let's not ruin it for her."

Lauren was suddenly awake. "Oh, I forgot. Of course we won't ruin her day." She threw back the covers and found her robe. Aware that Jackson watched her from where he lay on the bed, she tied her robe and went to the door without another word. She hated that he was miserable, she understood, because she was miserable too.

Aunt Willa sipped from her favorite cup and saucer while standing at the windows gazing onto the gardens. She glanced over her shoulder when she heard Lauren at the buffet. "Good morning! Coffee's fresh. You're early—oh yes, today's the horse outing." She smiled when Lauren joined her to survey the gardens.

"I've often wondered how many hours I've stood in this spot in my years in this house."

Lauren relished the fragrant steam just inches from her nose. She breathed it in to help wake her senses. She reprimanded herself to put her own feelings aside today for Aunt Willa and Brooke's sake.

"Well, I dare say it has been time well spent. I, too, love standing here at dawn to watch the beginning of a new day."

Aunt Willa nodded, with a pleased expression. "Well put, my dear, well put."

They both turned when Jackson entered the room.

Lauren continued standing by the window after Aunt Willa went to refresh her coffee and speak to Jackson. She heard their conversation, even though they held their voices to a respectable early morning volume. Brooke was still asleep.

Lauren found it strange that Brooke and Mandy had been beside themselves with excitement the day before the outing, and now Brooke was sleeping in—strange indeed.

Aunt Willa had asked Jackson what time they planned to go to the riding stables.

He took a seat in the chair he usually sat in, across from Lauren's chair, as his aunt settled into her chair. "I'm not sure—around ten o'clock, I believe." He rattled his paper. "Is that right, Lauren?"

"Uh-huh. Ten o'clock. Mandy and her mother are meeting us there." Lauren wandered to the desk and examined the stack of mail from the day before. She browsed the envelopes, paused at the soft gray one with the bold handwriting. She sighed, and placed it back. She didn't want to hear what Max had to say— not now. The memory of Max and New York was a bitter one. Besides, Max had called the afternoon before and explained all about Simon Lankford. Lauren got the feeling that the two of them had hit it off great, so what was she writing about?

Jackson's paper rattled. "Uh, did I see something from Max?"

"Looks like it." Lauren sat in her chair. "Aunt Willa, why don't you come with us this morning?" She smiled. "You know, you might enjoy watching Brooke take a trial ride."

Aunt Willa laughed. "I'm sure I would, if it didn't unnerve me to watch her on one of those huge animals."

Jackson glanced up and dropped the paper to his lap. "Speaking of Brooke, I can't believe she's not already dressed and begging to go—you suppose she's getting cold feet?"

Lauren remembered Brooke worrying about falling off the horse. "I don't think so. We talked about riding and being nervous at first, but she seemed okay afterward."

Aunt Willa glanced at the clock on the desk. "It's still early. She may not have fallen asleep until late and is making up for it."

They all turned when Brooke padded quietly into the room.

Jackson lowered his paper again. "Good morning, Pumpkin! Are we all set to ride this morning?"

"Morning. Uh-huh."

Relief at Brooke's presence was evident in Jackson's voice. Was he having second thoughts about the riding lessons, too? Would he be just as happy if she did back out?

Brooke headed straight to Lauren and climbed into the chair with her and nestled her face against Lauren's shoulder. Making a pretense of pushing the sleep-tousled hair back from Brooke's face, Lauren touched her forehead for signs of fever, but the small face was cool to her touch. She glanced at Jackson, and a nod that went unperceived by his aunt or Brooke, told him not to worry.

Jackson thanked her with his eyes and rustled the paper into a sloppy fold. "Better have a good breakfast—gotta stay strong." He motioned for her to come to him.

Lauren sensed Brooke's reluctance, but she went to her dad. Something *was* wrong. Was Brooke afraid of the horses and ashamed to admit it? That didn't fit Brooke's character though—never had she hesitated to confess any fear or doubt to Jackson.

Lauren startled at hearing her name.

"Lauren—wake up—wake up!" Aunt Willa was waving her hand and laughing. "Maybe you got up too early."

Lauren nodded. "I . . . was just thinking." She smiled. "What were you saying?"

"I'd like to come watch Brooke ride, but I don't want to be gone long. Thelma and I are running out to the nursery." She smiled. "Claude told us they have a new shipment of fall plants. Should I drive my own car?"

"Well . . . you may want to drive, since we can't know exactly how long we'll be there."

"Okay." She stood. "I may see if Thelma would want to go too."

Brooke perked up for the first time. "Oh, I'm glad you're coming, Aunt Willa—and bring Thelma!" She jumped up from her dad's chair, and clinging to her great aunt's arm, she walked with her to the kitchen.

Lauren bit her lip. Odd that Brooke would want an audience if she feared she might fall and embarrass herself . . . no, it had to be something else

# CHAPTER TWENTY-THREE

# Riding Lessons

They arrived at Silver Cup Stables right on time. Mandy's mother drove into the parking area just as they did. Jackson barely came to a stop before Brooke was running across the gravel to greet her friend. He shook his head and glanced at Lauren. "To be so excited now, I thought for a while this morning she might change her mind about the whole thing."

Lauren nodded and reached for the door handle. "Her behavior was odd—"

"Lauren, thank you . . . for making this a fun day for Brooke."

She shrugged and opened the door. "I haven't done anything." She stepped out.

Jackson sat for a second longer and watched Lauren walking toward the others. There had to be a way to make her see how important her health and safety was—for the baby's sake as well as hers.

He sighed. "Who am I kidding?" He rubbed his hands over his eyes. It wasn't just what she and Max had done—or tried to do. Dr. Stinson had assured him that Lauren and the baby were both very healthy. It was everything—that Lauren didn't take her condition seriously, but just as much that she didn't *share anything* with him.

The four chattering girls were approaching the front of his vehicle. He stepped out of the Range Rover. "Morning, Mandy!" He smiled. "Are you all set to ride?"

"Yes, sir. I can't wait!"

Mandy's bright eyes and ready smile backed up her words. He nodded to Jill, Mandy's mother. "Couldn't you get Harry to come?" He grinned. Jill and Harry Rush were ten or twelve years older than him. He'd heard that they had given up on having children when the miracle now known as Mandy, had happened.

Jill laughed and patted at her short curly hair. "Harry had business out of town. He told her to break a leg; I asked him to please not ever say that again."

He and Jill were laughing when Lauren rejoined them. She'd left the girls at the front of the arena to wait for Steven, the stable owner.

She smiled at Jill. "I believe they're excited about this."

Jill nodded. "I can't tell you both how grateful Harry and I are that you invited Mandy to come. It would never have occurred to either of us that Mandy might enjoy learning to ride. And she needs more physical activities like this."

"Riding lessons were Jackson's idea."

Jackson dared a glance at Lauren, but she was being nice and not showing a sign that she remembered he'd questioned inviting Mandy to come with them.

At that moment Steven Ryder hurried out of the riding arena and waved to Jackson, his long strides carrying him toward Brooke and Mandy. Jackson grinned at Lauren and Jill. "We better join the girls."

When they drew close, Jackson smiled. Steven had both girls in wide-eyed rapture of the joys and responsibilities of horsemanship. Jackson stuck his hand out. "Morning, Steven! You've got two live ones here."

Steven pushed his cap back an inch on his red hair and shook his head slowly. "I see blue ribbon winners."

The girls faced each other, eyes big, in unison they mouthed, "Blue ribbon winners!"

Steven said, "Yep, winners for sure. But winning takes a lot of hard work, and determination. Remember that." His glance included Lauren and Jill as he said, "Are we ready for the ten-cent tour and a look at the horses?"

"Yes, sir, we are!" Brooke and Mandy turned to each other and hopping about did the praying mantis thing with their hands that they seemed to do at regular intervals. Jackson glanced at his watch. "My aunt and a friend were supposed to be here. She said they might be a little late, but—oh, here they come!"

The small group waited for the late arrivals.

"Sorry we're late! I hope we're not holding you up." Aunt Willa huffed toward them while holding onto her wide-brimmed hat, with Thelma fast on her heels.

Steven smiled and doffed his cap. "You ladies are fine, we're just about to head out." He led the way into the large, long structure, the indoor riding arena. "Classes can take place even in rainy weather." Three students were having a class when they walked in. "This is a semi-private session." He nodded to Lauren and Jill. "Private or semi is up to the student.

They watched for a while with Steven explaining the exercises."

A look at the facilities made the first half of the tour, which took thirty or forty minutes, and then Steven winked at the girls. "We save the best for last—the horses." They headed for the stalls. "Some students prefer to have their own horse and stable them with us, but many students work with our school horses."

Jackson had never been around horses much—a friend in college had lived on a horse ranch, Jackson visited the ranch several times, and that summed his experience with horses.

The smells of the stables were a confusing mix. Bales of clean, sweet smelling hay stacked in a shadowy corner of the huge stable mingled its fragrance with the sent of stall shavings, mineral blocks—and horses. Jackson laughed at Aunt Willa as she held a tissue to her nose.

Lauren, Brooke, and Mandy were stroking a pretty white mare that a handler had brought out of its stall. The three of them were mesmerized; a look of wonder lit their faces. The semi-private class must have ended, since the horses and students were filing into the stable. The instructors chatted with their students, giving pointers and advice about their lesson.

Steven called to a young woman; an instructor who'd just finished a class and motioned her over to where they were. He introduced her as Lindy. "I see that Allison hasn't put her horse up yet, ask if she'd meet us in the arena."

"Sure," Lindy said, "I'll send her over." She hurried away.

Steven led the white mare toward the large arena.

"The student that's coming to help is an excellent rider. She can show you girls how it's done."

Lindy, the same instructor as earlier, joined them in the walk to the arena. When the student rode into the far end of the arena on a tall sleek, deep reddish colored horse, the instructor went to meet her.

Mandy turned to Brooke, her eyes wide. "That one is *tall*. I wonder what kind is it?"

Brooke's eyes widened. "Uh-huh. It is tall. What if you fell off?"

Mandy inched closer to her mother.

Steven overheard their comments. "That's a Thoroughbred. Don't worry, girls. That horse belongs to the student, and she's been riding a long time. You girls will start out on gentle school horses, like Sweet Star." He patted the white mare.

They both sighed happily and gazed up at Sweet Star.

He pointed to the other end of the arena. "Watch what a good rider and horse can do with hard work, patience—and time. Lindy will call instructions to the student, who'll then put her horse through the moves."

When the demonstration ended, everyone clapped at the show of impressive riding. When Steven called to the instructor, she said something to the rider, and the two of them headed toward Steven and the group.

Steven took hold of Sweet Star's lead rope and glanced to the girls. "Who wants to go first?" They giggled and shrugged.

"Okay, tallest first."

Mandy smiled at Brooke and stepped forward to be helped into the saddle. She smiled from ear to ear. "Ohhh, this is fun!"

Jackson said, "Mandy, you look like a horse-woman already." Everyone agreed.

Brooke clasped her hands and bounced on her toes.

Steven motioned to the young girl on the thor-oughbred and she rode over to a wooden mounting block and dismounted. Lindy took the lead rope and started back to the stables with the horse in tow as the student walked toward Steven.

"Allison, thanks for helping. I want you to lead Sweet Star in a slow walk halfway around the arena, then walk her back."

Mandy stiffened. "I . . . I don't want to ride." She looked at her mother. "I want down!"

Jill hurried toward Steven as he hurried to help Mandy off the horse and said, "Of course. You don't have to ride, maybe another time?"

She shook her head and moved to stand close to her mother, as Brooke hurried to her side, where they whispered excitedly.

Steven patted Sweet Star and glanced at Brooke. "Brooke, you want to—"

"No, sir." Quickly she shook her head.

Jackson ran his hands through his hair. "Brooke—why do you not want to ride all of a sud-den? Are you afraid?"

"No, sir. . . ."

Jill was trying to get something out of Mandy with no success either.

Jackson looked around for Lauren. She was awfully quiet. She had walked over to the girl, Allison, and was speaking to her.

"Lauren—"

She shushed him with her hand and continued talking to the girl who still held Sweet Star's lead rope. Jackson looked helplessly from Brooke to Mandy and back to Lauren, who motioned him over.

"Jackson, this is Allison. She goes to school with Mandy and Brooke. They're in the same class. If the girls aren't going to ride, we should all go have an ice cream and get acquainted. Would you like to go with us, Allison?"

She glanced toward Brooke and Mandy and shook her head. "No, thank you, my aunt will be here after awhile."

Lauren persevered. "Oh, come have ice cream with us. We'll call your aunt, and we will take you home afterward."

Jackson glanced to where the girls huddled near Jill. They had their backs to him. He said, "Yeah, we'll take you home." This seemed important to Lauren.

Allison rolled her eyes toward the girls. "They wouldn't want me to come with you," she said primly.

Jackson frowned. His patience had been tested too many times the past few days. "Uh, and why would they not want you to come with us?"

Allison ducked her head and kicked the arena sand with her paddock boot. "They don't like me."

Jackson made an exasperated sound and pushed his hands into his pockets. "Anyone who rides like you do—they'd be foolish not to want you for a friend."

Her face whipped up, smiling and flushed pink, before she quickly looked down again. He'd said the right thing. He glanced to get Brooke and Mandy's attention, but caught Aunt Willa's eye instead. She pointed at her watch, letting him know that she and Thelma had to go. He nodded and waved. He heard Lauren coaxing a few words out of the girl about riding.

He sighed and called out, "Brooke—Mandy, over here please." They stared in his direction as if he had just landed from Mars.

"Come here—*Please*."

Jill wore a worried expression as she shuffled the girls, half pushing them in his direction. They seemed unable to pick their feet up.

He curbed the rise of impatience—women!

Lauren made a noise and when he gave an inquiring look, she threw him a warning shake of her head that said *tread carefully*.

"Why don't you girls invite Allison to come with us to get an ice cream? She can tell us how she got to be such a good rider." He glanced at the girls. "What do you think?"

Lauren stepped up. "That's a wonderful idea, Jackson!" Ignoring the wide-eyed stare on both girls' faces, she turned to Allison. "I hope you'll go with us, Allison. I'd love to hear how long you've been riding and what was the hardest part when you had your very first lesson."

Jackson watched interest creep into Brooke and Mandy's eyes in spite of themselves.

Allison bit her lip and lifted her face just enough to get a sidelong look at Brooke and Mandy. She shrugged one shoulder and said, "If *they* want me to."

Jackson clapped his hands together, doing a dry-hand wash, and said, "Good! Of course they want you to come with us. That's all settled."

Brooke tugged on his sleeve. "Da-a-d-d—you don't understand—"

Jackson ignored her, as Lauren seemed to be doing too, and stepped toward the equally puzzled stable owner who didn't know what was going on—well, neither did Jackson. But Lauren's eyes were firing signals as fast as bullets.

He walked over to Steven's side and lowered his voice. "Sorry about all this—ask again and see if Mandy will change her mind about that ride."

Steven nodded, pulled his cap back down and gently ran his hand down the side of Sweet Star's face, and said to Mandy, "She's awfully disappointed you didn't want that ride. Sure you won't change your mind?"

Mandy's eyes darted to Allison and then up to Steven. "If you'll lead her for me."

Steven looked surprised, but said, "Sure, I'd be happy to lead you." He reached to take the lead rope from Allison.

She held fast to it. "I'll go slow—and careful, Mandy."

Jackson didn't miss the hint of scorn in Allison's voice and Lauren's quick glance said she hadn't either.

When Mandy looked doubtful, Allison added softly, "I promise."

Mandy bit her lip and looked at Steven and back to Allison. "You promise?"

Allison's body relaxed and her eyes brightened, she nodded. "I promise, really."

Steven helped Mandy back on Sweet Star and showed her how to hold the reins. With Allison leading at a snail's pace, they headed out to the middle of the arena.

Jackson watched Mandy being led away. After a couple of minutes, he leaned his shoulder against Lauren's and said, "Now—can you please tell me what's going on?"

Lauren's look was one of resignation; she said dryly, "Later, it's another long story that I didn't bother to share with you."

He didn't have the energy or the nerve to pursue that remark.

# CHAPTER TWENTY-FOUR

# Horse Love

Drained, exhausted and weary, Lauren smiled—a satisfied smile. There should be no more trouble at school, anyway not with Allison. They called her aunt and got permission for the ice cream outing.

The first thirty minutes or so had been awkward when all three girls climbed into the Range Rover at Lauren's suggestion.

Mandy's mom followed to the ice cream shop in her car.

Breaking the ice had taken a little time, but lingering excitement of the horse ride, signing up for weekly lessons, and learning that the new girl wasn't so bad, and she was an excellent rider, they gave her a chance. The morning had proven to be successful.

Jackson said, "I don't know what happened at the stable today, but the look on your face tells me you're pleased." He casually draped his tall frame into his chair and looked down at the gardens where his aunt and Thelma were involved in a lively discussion of planting and transplanting.

Lauren said, "I'm happy for the girls. Sometimes, friendships that have the rockiest starts, last the longest."

He turned his attention from the scene in the garden. "I know, look at us." He grinned. "I'd be interested in hearing about it."

Lauren sat opposite him. "Well, the girls have been having trouble at school with Allison. She was bullying them, mostly Mandy."

He frowned. "I find that hard to believe."

Lauren shrugged. "I would have too, but I saw it with my own eyes."

"Why didn't you—"

"Jackson! Before you even start—I didn't tell you because you were already worried about Brooke, and I thought that was something I could take care of without worrying you. If that makes me a bad person, then I'm sorry—I'm a bad person."

He sighed. "Why do you suppose she picked on the girls? She said *they* didn't like her."

"That's kids for you. I believe she wanted to be friends, but they paid her no mind." She smothered a yawn. "I imagine Allison really thought they didn't like her. Brooke and Mandy have each other, it never occurred to them to reach out to the new girl in school.

"They didn't snub her on purpose, they just never thought about it." Lauren raised her brows. "And you know what they say, bad attention is better than no attention. I'm sure that's all it was on Allison's part."

Jackson pressed his lips together and nodded. "I hope so. How did you know it was the girl from school?"

"I didn't at first. The riding helmet covered her hair." She smiled. "The girls hadn't recognized her either. Steven called her name and Mandy got a look at who was going to lead the horse." Lauren sighed. "I could tell she was really afraid, so I took a close look at the girl and then I recognized her."

Jackson was smiling and shaking his head. "You're something else, you know that? The ice cream was a great idea."

She shrugged. "I wanted the girls to have a chance to see each other in a different setting than school." Lauren bit her lip. "I'll bet they become fast friends—through the horses."

"I hope so. Brooke and Mandy really could be encouraged and learn from Allison. She's amazing on that giant of a horse she rides." He smiled. "I heard her correct Brooke when she referred to the color of Allison's horse as reddish brown." He smiled. "Allison informed Brooke that the color was chestnut."

Lauren nodded, smiling. "Uh-huh, the girls were soaking it all in as their ice cream melted." She yawned again. "Let's keep our fingers crossed that the weekly riding sessions will bring them together."

"Maybe so. Did you hear what the trainer called Allison's horse as she led him away?"

Lauren frowned. "No, I didn't."

"Destiny, " Jackson said with a knowing grin. After a long pause they both laughed.

Lauren laid her head back on her chair, still smiling. "How appropriate." She yawned.

Jackson rose from his chair. "I think you better get a nap. And as much as I hate it . . . I need to have a talk with Brooke about the trip." He glanced sidelong at Lauren.

She shook her head. "Don't even think about asking. I'm not about to break that news to her." She stood and headed toward the bathroom, but stopped and tilted her head. "You won't reconsider her going with me?"

He sighed. "Lauren, you'll be run ragged while you're there, I wouldn't rest a minute for worrying about both of you."

"Fine. I understand, but you do need to go tell her. Lauren went into the bathroom and closed the door. She heard Jackson leave their room. She sat on the stool in front of her dressing table and beat herself up for not making it easier on him. If nothing else, she might be a comfort to Brooke. Grumbling to herself she hurried from the bathroom to Brooke's room. Lauren approached the open door and heard Brooke's raised voice; she halted.

"But Dad, why can't I go anyway? Did Lauren say I couldn't?"

"No, no, sweetheart, of course Lauren didn't say that. It's just that since I can't go—"

"You could go—Uncle Matt can run the gallery, can't he?"

She heard Jackson sigh. This had been a hard day for him.

"Brooke, you and I are not going. I'm sorry, but there'll be another time for us."

"No, Dad. I want us to go this time."

"It's out of the question, Pumpkin. What has come over you?" Lauren heard desperation and frustration mounting in his voice.

Brooke started to cry. Lauren didn't know whether to go in and try to help or quietly slip away. Jackson said something else that she couldn't make out, and Brooke's voice rose again.

"You're not fair! You told me to be fair about Mandy when we got in trouble, but you're not fair about Lauren. She's not irr . . . irrsponsi . . . irresponsible. She talked to my teacher about . . . about bad things at school." Brooke sobbed so hard Lauren couldn't understand what she was saying. Moving as quickly and quietly as possible she fled back to their room and hid in the bathroom. She didn't want Jackson to know she'd overheard the conversation. She turned the shower on just as the phone began to ring in the bedroom.

Hurrying to answer it, she muttered, "Please be Nicolas canceling the exhibit, please!" "Hello—oh, Clair, it's you!"

"You were expecting someone else? And I'm a disappointment?" She laughed.

"Of course not." Lauren glanced at the clock. The day was dragging. It should be bedtime by now but the sky was still blue. "What are you up to?"

"I thought I'd share something touching and make your day. Caroline has mentioned several times the last few days what she might wear to the event she and Dad are attending this evening. I've never before heard her fuss about what to wear. I think she's nervous to please Dad." Clair laughed delightedly. "I saw Dad this morning and he'd had his hair trimmed and a manicure. I think they're both looking forward to the evening."

"I hope so, that's what we all hoped for. Are you pleased?"

"Oh, of course. I love them both and if they should have enough common interest to enjoy one another's company, then fine." Clair paused. "You sound tired. When do you see the doctor?"

"I'm fine." Lauren scrunched her face. "I have a doctor visit first thing on Monday."

"You better rest up before the exhibit, that'll drain even the bunny that keeps on going."

Lauren laughed. "I know, and I'll get there rested if it kills Jackson." They giggled at Jackson's expense.

Clair couldn't know that Lauren's heart was breaking for him at the very moment. "Will you guys be here for church Sunday?"

"We can't make it Sunday, Dad has plans for us Sunday afternoon." Clair was quiet for several seconds. "Well, I'll let you go, but expect to hear a detailed account of how the evening went. I will press Caroline for *everything*."

"I'll be waiting, but do go easy on her." They said goodbye and ended the call.

Lauren went to the door and peeked into the hall. No sounds from anywhere. Jackson must have gone walking after speaking with Brooke; he wanted to be alone.

Moving quietly across the upstairs gallery toward Brooke's room, Lauren opened the door an inch. Brooke was asleep, curled on her side with her hand to her mouth; her fair skin still blotched from crying. Lauren swiped at the tears blurring her own vision, remembering how Brooke had stood up to her father for her. She gazed tenderly upon the small face. "Don't give up, Brooke," she whispered. "Now it's my turn to stand up for you."

As quietly as she had entered Brooke's room, she crept back to her own. She took off her boots and jeans, and pulled the turtleneck off over her head and slipped on her robe.

Snug in the warm fuzzy robe, and ready for a nap, Lauren huddled on her side of the bed. What had Brooke meant when she told her dad that Lauren had talked with her teacher? How could Brooke possibly know of Lauren's talk with Mrs. Flowers?

She recalled a conversation she'd had with Dr. Brickman just before she and Jackson were married.

Still afraid and unsure of being a wife and mother, she'd explained to Dr. Brickman her fear of not having the wisdom to be an authority figure, a parent. What if she was weak and couldn't make a decision or take a stand when it was imperative that she do so? Dr. Brickman had kindly shook her head, and said, "Each of us live with that fear daily."

To which Lauren had complained, "That's no help—I need answers. Before, it was only myself to suffer the consequences of my actions. . . ."

Dr. Brickman had said, "The only answer I have is to pick your battle wisely, view it from every side; be fair and pray for guidance."

Lauren yawned, and relaxed, allowing sleep to claim her body and dull her thoughts . . . she was glad she'd remembered that time with Dr. Brickman . . . it helped with her decision. Pick my battle wisely . . . be fair . . . and pray . . . .

At one time she thought someone had opened the bedroom door, but she couldn't rouse herself; either she'd dreamt it, or they went away. She turned and twisted; her feet and legs felt as if they were tied.

Gradually, the much-needed rest restored her body to the point that she woke. The room was dark.

Her legs were tangled in the throw from her chair. Jackson must have covered her.

# CHAPTER TWENTY-FIVE

# Lines Drawn

Once she'd freed her legs from the tangled bed throw, Lauren was fully awake, and the events of the day were still crystal clear in her mind. So was her determination that Brooke would go to Italy with her.

Jackson had better come up with something better than the excuse that she was having a baby. Her health was good and he knew it.

If worse came to worse, Clair would be happy to travel with them, she'd mentioned going anyway, so it wouldn't be difficult to persuade her.

Standing in her closet, deciding what to wear, Lauren finally just reached for the new, long white top she'd bought like the one Ally had worn so often before Eli was born. Wiggling into black skinny jeans and slipping on black suede loafers, she gathered her long hair into a loose ponytail. Viewing herself in the mirror, she wondered if Jackson had noticed that she had let her hair revert to its more curly state?

Max had advised it—easier on the hair and a lot less effort than blow-drying to straighten it. She would appreciate less effort once the baby got there. Lauren thought it odd that neither he nor Brooke had noticed her hair.

On her way to the stairs, Brooke's door was still closed. Wanting to peek in to check on her, Lauren tried the door. It was locked. She tried it again. Brooke had never locked her door. Heading to the kitchen, she glanced into the morning room as she passed the wide-open entry. No one was there. Gratefully, she heard Aunt Willa in the kitchen. But it turned out to be Jackson.

Her heart wrenched at the drawn, tired look on his face. "Oh, I thought you were Aunt Willa."

"She had a bad headache, I sent her to bed."

Lauren glanced at the sandwich fixings on the bar. She stepped around to where he had piled everything. "Let me do that."

"Thanks," he said and moved to the other side of the bar. He took a seat in one of the bar chairs and watched as she made two sandwiches.

"Jackson, I know you're probably not up to this, but we have to talk about the exhibit and Brooke." She cut his sandwich in fourths the way he liked and stacked it on a plate with chips and pushed it toward him.

"Thank you." He pulled the plate in front of him. "We can agree on that—I'm not up to it now." He bowed his head for a moment before lifting the sandwich to his mouth.

She cut her sandwich, stacked a small handful of chips on her plate, poured two glasses of tea and took the seat next to his. "We have to talk and putting it off won't make it easier."

Jackson reached for his tea and took a long swallow. "I know you and Brooke are upset, and I'm sorry, but I can't see any other way."

"You could ask Matt if he couldn't handle the new contract without your help—I'm sure he'd be happy—"

"No. I won't put it all on Matt. Of course he'd tell me to go on, he's like that."

An expression crossed his face, guilt? He'd glanced at her and quickly down to his plate. Yes, he looked and acted, guilty. She sighed. So that was it, Matt had already offered to take care of the new job. Jackson *wanted* to stay and be a part of the project.

The sandwich had begun to taste like cardboard, but she hadn't eaten all day and needed the nourishment. Jackson had only eaten half his sandwich and most of the chips, when he pushed the plate away.

"The sandwich was good, but I can't finish it." He ran his hand through his hair. "I need a shower." He rose from the bar.

Lauren didn't look up, or move. "If it would make you feel better, Clair would be happy to go with Brooke and me." She rushed on. "She really wants to go anyway and traveling with us would give her a good excuse to go." She held her breath. Jackson was taking so long to answer she first thought he wasn't going to.

"No. I'm . . . I'm sorry, honey."

Lauren gave a loud huff, and unaware that Brooke had entered the kitchen, she raised her voice, "What would Jenna think of you depriving your daughter of this opportunity?"

Jackson made an odd sound. She turned and looked over her shoulder. Brooke was standing just inside the kitchen, she'd heard. Her round eyes stared at Jackson for a split second before she turned and ran, flying back up the stairs.

"Oh, Jackson! I'm so sorry. I'll go talk to her—"

"No!"

"But, I'll explain—"

"Leave it alone!"

He made for the stairs and thundered up them, two at a time. With a heavy heart Lauren put the kitchen back to order.

Between her and Jackson they'd managed to put a sorry end to Brooke's fun day.

She sighed, retrieved her cell phone from the bar and went to the mudroom where she shuffled into her garden boots. In the dimly lit mudroom, she fumbled among the sweaters on the hooks. She pulled on the first one to come off the hook; it didn't matter which one she wore.

As she was about to step outside, Winslow came running with Winnie right behind him. "Oh, okay, you two, come on. But be warned, I'm not good company tonight." In her mind she finished with, *just ask my husband.*

The gardens were so familiar that Lauren could have walked every inch blindfolded, and she might as well have for all she saw. The fragrance of Thelma's roses guided her, as they showed no signs of knowing that fall was nipping at their petals. Winslow halted a few feet ahead of her and growled low in his throat.

"Silly boy that's just a rabbit looking for an evening snack." He shot after it, but Winnie stayed close to her. "You're a smart girl—" The phone in her pocket rang. She pulled it out and glanced at the lighted screen; it was Clair. Lauren made an effort to sound cheerful as she said, "Hello, how did the date go?"

"Who would know? They haven't come in yet."

Lauren detected a touch of annoyance in Clair's voice. "It's still early." She laughed. "You didn't set a curfew, did you?"

Clair laughed. "No, but I wanted to. Dad's too old to be staying out so late."

"Clair! Don't ever say anything like that to Charlie—he wouldn't like it one bit."

"Oh, no, no, I'd never say anything." She paused a second. "But that's not what I called about."

"Oh—?"

"Is there anyway you could find time to come to the city for a few days?" Clair hesitated several seconds. "I know with the exhibit and all you're terribly busy, but I really could use your help."

"Well, of course, what kind of help do you need?"

"It's a silly thing, really, but important to me." She sighed. "One of Drew's elderly aunts, the one from Ohio, that I've only met once, at our wedding, is going to spend a week with us—the week that Drew will be out of town the first three or four days." Clair sighed. If you could just come for those few days that Drew's gone."

Lauren pulled the sweater closer to her body. The evening air was turning cooler by the minute. "How can I help by being there?"

"Just that—by being here. I don't know what to do with an elderly woman—if it was an uncle, I'd just treat him like I do Dad, but, you know."

"What makes you think I'd know what to do with Drew's aunt?"

Clair pleaded. "Surely the two of us could figure it out better than I can by myself. I thought it might be easier if we entertained her together."

Lauren hated to say no, she couldn't say no, but this was the worse time ever for her to be gone. She was tempted to tell Clair the latest, but thinking about trying to explain the mess she was in made her head throb. "When do you need me?"

"I know you go to the doctor on Monday—you said it was early?"

"Yes. Eight-forty-five, a.m."

"Could you head this way as soon as your appointment is over? I'm picking her up at the airport at noon." Clair sighed. "I thought we could take her to lunch . . . unless something else would be better?"

Lauren bit her lip. "She might have lunch on the plane, and if she's elderly she may want to go to your place and rest, do you suppose?"

"I don't have a clue. All I know is that I would feel better if you were here, too." She gave a short laugh. "I would feel the same if Ally asked me to keep Eli for three days—I'd be at a loss as what to do with him."

Lauren laughed and said, "I'll remember that when my baby gets here—" Jackson had turned on the outside lights and was looking for her. "Clair, I'll come, but I have to go now. I'll call you later."

"Of course, and thank you a million times over."

They ended the call as Jackson ambled up and sat beside her on the cold stone bench.

"What are you doing out here in this cool damp air?"

Lauren heard his question, and weary of his worrying, she suddenly wanted to be with Clair. Jackson was going to worry no matter what. "The cool air feels good," she said. His eyes swept her clutching the old sweater close to her body. She relaxed her grip and said, "But I'm ready to go in." She rose from the bench. "That was Clair on the phone. She asked me to drive in and spend a few days with her."

Jackson drew a sharp intake of breath. "This is not a good time—"

"I know. But a houseguest is arriving and Drew's out of town. She seems to think I'll be able to help her entertain this person."

In the dim lighting of the garden he nodded. "And you probably need a break."

As they walked side by side, she glanced up at him. "I don't need a break, but I couldn't say no to Clair. She would do anything for me, so I have to go." Lauren kept her head down as they neared the house. "I seem to be making things worse here anyway."

"Don't be silly. And of course, I understand about Clair." He ran his hand through his hair. "I had a long talk with Brooke."

"I'm sorry for saying that about Jenna—" Lauren darted a glance in his direction.

"It's okay. She's fine. She wants you to come to her room before you go to bed."

Nodding, Lauren said, "Yes, of course." She sighed. "I'm glad she still wants to see me."

They were at the door to the mudroom when Jackson slowed his step; he turned and pulled Lauren into his arms. "I love you. Don't ever think I don't."

She lifted her face to his. "I love you, too, Jackson! Even when it may seem like I don't—I could never stop loving you." She tightened her arms in response to his. "Never, ever could I stop loving you."

Winslow and Winnie waited patiently at the door, poised to shoot inside.

Jackson opened the door and shook his head, he grinned at Lauren as the dogs tumbled inside and stood waiting while she changed back to her shoes and hung the sweater on its hook.

Warmth from the kitchen dispelled the chill from the night air, and Lauren thought again how winter was creeping close and that Thanksgiving would be upon them in a flash. She groaned to herself, in the events of the day, she'd forgotten to open Max's letter!

"Walking in the garden at this time of evening?" Aunt Willa sat at the bar having tea and a sandwich.

Jackson went around the bar and sat next to her. "Yeah, partaking of the fall air. I'm glad to see you feeling better. That headache all gone?"

She smiled and set her cup down. "It is, thank goodness." She glanced at Lauren. "What did you all have for dinner?"

"Sandwiches." Lauren remembered that Brooke had come down to the kitchen, but heard them talking and ran back to her room. "Jackson, I'm afraid Brooke hasn't eaten yet—"

"Yes, she has. Milk and cereal was all she wanted. I allowed her to have it in her room."

Aunt Willa frowned. "I hope she's not coming down with something. She's had a busy day."

"Nah," Jackson said. "It's just the excitement of the day."

Lauren stood and said, "I think I'll run up and look in on her—" And on the way she'd stop in the morning room and grab the envelope from Max.

Jackson stood also. "I'll go with you. Goodnight, Aunt Willa, see you at breakfast."

She was pouring hot water over a tea bag. "Goodnight, both of you."

Lauren nodded. The letter would have to wait until later. They reached the stairs and Lauren took the lead. She hesitated at Brooke's open door. Under her breath she whispered to Jackson, "She had it locked earlier, did you know that?"

He nodded and lowered his voice, "Yes. She was angry and hurt."

Lauren knocked lightly on the doorframe, "Brooke?"

Her cheery voice called, "Come in! Come see what I'm drawing."

Lauren raised her brows at Jackson and whispered, "She sounds okay."

He laughed quietly. "I told you she was fine."

Lauren entered the room and sat on the bed. Jackson stayed at the door leaning against the doorframe.

Brooke was sitting in the middle of her bed coloring. "Look, it's Allison's horse."

"You certainly have a good likeness." Lauren took the paper in her hand. "Is it for Allison?"

Brooke nodded shyly. "If she wants it."

"There'll be no doubt of that!" Lauren pursed her lips. She caught a signal that passed between Brooke and her dad. What were they up to?

Brooke said, "I have a surprise."

Lauren widened her eyes and glanced at Jackson then back to Brooke. "Do I have to guess?"

Brooke giggled and bounced on the bed, her eyes full of mischief "You'd *never* guess."

"No, I'm not good at—"

"We're going to Italy! Brooke clasped her hands under her chin; her eyes as big as saucers as she waited for Lauren's reaction.

Lauren half turned to Jackson. "What—?"

"Not *we* as in all of us, just you two, Pumpkin." He glanced at Lauren. "I've reconsidered, and Brooke promised—"

"But, Da-a-a-d, I thought you were going, too!" Brooke's wail hung in the air as she folded her arms on her chest and her eyes threatened tears.

"No, sweetie, that's not what I said."

"But I thought . . . I want you to go, too."

Jackson jammed both hands into his pockets. "I never said I was going, just you girls. Remember, I have a commitment here at home." He waited, but Brooke remained silent. He glanced at Lauren. "And I would feel better if you could get Clair to go with you—"

"I don't want to go." Brooke began gathering her pencils and placing them back in their box. She looked up; her tear-filled eyes glistened. "I'm . . . sorry Lauren."

Lauren rose from the side of the bed. "It's okay, honey." Lauren bent to kiss her. "I don't think I want to go either." She gazed at Brooke for a moment. "Well, goodnight." She brushed past Jackson and hurried to their bedroom and into her closet. She grabbed a robe and was headed to the bathroom as Jackson entered the bedroom.

"Would you please go and talk to her." He raked his hair and paced to the windows and back. "I've tried to be fair and nothing I do seems to please anyone." His eyes pleaded.

"By anyone you mean Brooke and me?" She gazed at him. "And even though I mentioned Clair going with us, I find it really bothers me that you'd feel better about Brooke going with me if Clair is along." She sighed. "And no, I won't talk to Brooke. I'm tired of talking about the trip. I'll go alone and get it over with and never mention it again."

With a glance at Jackson's stricken face, she turned and stepped into the bathroom and leaned against the door. *It would be good to be with Clair in New York for a few days.*

When she heard Jackson leave the room, she changed into her pajamas and robe, thinking she might slip down to the morning room and retrieve Max's letter. Jackson wasn't in the room when she came out of the bathroom.

There were no lights on downstairs in the morning room, so Lauren made her way by the light that filtered from the kitchen. The pale gray envelop lay where she had tossed it that morning. She carefully tore the flap open and there in the dim light, read the note. Her heart sank even lower than it already was.

Max and Whitney wouldn't make it for Thanksgiving after all. Whitney's building project was running over time and the owners were in a panic. She'd promised not to leave until their home was finished. Max was vague about why she couldn't come, just other commitments. Lauren sank into one of the big chairs and the tears came.

Disappointment over Max and Whitney was the last straw. She cried for all the miserable events that had happened the last few weeks.

## CHAPTER TWENTY-SIX

# Off to New York

Jackson stood in the shadows near the windows in the dark room. He'd been reasoning with himself, trying to understand the two girls he loved more than his own life, when Lauren came in. Not bothering to turn on a light, she had picked up the letter from Max.

He was afraid to breathe for fear she would discover him. He observed as she read the note. It was all he could do to not go to her when she cried as if the world was on her shoulders.

What had Max written to cause such a flood of tears?

His feet felt frozen to the floor, and he didn't move for the longest time after Lauren had wearily risen from the chair and made her way back upstairs.

He stood in the dark, puzzled, until he heard Aunt Willa moving about in the next room, making her hot chocolate. He breathed freely again and headed to the kitchen. When he came out of the morning room, his aunt jumped.

"Mercy—you startled me. Were you sitting in there in the dark?"

"Yeah, sometimes the dark makes it easier to sort things out."

She nodded. "Very true. I like to sit in my bed-room chair sometimes when it's dark and look out onto the gardens and across to the woods, it's restful—and especially when it's raining or on a full moon." She stirred the chocolate. "Would you like a cup?"

"No thanks, it's about my bed time, or I'll have a hard time staying awake in church tomorrow."

Aunt Willa sipped her hot drink and watched him over the rim of her cup. "How did it go at the stables after Thelma and I left?" She smiled. "Did the girls finally take a trial ride?"

"Yeah, they finally did. Turns out the girl that rode that giant of a horse, is a classmate at school." He stifled a yawn and rose from the bar chair. "I'll say goodnight and drag myself upstairs."

"You look tired, Jackson. I'm glad you're going to the exhibit with Lauren. You need a break."

He halted and turned around to face his aunt. "I haven't had a chance to tell you, but I'm not going with the girls."

"What?" She sat her cup on the bar. "I understood you were going."

"I was at first. But we got that contract to supply the artwork for a huge corporation that's doing some major redecorating, it's very important. I need to be here."

She pursed her lips. "I'm sure that was a big dis-appointment to Lauren."

Jackson ran a hand through his hair. "Aunt Willa, I already feel like the Lone Ranger in this. Lauren and Brooke are both upset with me—please, don't you take sides against me too."

"I'm not taking sides with anyone, but as Lauren said at the beginning, it's not two weeks or a month—just four days. What can happen in four days?"

Jackson shook his head, threw his hand in the air and headed for the stairs. "There's no use talking to you women!" If he wasn't mistaken, it sounded like his aunt was chuckling as he stormed from the kitchen.

He reached the top of the stairs to find Brooke's door closed. Had she locked it again? He'd rather she didn't start that habit. He closed his fingers around the brass knob, but slowly he pulled his hand back without trying it—he would assume the door wasn't locked. He moved on to his own room and appreciated the small lamp Lauren had left on for him.

She was already sound asleep, flat on her back. She was worn out just as he was. He stood by the bed and studied her face. She hadn't braided her hair and it fanned out around her head. He noticed again that she'd let it go curly—it was pretty, but not Lauren—more of Max's influence.

Jackson was amazed that she slept so soundly in that position—didn't the weight of the baby bother her back? Lauren stirred in her sleep and turned on her side.

He went to the bathroom and started the shower. He missed Lauren already for the three days she'd be in New York with Clair.

\*\*\*

Sunday morning arrived with a snappy fall breeze in the air. The elms gently scattered golden leaves across the lawn and swirled them onto the flat stones of the patio. Jackson and Aunt Willa sat at the table in the dining room. The table was near the wide French doors that led out to the patio. He glanced at his aunt. "Claude should be happy, there's nothing he likes better than burning leaves."

Aunt Willa laughed. "He got that from his dad. Claude used to help his dad burn leaves when he was a kid."

Brooke padded barefoot past the dining room door on her way to the kitchen, Winnie trotted along with her. After awhile when she hadn't made an appearance in the dining room, Jackson sighed. "I guess she's still upset with me."

"Give her time, she'll get over it."

He nodded, and said, "Yeah, in time, Lauren will too, I hope." He was worried; she had tossed and turned all night. Every time she switched from one side to the other, he woke up. He hadn't gotten much sleep, so he knew she hadn't either.

After twenty or thirty minutes, Brooke started past the door again, wiping her mouth on the back of her hand. She'd apparently had a bowl of milk and cereal at the bar.

"Brooke! Come say good morning to your aunt and me."

She backed up, paused, did a tentative wave, and said, "Good morning, Aunt Willa . . . Dad." She bunched the front of her gown in her hands, cutting her eyes from one to the other, then hurried on. Winnie looked across the room at Jackson as if to say, "sorry, I have to go where she does," and padded after Brooke.

Aunt Willa refreshed their coffee. "She's very disappointed about the trip, she just has to get over it. Don't worry about it, or change your mind and go." She moved the breakfast quiche closer to tempt him.

"Please, let's not get into that this morning—"

"Good morning!" Lauren came quietly into the dining room, still fastening her watch on her wrist. "Something sure smells good, and I'm starved." She took her customary place at the table next to Jackson and said, "Has this food been blessed?" as she reached for the quiche.

Jackson couldn't believe how rested she looked. He reached for his aunt's hand and caught Lauren's in his other hand. "It will be in a moment." He returned thanks, and he too, was hungry now.

Lauren moved her cup and saucer toward Aunt Willa for her to fill from the coffee carafe. "Thank you." She smiled at his aunt and spread her napkin in her lap. "I love this weather."

Aunt Willa glanced out the window and nodded. "Yes, it's perfect."

Whether it was the weather, or that she was going away from him for several days, *whatever*, Jackson was deeply grateful that Lauren seemed more her old self than she had in days and that she wasn't going to pout and punish him. Suddenly, he wasn't just hungry; he was starved.

"Jackson, you remember I got a letter from Max the other morning?"

He glanced at her. "Uh-huh." Was she going to tell him why she cried after reading it? "Umm, what did she have to say?"

"Well," she said, and finished chewing and touched her lips with the napkin then continued. "She and Whitney can't make it for Thanksgiving. I was terribly disappointed at first. But the more I think about it—it might be more fun to have the big party at Christmas instead of Thanksgiving anyway." She took a sip of coffee. "Max said they would definitely clear their schedules for Christmas if it worked for us as well. What do you two think?" She glanced at Aunt Willa and back to Jackson.

He nodded. "Or, if you want to, we could do both."

With her mouth full again, she shook her head until she could answer, "No, two big parties that close would be too much."

Aunt Willa said, "I agree. People are so busy that time of year, one party should do." She smiled at Lauren. "I personally like a big Christmas party for family and friends."

"So," Jackson said, "Thanksgiving will just be us and maybe Thelma?"

Lauren glanced at Aunt Willa; they nodded. "Yes."

Jackson drew a deep breath, relieved that Lauren appeared to be just fine. But had she cried her eyes out the night before, simply because Max couldn't come for Thanksgiving?

He gave a sidelong glance. She looked happy enough now, but it didn't make sense.

A shadow of doubt darkened his thoughts about his decision not to go with her.

# CHAPTER TWENTY-SEVEN

# A Breather

Sunday afternoon passed swiftly in a swirl of activity. Lauren completed the many small tasks that needed to be done before she left for New York the following morning. She'd returned the call to Nicolas.

He'd asked her to rush ship another three small canvases. His thinking was to have more small canvases to offer those collectors who enjoyed collecting, but who were not ready for another large piece at the time.

Nicolas assured her the gallery would of course pay the exorbitant shipping costs, but Lauren offered instead to carry them in her luggage when she came. With that settled, all she had to do now was decide which three to take. And that could wait until she got back from Clair's.

She ticked off completed items from the list until she came to Brooke's dental appointment. She'd better remind Aunt Willa. The appointment was Wednesday after school and Lauren wouldn't be back in time to take her.

Seeing again the disappointment in Brooke's eyes, Lauren couldn't stop the sudden fatigue that slumped her shoulders. She made her way to the chairs in the sitting area of their bedroom. Why couldn't Jackson see how important this was to his child? Her head throbbed, she must not think about it—her anger resurfaced the moment she allowed her thoughts to question Jackson's reasoning.

He must really believe she was incapable of keeping Brooke safe. Lauren had traveled the world over from the time she was a child . . . Jackson knew it.

Lauren rose from the chair; a nap would make her feel better. She pulled the lap throw off the back of her chair and staggered to the bed.

Waking hours later to a dark bedroom, she quickly glanced at the bedside clock. Church would be half over, had the others gone without her?

She threw the cover back and hurried barefoot down to the morning room first and then on to the den. Ambling back to the morning room, she stood in the middle of the room. Jackson wouldn't have been able to force himself to wake her; he knew she was tired. She wandered over to his chair by the windows and sank into it.

She had needed the rest.

Although she had lived most of her life alone, only now did she understand loneliness. Could she stand three or four days in New York? And no sooner get home than it would be time to repack and leave for Italy? If only Brooke was going with her.

Sitting in the growing darkness, Lauren relaxed her head against the chair, and played out several scenarios in which she demanded that Jackson accompany her and Brooke to the exhibit. Would she have the nerve or the courage to go through with it? The worst he could do was say no.

Mentally studying her calendar, she ticked off the days she'd be gone the following week, arriving back on the weekend—not a good time to start something. It might be best to wait until the following week to force Jackson's hand. Just in case her plan was successful, she'd be ready and prepared to help Jackson and Brooke pack at the last minute.

The alarm that the garage door was going up jerked Lauren to her feet.

Jackson would think something was wrong if he caught her sitting alone in the dark.

She hurried to put on several lamps in the morning room and ran to the den and switched on the TV, turned on lights and was relaxed on the sofa when he entered the room.

"Well, did you have a good rest?"

"Yes, I did, but why didn't you wake me in time for church?"

Jackson pushed his hand through his hair and took a seat on the leather sofa beside her and reached for her hand. "You needed the rest."

"Yes, I probably did." She glanced down at his large hand holding hers and wished he could know how much she loved him. But words can't convey the depth of feelings, and it grieved her heart that he would never truly know how deeply she loved him.

He put his arm around her shoulder and pulled her close. "I'll miss you. Would you like for me to drive you to the city in the morning?"

Lauren shook her head. "Thank you, honey, but I'd rather drive myself."

"Okay." Jackson sighed. "Will you stop by the gallery on your way out?"

Snuggling closer into his arms, she said, "Of course, I'd planned to. I would like to take Brooke to school, if you don't mind."

"Of course, I don't mind." He brooded for several seconds. "Anyway, Brooke would rather you take her. She's still being cool to me. I would never have be-lieved Brooke would stay this upset and for so long."

Lauren's heart jumped—here was her opportu-nity, but at the very thought of mentioning the exhibit again, her breath almost squeezed off and, she begin to hyperventilate. No . . . she hadn't prepared or thought it out . . . plus the very thought of demanding or threat-ening Jackson about the trip gave her a sick stomach. But it was for Brooke. "Jackson I feel—"

He had risen from the sofa still holding her hand. He frowned, saying, "You feeling bad? What's wrong—are you hungry?"

Lauren took the coward's way out. "Yes, I . . . feel hungry."

Jackson pulled her to her feet. "Well, we just had a light snack before church. I could snack again."

They made their way to the kitchen, where Aunt Willa had prepared a tray with cheese, crackers, cold ham, and a bowl piled with red and white grapes. "I thought we might all need a snack before bedtime."

She went to the stairs and called up, "Brooke! Snacks are ready." Smiling, Aunt Willa strolled back to the bar. "There's a good movie coming on. Anyway it's supposed to be a good one." She glanced at Lauren and Jackson. "Why don't we watch it together?"

Jackson raised a brow toward Lauren. "Sounds like fun."

"Yes." Lauren nodded. She was breathing freely, having recovered from the close call of possibly pushing Jackson to a point that she didn't really care to witness. How did she ever hope to stand firm and demand anything of him?

Brooke hopped down the stairs with both dogs at her heels. She went to Lauren and put her arms around her waist. She leaned her head back and smiled up. "You feel bigger!"

Lauren smiled and brushed Brooke's hair away from her face. "I am bigger. I've gained three pounds this week. Dr. Stinson will be happy that I didn't gain ten pounds."

Brooke giggled. "Will you and Clair stay on a diet when you go to New York?"

"I can't speak for Clair, but I'll try to stick to my diet." Lauren frowned. "I wish I didn't have to go."

Brooke continued looking up into Lauren's face. Her expression became serious. "Why are you going then?"

Lauren hesitated. "Well—"

"Come on girls," Jackson said, "Let's ask the blessing, you can talk later."

Afterwards they chatted about the movie they planned to watch and about the weather for the following week, until suddenly Brooke turned to Lauren.

"Why are you going to Clair's hotel when you don't want to go?"

The question startled Lauren. "It's not that I don't want to go. I love being with Clair, but I have things here I need to do and . . . she glanced at Jackson and Aunt Willa . . . and I miss you guys."

Jackson nodded, pleased, and said, "And we don't always get to do exactly as we wish to do. We have to consider other people and what's best for all concerned—"

"May I be excused, please?" Brooke asked.

Jackson controlled his exasperation, but Lauren watched it rise in his face. Just as she'd seen Brooke's eyes glaze over while Jackson spoke. Brooke recognized a lecture.

Wearily he said, "Brooke, you were rude just now."

"I'm sorry, Dad."

"Yes, you may be excused."

Lauren bit her lip to hold back a smile as she and Aunt Willa began to clear the bar and load the glasses and snack plates into the dishwasher. In a low voice Lauren said, "Brooke may be just like Jenna, but she got a good dose of the Montgomery side, too."

Aunt Willa directed a knowing smile at Lauren and nodded before saying, "Jackson, why don't you go ahead and check the movie channel and get us ready to watch."

Jackson's exasperation lingered, he directed it at his aunt this time in a clipped question. "I have no idea which movie you were talking about—may I know the title and which channel it's aired on?"

Aunt Willa said pleasantly, "The eight o'clock movie on channel eight, easy to remember, but I don't recall the title."

Jamming his hands deep into his pockets, Jackson wandered toward the den.

"I sense an unrest in this house; between all of you. I'm sure Brooke's disappointment at not going with you, Lauren, is part of it, but is that all?"

Lauren lifted her hands in a futile gesture. "I . . . I'm not sure either. The exhibit is the biggest problem right now, but there's something else going on with Jackson." Lauren shrugged. "I guess the problem at school, and me running around in New York with Max." She glanced at Jackson's aunt. "I really don't know, but I wish you wouldn't worry. We'll all be okay—we love each other."

Aunt Willa laughed. "I'm not worried, I just want to help if there's anything I can do." She hesitated as if she didn't know whether to speak or not. "Jackson *is* nearing forty. He has a daughter who's growing up, one who has a mind of her own, there's a new baby on the way—and—your career may take you away even more after this show in Italy." She studied Lauren for a moment. "Just think about all that."

Lauren nodded slowly. "Yes, I see what you mean; so many changes, and all so close together.

As they walked from the kitchen together, Aunt Willa slipped her arm around Lauren. "Jackson is a good person. He's level headed, he loves you and Brooke more than his own life, but he's human."

They were nearing the den and Aunt Willa glanced sidelong at Lauren. "At times even strong men must wrestle the demons of doubt and insecurity.

\*\*\*

Aunt Willa's idea to watch the movie had been a good one. The story had all the elements that make a great movie. They laughed, cheered, and cried through the struggles of a little boy who'd been born on a farm. He and his mother were forced to live in the city with an aunt after his father went to war.

Brooke walked on her knees to Aunt Willa's chair, "That wasn't fair that Teddy had to leave his pony and live in a place he didn't like."

"There are times, Brooke—" Jackson started.

"Um, sorry you two, but it's too late to rehash the movie." Lauren recognized the expression on Jackson's face—another lecture loomed. "It's bedtime, Brooke. We all have a busy day tomorrow."

Jackson raked his hand through his hair and looked thoughtful as Brooke hugged her great aunt goodnight and jumped up to run hug Lauren, who in turn gave Brooke's arm a firm grip that steered her toward her dad before she had a chance to flee the room.

"Goodnight, Dad." She allowed him to pull her into his arms for a long tight hug.

"Goodnight, Pumpkin."

Lauren cast a covert glance at Aunt Willa, who had a pleased smile on her face as she said, "Will I see you in the morning for coffee, dear?"

"Oh yes, I'll have time for coffee before I leave. Goodnight."

"Goodnight, you too, Jackson."

"Goodnight Aunt Willa."

Jackson and Lauren were left to turn out lights.

"Well, I think Brooke may be coming around," Jackson said. "Don't you? She hugged me for the first time since . . . since . . . you know."

"Yes, I know."

They climbed the stairs without further conversation.

Later, in bed, Lauren snuggled in the comforting protection of Jackson's arms. He held her as if she planned to be at Clair's for a month instead of a few days. She fell asleep formulating a plan to get him to Italy

.

# CHAPTER TWENTY-EIGHT

# Doubts

Jackson was the first one downstairs the next morning. But as usual his aunt was ahead of him and busying about. Her suite was just off the kitchen, so no one else ever beat her to the coffee maker.

She had placed the carafe on the serving bar in the morning room when he entered the room. "Good morning! Something smells good, and not just the coffee." He lifted his brows in a questioning way.

"Just plain old strudel. The same I always make." She straightened the stack of white china breakfast plates and situated the silverware next to them. "Maybe you're especially hungry."

"Maybe, sure smells good." He wandered across the room to the windows, checking that all was well with the world outside. Standing at the floor to ceiling windows first thing in the morning was something he'd seen both parents and his aunt do every morning as he was growing up. Now he and his aunt carried on the tradition. He'd noticed that Lauren had also acquired the habit.

"Hmm, looks like Lauren got a letter from Max." Aunt Willa had gone to the desk that caught all the mail. She held a couple of envelopes and her paper in one hand. "I'll leave Lauren's on top. I'd hate for her to go off and not see it."

"Humph." Jackson walked away from the windows toward the food.

Aunt Willa tucked her paper under her arm and poured two cups of coffee. "I thought you liked Lauren's cousin. I know I certainly did."

"Of course I like Max. It's just that Lauren was different when Max was here." He returned his aunt's gaze with a defiant air. "Well, I like Lauren the way she is. I see no reason for her to change." He helped himself to fresh strudel, and along with his paper and coffee he proceeded to the round oak breakfast table.

Aunt Willa followed him. "I didn't notice a change in Lauren while Max was here."

They sipped and read in silence for several moments.

Jackson glanced from his paper. "Have you not noticed Lauren's hair style lately?"

Aunt Willa frowned a little. "She seems to be letting it grow longer."

"And curly—like Max's."

"Girls do different things to their hair all the time, that doesn't mean anything—nothing to do with Max, I'm sure."

Jackson nodded. "I'd bet you a dollar it has something to do with Max." He went back to his paper for a few seconds then he said, "I didn't even know Lauren *had* curly hair. She's just been different ever since Max was here."

"To be fair, you've been different, too, Jackson."

"What do you mean?"

"A lot has been going on lately and you've been a little testy. You must remember that Lauren has always been her own woman, dependent on no one but herself—not having to answer to anyone. Marriage has been a big change for her."

Jackson rattled his paper. "She's still an independent woman." He had a sudden recollection of times she'd sigh and look weary when he worried about her activities or pressed her about resting more. Well, was he not supposed to be concerned for his wife's safety and wellbeing?

Aunt Willa went to the serving bar to get the coffee carafe. She returned and refilled their cups. "Lauren wants you to be happy. She wants Brooke to be happy, and her galleries, and of course all the many other things—"Oh, good morning, Lauren!"

"Good morning, Aunt Willa, is the coffee over there?"

"Yes, dear, grab you a cup. And there's a letter from Max. I put it on the top."

Lauren glanced at the stack of mail. "Oh, thanks."

Jackson glanced to see if she would read it now or tuck it into her pocket. She was carrying it to the table.

"Good morning, Jackson, did you sleep well?" She tossed the envelope on the table.

Jackson smiled and folded the paper. "Good morning. And I did sleep well—you?"

She nodded. "Uh-huh, very well. I didn't mean to sleep this late."

He glanced at his wrist. "Yeah, you may have to hurry a bit." He quickly reframed from reminding her to not leave in a hurry and drive too fast.

"Oh, I should be okay. I'll just have to wait when I get to the doctor's office anyway." She opened the letter from Max and read for several minutes. "Oh, Max is going to New York again soon—"

"Max is coming again? When? Will she come stay with us?" Brooke had entered the room just in time to hear Lauren's news. She hurried to stand at Lauren's side. "When will she be here?"

Jackson laughed. "Hold on, Brooke. Give Lauren a chance to tell us." He wanted to know all about Max's visit too.

Lauren glanced at the note in her hand, and said, "I don't think we'll get to see her this time."

"Awww, no fun." Brooke slumped into a chair and Aunt Willa reminded her there was milk and cereal on the serving bar.

Jackson's brows rose, he said, "More business with the same gallery?"

Lauren gave him a funny look. "More business, yes, but not the same kind of business." She smiled and continued to have the funny expression on her face. "She has a date with the gallery owner next weekend."

"A date? Is she sure that's wise? After all, her first impression didn't sound so good—"

"Jackson, the owner is Simon Lankford."

She sat gazing at him as if the name meant something. Suddenly he remembered the name. "Simon Lankford? The Simon Lankford who owns a gallery in New York? Is that the gallery she was having trouble with?" He sat stunned. "I went to college with

Simon—we were friends." He glanced at his aunt and then to Lauren.

"Yes, I know. He told me that day when Clair and I met him in his gallery."

Jackson frowned. "You met Simon and he told you we were friends? Why didn't you tell me?"

Lauren glanced at her watch. "I was trying to that evening when you became angry and jumped in cutting me off and we had an argument. I haven't have a chance with everything. . . ." She shrugged. "And I forgot all about it."

They sat looking at one another. Aunt Willa rattled her paper and began studying it.

"Who's taking me to school this morning?" Brooke's voice broke the tension.

"I am." Lauren got up from her chair. "And it looks like we're both ready to go, so let's hit the road."

"Hit the road?" Brooke giggled. "*Hit the road*?" She continued giggling as she hugged her great aunt and moved on to hug Jackson. "I never heard of hitting the road."

Absentmindedly Jackson returned her hug, saying, "Settle down, Brooke." How could Lauren forget to tell him something like running into an old friend of his? Okay, he had barked at her when she tried to tell him about visiting the gallery in New York and she'd clammed up. But she should have told him. He sighed.

Aunt Willa nudged him.

"Jackson? Jackson, did you hear me?" Lauren was standing by the door.

"I'm sorry!" He rose from the table and quickly crossed the room to where she waited. "What were you saying?" He circled her waist, and pulled her close.

"You were miles away." She smiled up at him. "Anywhere exciting?"

"Uh, work I suppose. I didn't catch what you said."

"Just that I'd see you later when I'm finished at the doctor's office, okay?"

"Okay, and I want to hear all about the meeting with Simon—is that all you're taking?" He nodded at the small soft-side bag in her hand.

She lifted it higher. "It holds more than you'd think—plenty for three or four days."

"Three or *four*? I thought it was only three—"

"Da-a-d-d, we have to go! I'll be late—"

"Okay, okay!" He kissed Lauren. "See you later." He watched until they were out and the door closed. Wandering back to the table, he sat back down and mumbled, "I was sure she said *three* days." He glanced at his aunt. No sympathy there, she just smiled and turned to look out the windows.

"Claude and I may do some transplanting today."

"Well, you and Claude have fun." Jackson rose from the table. "I'd better get to work." He glanced at his aunt as she stood also and began to stack things onto a tray.

"Yes, me too. Claude will be getting here soon."

\*\*\*

He'd suffered depression only once in his life; after Jenna passed away. He never believed it to be a true depression, but a grievous sadness and loneliness, which to him was natural and unavoidable when you'd lost half of yourself.

But as he guided the red Range Rover along the road into Valley Ridge, this beautiful fall morning, he suspected the onset of depression—and he couldn't put his finger on why or where it was coming from.

Matt's car occupied its private spot in the parking lot when Jackson parked in his place next to it.

"Good morning!" The office smelled of fresh coffee.

Matt finished whatever it was he was typing and swiveled his chair toward Jackson. "Yes, it is a good morning." He smiled. "The phone's been ringing."

"Oh? Who's calling this morning?" Jackson sat in his chair, pulled some files from his briefcase and set it on the floor by his desk.

"TechRom called as I was unlocking door. They liked everything in the files we sent and said they were leaving the selection up to us." He grinned. "That made Maggie's day. She's taken a tour through the new offices and boardrooms and made a list of her picks already."

"Great! That's good." He nodded and powered on his computer. "I don't know if I told you are not, Lauren's going to New York for several days. Clair needed her help with something."

Matt turned back to his computer, over his shoulder he said, "No, I don't think you told me. Is everything okay with Clair?"

"Oh, sure. No problem, just girl stuff." He laughed. "You know. . . ."

Matt chuckled. "Uh-huh, I do. How long will she be gone?"

Jackson glanced up and shrugged. "Just a few days." He hoped no longer than three. "She's coming by this morning after her doctor's appointment." Jackson turned his chair toward Matt. "I wish she wasn't going, but she felt like she had to."

Matt turned from his desk too. "She'll be okay. The time with Clair may be good for her right now."

"What do you mean?"

Matt shook his head and lifted one shoulder. "Nothing in particular—just that she's had a busy summer, and the exhibit is coming up—a break right now might be nice."

"You're probably right." He smiled at Matt, and immediately felt better. He glanced at his watch. Lauren should be along in an hour.

Matt pointed to his mug. "There's coffee. Just finished making it before you walked in."

"Hmm, sounds good." Jackson got to his feet. "You need a refill?"

"Yeah, but I'll walk back with you." Matt grabbed his cup and they wandered toward the break room.

Another hour and twenty minutes passed before Lauren breezed into the office. "Hello, guys! Ohh, it's so beautiful outside!"

Matt nodded. "Yes, a perfect day to be outside. But alas, we're stuck inside."

Jackson stood and hugged her. "Was doc's office crowded? Is everything as it's supposed to be?"

She nodded and sat in the chair by Jackson's desk as he sat down, too. "Doctor says I'm the picture of health. The waiting room was full of women. A little child threw a temper fit and that entertained us for awhile."

Jackson lowered his voice a bit. "I'm glad to hear that all is well, and I'd also like to hear about how you met Simon—"

"Honey, there's no time to go into that now. When I get home I'll tell you all about it. I really should be going. Clair and I are picking the aunt up—" She glanced at her watch. "In about three hours. That just leaves me time to get to Clair's and then on to—"

Jackson held his hand up. "I get it, you need to be going. Okay."

"Yes, I do. Sorry the doctor took so long."

They both stood and Jackson said, "That's okay. Please be careful. I love you."

She tiptoed to kiss him. "I'll be very careful, and I will call you when I arrive at Clair's." She looked into his eyes. "I do need to talk with you when I get back."

Jackson walked with Lauren to her vehicle and watched her drive away. He hadn't been able to read the expression in her eyes. She *needed* to talk with him when she got back? He hated it when she did that . . . .

# CHAPTER TWENTY-NINE

# A Job Done

Leaving the traffic of New York behind, Lauren welcomed the open road to Valley Ridge as her thoughts turned homeward. She would gratefully embrace the regular routine of the Montgomery household once more, even though the days with Clair had passed swiftly.

Drew's elderly aunt had turned out to be a lively and entertaining lady, Aunt Trudy.

Soon after meeting at the airport, Lauren and Clair both dropped the aunt part and called her Trudy, as she had immediately become a girl friend.

The last three days they'd all had great fun shopping, having lunch out, with hours, and hours of girl talk—and even with the constant running around, it had been relaxing.

Lauren stayed four days, but since she was arriving home early on the fourth day that made the trip

really just three and a half days. As she drove homeward her thoughts turned to a conversation they'd had
with Trudy.

One evening as they lingered over dinner, the
conversation turned to the exhibit. Clair explained to
Trudy the honor entailed upon Lauren in being selected as the featured artist. Trudy had smiled and
commented that Lauren and Jackson might consider
the trip as a second honeymoon. When Lauren told her
that Jackson wasn't going. Trudy expressed genuine
shock at the idea.

Patting her silver curls, Trudy had straightened
her back and said, my husband would have accompa-
nied me to Europe, or I'd have resigned my status as a
designing and persuasive woman."

Lauren and Clair had both laughed and Clair said,
"Trudy, Lauren's done everything short of begging
Jackson."

"Girls, there's no shame in begging. And it's still
a notch above the last resort."

They had laughed and enjoyed Trudy's independent spirit and off the cuff advice. Clair asked, "What *is*
the last resort?"

"Throwing an all out fit." Trudy smiled.

"I don't know about that . . . did you ever throw a
fit?" Lauren asked.

"In the fifty years Harry and I were married,
twice, I resorted to the last resort." She eyed them with
a wicked smile. "It concerned something *very* important to me." Then Trudy focused her attention on Lauren, with a smile, she said, "You must decide how
important it is to have Jackson with you."

Lauren, caught off guard had said, "Well, it's important. I want him to be there very much."

Trudy sipped her tea and then carefully set the cup down. "Is it impossible for him to get away? Would his business suffer with him away? If the answer is no to those questions, I wouldn't allow pride to stand in the way of a once in a life-time event, if I had to, I'd throw a fit." She smiled. "That is if you have the nerve and are prepared to live with the consequences after the exhibit is behind you."

Later that evening Lauren and Clair had puzzled over Trudy's words. And now the words echoed again in Lauren's head as she sped along the interstate.

What consequences? What had Trudy meant?

She tried to imagine the look on Jackson's face if she threw a fit and insisted he come with her. Temper fits had never been allowed in her upbringing and she doubted she could pull off a convincing one at this late date . . . *but* as a last resort.

Lauren glanced at her watch. She would be home by two o'clock. The drive from the city had a way of clearing her thoughts and helping her sort things out. She and Jackson hadn't gone to dinner alone in quite a while—it was time for a date. She would employ Trudy's persuasive and designing tactics before considering the last resort.

When she arrived home, Aunt Willa and Claude were up to their elbows in transplanting an old variety of long stemmed daisies, an important staple in the cutting garden.

"You guys have been working! That bed was full and you've picked it nearly bare!"

Aunt Willa looked up and groaned. "Since about nine o'clock this morning."

Claude sat back on his heels. "I tried to get her to quit three hours ago, but you see how successful I was."

"It's been good to dig in the soil." She glanced at Lauren. "I have a roast cooking for dinner—"

"Ohhh, I'd hoped to catch you before you started dinner. Jackson and I will be dinning out tonight."

"No problem, we'll have roast beef sandwiches tomorrow night." She looked at Claude. "I'll send half of it home with you—call your wife before she starts dinner."

He grinned and nodded. "Thanks, we appreciate it." He whipped his phone out.

Aunt Willa called out as Lauren started to the house. "Brooke's dental appointment went well, no cavities."

"Great! I'll pick her up from school since I'm home."

"Thank you, dear." She went back to the daisies.

Lauren retrieved her bag from where she'd placed it by the door and headed up the stairs, one step at a time. How wonderful to be home in her own bedroom.

She got her phone and settled comfortably into her chair by the window and called to the dogs as they came puffing into the room. "Hey, come here you guys! I missed you." They plopped contentedly at her feet. She scratched each one's back before taking a deep breath and calling Jackson. "Hi! Are you busy?"

"Not now. Are you coming home."

She laughed. "I'm home now. And I was wondering if you would you mind having dinner out tonight, just us so we can talk?"

"Of course I wouldn't mind. I'd like that."

"Good, I'll make reservations." They chatted briefly and ended the call.

Scooting down into the chair Lauren calculated the time for a short nap before picking Brooke up, and to be safe, she set the timer on her phone to thirty-five minutes.

Winnie and Winslow were still nestled at her feet. While she dozed her mind worked on, sorting and planning. But when her thoughts touched on Trudy's *last resort,* something deep inside her recoiled with such clarity that it woke her from napping. When she sat up the dogs stirred too—just as the timer went off. Winslow jumped up and barked.

"Quiet, silly boy, it's nothing that'll get you." She slipped into tan leather moccasins and grabbed her purse. "Let's go get Brooke! Come on!"

She waved at the two daisy diggers as she went out the drive, and confided to the dogs. "Aunt Willa will probably need to stay in bed tomorrow." Winnie studied Lauren's face as if she was suddenly alarmed for Aunt Willa. Lauren laughed and stroked Winnie's sweet face. "Don't worry, dear, we'll take care of her!"

Lauren guided the Range Rover into the pick up lane, put the front windows down and cut the engine. Curiosity and hope that the girls would be interacting with Allison made Lauren train her eyes on the double exit doors.

No sooner had the thought entered her mind than the three of them, Allison in the middle, exited the school. The conversation flowed fast, and apparently serious as the three heads hovered together. When Brooke spotted Lauren waiting in line, she struck out in a run and the other two followed fast on her heels.

Brooke all but slammed her body against the door and jumped onto the chrome step-up.

"Lauren! I didn't think you'd be here—we have a plan! You have to say yes—please, please!" Mandy and Allison were also excited, as they crowded at the open window.

Laughing and holding her hand up, Lauren said, "I never agree to a plan before hearing what it is—and I need to pull out of the way, I'm blocking others." She pointed. "I'll park over there." The girls stepped back and ran to the parking place.

Hanging on the door once more, they all talked at the same time. "One at a time, please."

Mandy and Brooke looked to Allison, who hesitated only a second. "Since we all have riding lessons on Saturday at the same time, my aunt gave me permission to ask Mandy and Brooke to spend the night on Friday and she will take us to riding class."

"Please, please say yes—please, Lauren?"

"I'm sure that will be okay, but let's ask your dad first. I need to get you aunt's phone number, Allison. I'd like to meet her, too."

Allison nodded. "Yes, ma'am." She bent down and searched her backpack for a scrap of paper and scribbled a name and a number on it. "My aunt is always at home."

Lauren took the paper. "Thank you, I'll give her a call." The aunt's name was Sandra Hampton.

Mandy spoke for the first time. "My parents already said I could spend the night. I hope Brooke can too."

"I'm sure it will be fine, but Brooke needs to ask her dad anyway." She didn't need to remind Brooke that she'd been less than agreeable with him lately.

They chorused okay and Brooke clambered into the Range Rover. While the other two ran to the bike rack.

Lauren glanced at Brooke as she backed out of the parking spot. "I'm so glad you girls got to know each other and are friends now."

Brooke nodded and brushed stray hair from her face. "Uh-huh, me too. Allison is bossy, but she's real smart and she knows everything about horses. I feel sorry for her." Brooke continued searching for something in her bag.

"Oh, what makes you feel sorry for her?"

"She doesn't have a regular mom and dad." Brooke finally found an envelope, the thing she'd been looking for. She handed it toward Lauren. "Mrs. Flowers said to give you this."

Lauren took it. "Thank you." She raised her brows at Brooke. "Maybe it's party time?"

Brooke giggled. "I hope so!" Then her eyes got big. "I hope it's not about my grades!"

"You make excellent grades, why would you worry about that?"

Brooke laughed. "It's just always scary when Mrs. Flowers is passing out grade cards. I think mine will be bad and when it's not I'm happy."

Lauren laughed until Brooke got tickled, too. "I know what you mean. I do that when I go the doctor."

Brooke grew serious. "Are you afraid he'll tell you something bad about the baby?"

"No, it's like you with your grade card. I know I'm healthy and so is the baby, but I'm really happy and relieved each time Dr. Stinson tells me so."

They enjoyed visiting and making up for the last few days that Lauren had been gone. But lodged in the back of her mind, was the comment that Brooke made about Allison's parents not being *regular* parents, it kept popping to the front of her mind. "Brooke, what did you mean about Allison's parents not being regular parents?"

Brooke continued drawing and with a shrug of one shoulder, answered, "They live in London and Allison lives here with her aunt." She glanced up. "That's not like regular parents is it?"

"No, I suppose it's not. Does Allison seem to mind the situation?"

"I don't know." She glanced up at Lauren as if in warning, said, "She doesn't like to talk about it."

"Oh, I see. Well, best not to then." Lauren's curiosity along with her sympathy was roused for the young girl. With an effort she turned her thoughts to the evening ahead.

Back home, Brooke raced up the stairs explaining on the run that she wanted to get her homework done before dinner. Aunt Willa had retired from the garden a short time earlier and was fresh from her shower, and wearing a comfortable print housecoat.

Aunt Willa looked at Lauren. "Brooke and I are having a sandwich and then we may watch a movie." She rubbed her back. "We might both be in bed when you and Jackson get home."

"By all means, don't wait up for us," Lauren said. "We have a key." She had to smile as she thought that by the time they got home it might not be a good idea to run into anyone—depending on the way the evening goes. Her nerves grew more taut with each passing hour. Would it be asking too much that Jackson be in a generous mood and announce that he'd changed his mind and decided to attend the exhibit after all? Lauren smiled, yeah, that would be asking too much.

"Penny for your thoughts." Aunt Willa sat on the little barstool she'd had forever, steeping a cup of tea.

"My thoughts were that you might prefer being in bed when Jackson and I get home this evening."

Jackson's aunt laughed and lifted the tea bag out of her cup. "Oh, I assumed that your dinner was a pleasant outing to celebrate your return."

"I wish. I want Jackson to go to Italy with Brooke and me. I'm going to try to persuade him. There's no reason he couldn't be gone four days—four or five days! I'm not asking for a month!" She tried to read his aunt's face. "Am I being so unfair, so unreasonable?"

"No, of course not. But Jackson's pulled both ways. He's proud of you, he knows you've worked hard for this, just as he's worked hard to gain the recognition of the business world." She stirred her tea. "To bad both opportunities came at the same time."

Lauren bristled. "My opportunity came first—but it didn't matter to Jackson once that big contract came to him and Matt." She folded her arms across her chest. "I'm going to let him know how he's hurt me by being so stubborn and unfair."

Their gaze locked as the alert for the garage door sounded "He's home! I'm heading for the shower—wish me luck!"

Aunt Willa bobbed her head. "Yes, dear, good luck!"

# CHAPTER THIRTY

# Quiet Dinner

Lauren finished her shower and roughly toweled her body, venting her anger on her own skin. Why had she mentioned her intentions to Jackson's aunt? It wasn't fair to put her in the middle of their problem. Aunt Willa loved Jackson as if he were her own son.

When he was unhappy, his aunt was unhappy. The last four days were catching up with Lauren. Sudden tiredness sapped the energy from her body.

She'd have no energy left to match wits with Jackson. She dressed with care though her closet didn't offer much in the way of smart maternity wear. The one-piece, sleeveless, black swing-tail dress that Ally had loaned her would have to do.

She went to the trouble of straightening her hair as she suspected Jackson didn't like it curly. Her dark hair, swept into a low sleek ponytail, flattered her oval face. Slipping on suede ballerinas, she tucked some

Kleenex, a lip-gloss, and two aspirin into a small evening clutch and stepped from her dressing room.

Jackson had showered and dressed. Lauren's
heart swelled with pride and love for him. He didn't
realize what a handsome man he was. She looked
away; he was handsome, but he was also unfair and
stubborn. One of them would come home this evening
the winner in this battle of wills—it wasn't going to be
Jackson.

He walked over to her as he fastened on his
watch. "You look beautiful—how did I get so lucky to
catch your eye?" He kissed her forehead.

Her nerves were shot, but his compliments
boosted her morale. "As you said, luck I suppose, and
being alert to trespassers."

Jackson tilted his head back and laughed.

She smiled, enjoying the sound of his voice.

"This is nice. We should have a dinner date more
often. What do you say?"

She gazed at him and murmured softly, "I say
yes, I'd like that." When Jackson was dressed and
ready to go, the last thing he always did was run his
hand through his hair, as he did just then. She rose
from the arm of the chair where she'd been sitting.
"I'm ready."

"Me too. Where are we going, the club?"

Lauren laughed softly. "I forgot to tell you. We're
going to one of Matt's favorite places. The Colony, it's
very private."

He ushered her toward the door. "That'll be a nice
change.

Before leaving, they went to the den to tell Aunt
Willa and Brooke bye and good night. Brooke pre-

tended to pout. "No fair not inviting anyone else—oh, Dad! Can I spend the night at Allison's house—"

"Brooke, your dad hasn't the time now." Aunt Willa patted her leg.

"Pumpkin, can we talk about it in the morning?"

"Don't forget!" She shouted after them.

"I'm sure you won't let me," Jackson muttered and shook his head. "I think she gets louder everyday." He grinned.

"Well, she's growing up." Lauren had given her standard response before thinking.

"I hear that everyday—I *know* she's growing up."

Lauren laughed lightly. "Sorry, dear." They made their way toward the garage.

The beautiful fall day carried over into the evening. They were both quiet on the drive into town. What was Jackson thinking? His thoughts couldn't be as chaotic as hers. How would she bring up the dreaded subject? Lauren caught a deep sigh in mid breath—she'd been sighing every few minutes all afternoon. She sneaked a peek at Jackson. The wisest thing would probably be to forget mentioning the exhibit, just get it behind her and never—

"You're awfully quiet. Did you have a good time at Clair's?"

"Oh yes, we had a really good time, and I liked Drew's aunt." She sighed, again. "But I'm glad to be home, and it's wonderful to relax and enjoy the evening." She struggled to get her mind on something besides what she was going to say to win him over. "The drive from the city was pretty with the fall colors."

"I'm sure. I've always liked that drive in fall."

Jackson appeared to be relaxed, but still Lauren sensed a tension in the closed confines of the Range Rover. Did he have something on his mind just as she did? In the next several moments, she had her answer as he cleared his throat and his hands moved restlessly on the steering wheel.

"Lauren, I hate to keep on, but I do want to hear all about the time in New York with Max—when you met Simon. Is that what you wanted to talk about this evening?"

Not expecting that to still be on his mind, she said, "Oh . . . well, partly."

"I know it's my fault you didn't tell me at the time, I . . . I didn't give you a chance when I got so upset."

"It was no big deal, really—"

"It was and still is a big deal to me. I'm glad I didn't run into Simon in the meantime, it could have proven embarrassing that my wife met him and forgot to tell me about it."

Lauren's near resolve to forget everything and not mention Italy, quickly reversed. She stiffened. "I'm happy to tell you everything I remember, though it *has* been a while."

"I don't mean to upset you, and I said it was my fault, so please don't take offense."

She made her voice calm and spoke lightly. "No offense taken. You have a right to know *everything* you want to." They were nearing the restaurant and she was glad. Jackson glanced sidelong at her last words.

They were given a table out of the way, perfect for couples wanting to share private conversation, or to argue. Were ushers trained to spot troublemakers? The thought of her and Jackson being thrown out of a res-taurant was wildly amusing.

"What are you smiling about?"

She widened her smile. "Us. We are so funny. Is there any hope for you and me?"

"I certainly *hope* so." Taking her hand, Jackson said, "I missed you. The last four days seemed—"

"Three and a half."

Jackson laughed. "Okay, I'll give you the half." He held her hand. "It felt like a week."

"I know. It did to me, too." She sighed once more, and wishing she could stop sighing, she remem-bered an article she'd read. The article said constant sighing was a sign of tension, which caused shallow breathing, which deprived the brain of oxygen and made one sigh in an effort to supply the lack of oxy-gen—

"Lauren?"

"Hmm?" She pulled her thoughts back. Jackson's expression gave away that he'd recognized her mind-game of escaping a situation she dreaded.

"I've wondered if you missed me like I missed you—I didn't know if you would or not."

"What a thing to say. Of course I missed you. I love you, Jackson. You know that."

He slowly nodded as he gazed into her eyes. "I know you love me. But I often wonder if you'd miss me, if you need me like I need you. I don't know."

"What makes you believe you love deeper than I do?" Lauren wanted to understand his feelings, but the idea that he thought he loved more and deeper than she did was an amazing thought. "You believe you love our baby more than I do, too, don't you?"

Jackson leaned away from the table and stiffened his back. "Of course not!"

"You don't believe I'm capable of making wise choices concerning the baby, and wanting Clair to accompany Brooke and me, as if I needed an adult keeping an eye on me."

"You know I didn't mean anything like that. But, now that you mention wise choices, running up and down the stairs is not exactly a wise thing to do, is it?"

"I hold onto the rail now. I've run up and down stairs all my life, it's just a bad habit."

The waiter had tentatively approached their table twice already and Jackson had waved him away. He hovered nearby once more. Lauren smiled to encourage him.

"Have . . . have you decided?"

Jackson glanced at the young man. "What do you recommend?" He listened as the waiter named one thing after another. Jackson ordered without Lauren hearing a word of it. He handed the menus to the waiter, who made a hasty retreat.

"We'll enjoy whatever, the food is supposed to be very good—but maybe this wasn't a good idea, we could have argued at home." Lauren glanced down at her clasped hands.

"Are we arguing?" he asked.

She raised her face, and sure enough her breathing was very shallow, so much so that it threatened to become gasps. "I'm afraid we may." Before she lost her nerve she blurted, "Are you being fair putting a business thing ahead of my exhibit which was scheduled first?"

"Please—" Jackson sighed heavily. "That issue is settled. Let's not spoil the evening rehashing something that can't be helped—"

"But that's the point, it can be helped. You don't have to be there for the job to get done, your business wouldn't suffer at all with you gone those few days." She sat straighter and took a breath deep enough to suck oxygen into every corner of her starved lungs.

Jackson slumped and drummed a thumb on the table. "Why are we doing this in public?"

Lauren leaned closer to the table. The oxygen helped. Her breathing gained strength as she said in a soft voice, "Because in public, I thought we might have a discussion without either of us getting angry and end up not accomplishing anything." She took another deep breath.

Jackson pushed his hand through his hair and gave an exaggerated sigh. She wanted to advise him to breathe deeply also.

The waiter placed crystal goblets of iced tea on the table as they eyed one another across the white linen battle line.

"I'm sorry if I've made you feel that I don't respect your abilities, because I do. You've been the best thing that could have happened for Brooke." He smiled. "She told me you went to school and warned Mrs. Flowers about the bullying.

"How did she know? I asked Mrs. Flowers not to mention it—"

He shook his head. "No, not the teacher. David Holt was cleaning chalkboards for talking in class. He overheard the conversation and passed it on to Brooke."

Lauren rolled her eyes. "David Holt. I remember a boy being in the room . . . little ears."

"She stood up for you."

"She did, really?" Lauren couldn't tell him that she'd overheard part of his conversation with Brooke. "Well, now I'm doing the same for her. Brooke wants to go, but she's determined not to if you don't go with us."

Jackson huffed and glared as the waiter served the food. Poor man, he'd done nothing to deserve their bad manners and uncomfortable behavior. She smiled brightly in his direction, but feared a smile wasn't enough.

"Brooke is becoming a handful. She needs to learn that things don't always go the way she wants them to." Jackson glanced at the food in front of him. "This does look good."

"Yes, I'm sure it is. But Jackson, what you were saying about things not always going the way we want them to . . . that's all the more reason to grab those times and things that can go the way we want . . . there's so many of the negative times."

He kept his eyes on the food and didn't comment as he ate.

Lauren pressed on. "We don't have to stay over, just the four or five days I need to be there for the exhibit. Matt and Maggie are perfectly capable—"

Jackson pushed his plate away only an inch, but he might as well have shoved it across the table. "You're not eating, and I don't think you intend to. I've had enough. If you insist on continuing this, let's do it at home."

Lauren remained in her chair and picked up her fork. "I'm going to eat. You may leave if you want to. I'll take a cab home."

Jackson sat back. He reached for his tea goblet. "Well, so much for talking about meeting Simon in New York."

"We have more important things to talk about." She took another bite of whatever the stuff was on her plate, chewed and swallowed. "I want to share some advice I was given by an elderly woman who had been married over forty years when her husband died."

Without lifting his face, Jackson raised his eyes to meet hers. "I'm listening."

"She said if it was terribly important to have you travel to Europe with me, that I should do everything in my power to persuade you to go—even begging. And if that failed I should throw a temper tantrum."

Jackson all but rolled his eyes.

Lauren nodded. "I know. Well, I feel like I've begged. And I considered the tantrum. But I watched a child throw a fit in Dr. Stinson's waiting room last Monday—the child got her way." Lauren took a sip of cold tea to relieve her dry mouth. "But I'm not a child, and I don't think I should be reduced to acting like one. I'd have to live with myself afterward." She studied the gray-green eyes she loved so much. "I'm not asking an outrageous thing." She rubbed her forehead where a dull ache was starting. "I'll ask one more time, and then I'll never mention the exhibit or Italy again." She gazed across the table. "Don't give me your answer until tomorrow. I want you to pray about it."

"I have prayed about it." He hesitated before adding. "My conscience is clear."

"I'm glad." Lauren relaxed her shoulders and breathed evenly. Something a preacher said a long time ago flashed across her vision. He'd warned the congregation to take care and not push their conscience around in front of them as in a wheelbarrow, taking conscience where *they* wanted it to go.

She smiled at Jackson and pretended that the handsome face across the table didn't really resemble a spring thundercloud.

Jackson summoned their waiter. "I'm having coffee. Would you like a cup?"

"Yes, please. Thank you." Lauren sighed, but the sigh wasn't from lack of oxygen, it was born of relief. She had stood her ground, spoken her mind and had made peace with the outcome, whatever it might be.

CHAPTER THIRTY-ONE

# Love & War

Jackson fumed and gripped the steering wheel. Lauren's calm demeanor didn't help his state of mind. She had accused him of being unfair, and he grudgingly admitted to himself that what she said about the job was true.

It wasn't necessary that he stay home to oversee things. Matt and Maggie were perfectly capable of doing the entire job without him. Matt probably wondered why he wouldn't rather go with Lauren than stay and work on the TechRom project.

Jackson was having difficulty figuring it out too. He knew in his head that Lauren had a right to feel like she did—but why couldn't she sense his need? TechRom was the first really big corporate project they'd landed, after bidding on many, since the opening of the gallery. He should be there with Matt . . . but there was something else . . . something he couldn't put a name to that pulled at his heart.

If Lauren *had* thrown a fit and insisted he go, would he have given in? Honestly? Of course he would have, and he would be forever grateful she had chosen not to go that route. But he knew that she and Brooke would both get over the disappointment and everything would continue the same. He would make it up to them later.

"Don't forget to talk with Brooke in the morning."

Lauren's voice brought welcome relief from his thoughts. "Yeah. What's that all about?"

"Allison invited Brooke and Mandy to spend Friday night at her house and Allison's aunt will drive them to their riding class Saturday morning."

"Of course I don't mind if you're okay with it. We don't know the girl's home life, do you feel okay letting her spend the night?"

"I'm sure it will be fine. I'll meet the aunt on Saturday." Lauren was quiet for a moment. "Allison is very well mannered."

"Yes, but her treatment of Mandy still surprises me. Are you sure you don't want me to go to with you on Saturday? It's Brooke's first official lesson."

With a laugh, Lauren said, "Brooke would love for you to be there, but she can handle her first lesson. It's up to you if you want to come or not."

Jackson began to relax and feel better about the whole evening. He would definitely make it up to Lauren. "Matt has plans with Ally for Saturday morning, so I do hate to leave Maggie there by herself."

"I didn't realize Saturdays were that busy."

"They didn't used to be, but things have picked up the past few months. Matt and I have noticed an increase in sales on Fridays and Saturdays."

"What do you think the increased weekend sales are due to?"

"We haven't a clue. Our advertising is the same." Jackson slowed the Range Rover and turned onto the drive. "Lauren, I appreciate your attitude and I will make—"

"Not now." She touched his hand. "I'd rather talk tomorrow."

He nodded. "Okay.

As they pulled into the garage, Lauren said, "I hope your aunt's in bed."

"I hope they're both in bed and asleep." Jackson raked his hand through his hair.

They quietly and carefully entered the kitchen and listened for the TV. The house was quiet, so they headed straight upstairs. In the upstairs gallery, Brooke's door was closed and again no noise from within.

Casting a furtive glance at Lauren, Jackson whispered, "It's not like her to let us by without saying goodnight."

"Aunt Willa probably encouraged an early night." Lauren whispered. "She'll be ready for chatting in the morning."

When they entered their own bedroom, Lauren went straight to her closet and dressing room, she returned shortly in pale pink pajamas as she braided her hair.

"That was a quick change." Jackson observed her face. He searched for a clue to her present state of mind. He wanted to talk; there was no reason to wait until morning to tell her he was not going to Italy.

"I'm tired," she said and gave him a glance as if she'd heard his thoughts.

The impression hit him so hard, he blinked and looked away. "I'm . . . tired too." He trudged into his dressing room and sat in the chair Lauren had insisted be installed for the times when he might want a private place to be alone and think and pray.

The chair had been a good idea, and he was glad for it now. He had a need to pray, to talk to someone wiser than himself and someone who knew the needs of his heart.

He propped his elbows on the tops of his knees and bowed his head on his clasped hands.

\*\*\*

Morning arrived an hour earlier than Jackson was ready for it to. He'd tossed and turned half the night, struggling through weird dreams that seemed real, and to make it worse Lauren had fallen asleep the minute her head touched the pillow.

She'd slept with her back to him while hugging her side of the bed.

Jackson had missed the warm touch of her body through the night; he woke lonely. He stretched his arm across the king size bed only to find Lauren's side empty. The emptiness woke him completely. Throwing the covers back, he shaved, dressed and was skimming down the stairs in twenty minutes. He heard Lauren and his aunt chatting in the morning room. He slowed his step and wondered into the room at leisure.

"Good morning, girls. It smells good in here."

They both returned his greeting.

Jackson lifted the cover from a casserole dish. "Breakfast quiche?"

"Yes, it's sausage and veggies." Aunt Willa rose from her chair and strolled toward the serving bar. "I tried a new recipe, hope you like it." She refilled her cup.

Lauren wandered to the serving bar also and began to fill a plate. "I already know I'll like your new recipe." They carried their plates to the table. And minutes after being seated, Brooke bounced into the room with morning greetings. She got her milk and cereal and joined the others at the table.

"Dad, have you thought about if I can spend the night with Allison tonight—please?"

"I don't see why not—yes, you *may* spend the night. I have my fingers crossed that Allison's good grammar rubs off on you, along with her riding abilities."

Brooke giggled, totally unbothered to have her grammar compared to her new friend's. She wallowed in her chair and informed Jackson that she'd rather have Allison's riding skills rub off on her than her perfect grammar. "I'm a tomboy, Dad, and I can't help it." She grinned at Lauren. "He doesn't have his fingers crossed, either."

Lauren smiled back. "You're right, he doesn't. It's okay to be a tomboy, but tomboys can use good manners and good grammar, too."

"I know." Brooke hurriedly finished her cereal and skipped from the room to get dressed for school. "I'll be ready real soon, Dad!"

He called over his shoulder, "I'm ready when you are." He eyed Lauren. "How old before we can send her to finishing school?"

Lauren and his aunt both laughed. Aunt Willa said, "I don't think young girls today go off to finishing school."

"You mean we're stuck with her as she is?"

Lauren nodded. "She'd probably get expelled if you did send her off."

Jackson enjoyed the sound of Lauren and his aunt's laughter and chatter. A quiet talk with Lauren to get the exhibit trip settled once and for all—he wanted things back to normal. "Lauren, were you coming to the gallery this morning?"

"I thought I would. I have to run to the bookstore around eleven o'clock, I could grab sandwiches there and meet you at the park. Would you like that?"

He nodded. "Sounds great." He glanced at his watch and rose from the table. "I'd better call Tomboy." He walked to the foot of the stairs and called up.

"Time to go, Brooke!" He waited several seconds before she bounded down the stairs.

As always he enjoyed the time they had together on the days he dropped her off at school. She wasn't completely over giving him the cold shoulder, but she'd warmed. Excitement over the riding lessons had taken her mind off the trip a lot. They came at just the right time. Her new friend and the girls spending nights together helped.

"Dad, will you come watch me ride in the morning?"

"What time do you ride?" If the gallery was not busy and Maggie wasn't overwhelmed, he might run out to Steven's for an hour anyway.

"We have to be there at eight-thirty, but my lesson is at nine o'clock—can you come?"

"I'll plan on it, but if something comes up and I can't make it, I'll call and let you know. Fair enough?"

She smiled and nodded. "Uh-huh. I'll watch for you."

The drop off lane was empty for a change. Brooke leaned across the console, gave him a quick kiss, gathered her stuff and scrambled out of the Range Rover. "Bye, Dad," she said and banged the door. Jackson cringed. He watched her streak to the open doors of the school.

If things go as well with Lauren . . . he took a deep breath and began to relax when a vague snippet of the dream he'd wrestled with through the night teased his memory, only to vanish again. The rest of the way to the gallery he racked his memory, but the elusive dream continued to dodge him.

Matt was in the break room when he arrived at work. Jackson deposited his briefcase on his desk and followed the smell of freshly brewed coffee.

"Morning," he said.

"Good morning!" Matt reached for the two mugs they used every morning. They had a routine, or was it a rut? With mugs in hand, they strolled back to their office. Maggie stuck her head around the door just as they arrived in the office.

"Hey, guys!" She smiled from one to the other. "I'm running to the bank, does anyone need anything?"

"Um, Maggie, do you have lunch plans? I need to leave a little early. Lauren's meeting me at the park. Will that interfere with anything you have scheduled?"

"Not me, I have no plans." She glanced at Matt and scooted upon the corner of his desk where the three of them enjoyed an impromptu visit. Something they didn't do as often as they used to. After thirty minutes of light banter, Maggie stood. "You guys sure you don't need anything? She glanced from one to the other. "Okay, I'll be right back."

Jackson powered on his computer. A snatch of the dream he'd had the night before teased his senses again. He spoke over his shoulder to Matt. "Have you ever had a dream and know you dreamed, but you can't remember it for anything?"

"Yeah, I've done that. It nags at you until eventually you get a grip on it. Can't recall a dream you had last night?"

"Every now and then I get a wisp of memory, but when I try to remember, it vanishes into nothing."

Matt chuckled. "Well, you'll remember it. Your brain won't let it go until you do."

Jackson chuckled. "Yeah, and in the meantime I can't think of anything else." His thoughts turned to Lauren, and the dreaded talk. He hoped she wasn't thinking he would change his mind. He glanced at his watch. Not long before he wouldn't have to guess at what she was thinking. He and Matt worked in silence the next hour.

Matt did a sudden turn in his chair. "Is Lauren getting excited about the exhibit?

"I suppose so. She's prepared, no last minute rush to finish anything."

Matt frowned and tilted his head the way he often did when puzzling over something. "I still can't be-lieve Lauren's letting you get away with staying home." He was studying Jackson. "Well, at least Brooke is going with her."

Jackson scowled. "That's still debatable, she might not be going. She got upset when I said I couldn't go." He gazed at Matt. "Brooke decided that if I didn't go, she didn't want to go either. She's punishing me."

Matt shook his head and they went back to work. Another twenty minutes and Matt turned his chair again. "It's none of my business, but—"

"Matt, you don't understand, and I can't explain because I really don't understand it myself. I have this feeling that I *should* be there on the TechRom job. It's like. . . ." He ran his hand through his hair. "At the risk of sounding like I've lost my mind, I *need* to be there for Jenna. This was what we planned for and dreamt of for so many years. . . ." He heard Matt's weary sigh.

"Jackson, I'm no psychologist, I'll leave that to Dr. Brickman, but you don't owe Jenna anything, not anymore. We were young." He stood and pushed his hands deep into his pockets. "Jenna saw the gallery come to completion—and she was proud of it. You were there for Jenna when she needed you; she no longer needs you, but Lauren does."

Suddenly Matt's words released the memory of his dream, full force and crystal clear it flashed across his vision. . . . *They were all three in a foreign country, Brooke and Lauren kept running away in the dream, they laughed and taunted that they didn't need him.* Matt was saying something he hadn't heard, for Lauren and Brooke's voices had been as clear in his ears as if they'd been right there speaking.

" . . . you'll probably regret it if you don't change your mind." Matt's eyes were concerned and questioning.

Jackson raked his hair. "I . . . think you may be right." He glanced at the wall clock. "It's earlier than I planned to leave, but if you don't mind, I think I'll go." The feelings of sadness and loneliness from the dream had all come rushing back.

Matt had sat back in his chair. "Sure, but are you okay?"

Jackson nodded. "I'm fine."

"As you see, nothing's going on here, and Maggie will be back any minute. Have a good lunch with Lauren. I'll see you later."

Getting to his feet, Jackson said, "Thanks a million, Matt." He had the strangest sensation of wanting to cry and laugh at the same time. If he went on to the park, he might get in some walking and thinking time before Lauren got there. And he had a lot to think about.

The city park was only a seven-minute drive from the gallery, but that seven minutes spanned a lifetime.

His dream had robbed him of his rest last night because he hadn't wanted to consider that he might be a bit selfish, or the truth that Lauren didn't *need* him to go with her, she wanted him to go and share in her accomplishment.

Heaviness pulled on his heart, he wanted to be in on the start of the project at TechRom, but he also wanted to be there for Lauren when she asked something of him.

As he turned into the parking lot he saw Lauren's vehicle at the other end. She must have had the same idea of getting in some exercise.

He crept along and searched for her on the walking trail. He saw her and stopped.

She wasn't walking for exercise; instead she poked along with her head down and brushed at her eyes every few steps.

His heart wrenched. He'd practically told her last evening that he wasn't changing his mind. Speeding up, he guided his vehicle into a parking place next to hers and bumped the horn lightly. She glanced up and threw her hand in the air. She wiped her eyes and hurried her steps. Jackson wasn't dreaming now, as she ran toward him, not away.

They met and shared a kiss.

"The sandwiches are in the Range Rover," Lauren said.

As they strolled hand in hand to get the picnic lunch, he said, "You're early. . . . ?"

"Uh-huh, so are you."

He gazed into her eyes. "Remind me to tell you about the dream I had last night."

# CHAPTER THIRTY-TWO

# Lunch Date

Absorbed in thought, Lauren had first ignored the sound when a horn beeped close by. But then she'd glanced up and saw Jackson stepping from his vehicle. She threw her hand in the air and hurried to meet him. He looked weary.

She knew in her heart that he really felt bad about backing out on the trip. After greeting each other, they retrieved the food from her vehicle and strolled toward a table and bench she'd picked out earlier. After spreading a small tablecloth she had brought from home, Lauren proceeded to pour tea from a thermos and lay out the ham and cheese sandwiches.

"These look like Aunt Willa's sandwiches."

Lauren laughed. "That's because they are. She made them when I told her we were having lunch in the park." Lauren didn't share that she had told Aunt

Willa about the miserable restaurant dinner the night before. Aunt Willa was on Lauren's side.

"Jackson—"

"Lauren—"

Jackson chuckled. "Have you noticed how often we do that?"

She nodded. "Uh-huh, I've noticed."

"You go first," he said.

"Thank you, I will." She took a sip of tea, stalling, trying to remember the words she'd practiced in her head. "Well, first of all. I know you're not going, and I also know you feel bad about it." She gazed at him. "But I would appreciate if you would help me persuade Brooke to change her mind and go with me."

He gazed at her. "I think I can persuade her."

Lauren gave him a sidelong glance. "You may have to work at it. She's doing better, but she's still cool about the trip."

"Lauren, if you'll still have me," he said, "it would be my pleasure to go with you too."

"What . . . ?" She halted her sandwich mid-air. "What did you say?"

"I'll go with you and Brooke."

She laid the sandwich down. "Are you serious? Why did you decide to go? Is this time for sure? You won't change your mind?"

"I'm serious. I've had an eye-opener. You're more important to me than any job, even TechRom. I won't change my mind again."

She rocked back and forth several times and then threw her arms around his neck. "Thank you, Jackson! I love you so much, and we don't have to stay over any extra time—"

"Good, because there's a couple of conditions." he kissed her nose. "I don't think they'll be too hard to bear, though."

"I'll sign any contract—just tell me where!"

"After I left the gallery on the way over here, I called Matt back and asked him if he thought we could push the start date up several days so I can at least get in on the first phase. He's checking on it now."

"And what are the conditions?"

"I'll be on the phone a lot while we're there, and we must schedule to fly back as soon as you can get away."

She was still hanging on his neck. "Actually, I'll be ready to fly straight home. I'm ready to take a break and practice being a mother-to-be."

He hugged her. "Good! I'm ready for that, too. I'm sorry I've been thoughtless of your feelings."

"No, you had things on your mind, and I just wanted you with me so much that I didn't consider your feelings." She laughed and buried her face against his shoulder. "Brooke will be beside herself with excitement."

"Yeah, because she gets to fly on a big plane—"

"No! She's really excited to see the art work." Lauren drew back. "I see Brooke becoming a serious artist."

Jackson gave a thoughtfully look. "With you behind her, I can see that, too." He continued the thoughtful gaze for a couple more seconds before he said, "And, there is one more condition."

She smiled. "And, what is the last condition?"

"After this exhibit, you'll probably receive offers and commissions. I'm asking you to promise me you won't commit to anything that requires travel back and forth to Europe."

"But what if a really important client should—"

"Promise me. Besides, you'll have a small child to care for before long." He gave her several seconds. "Do you promise?"

She nodded, but her heart balked. "I promise."

***

After a tender kiss goodbye, Jackson went back to work and Lauren loaded the picnic things into the Range Rover and headed home. The vehicle kept trying to fly as Lauren's foot impatiently patted the accelerator. She pressed the cruise control button.

She must get in the habit of using it as Jackson constantly advised her to.

She couldn't wait to tell Brooke the news that her dad was going with them.

Repeatedly, she ignored the niggling irritation of the promise she'd made to Jackson each time it reared to interrupt her thoughts. The whole point of being selected as artist of the year was the recognition it gave the artist and their career. Jackson knew that, and yet he made her promise.

Lauren sighed. She'd worry about that later, and in the meantime she had to decide which three of her small paintings would travel in her luggage to Italy.

She turned onto their driveway and glanced across at the lake. The sparkling body of water reminded her of an eight by ten canvas she'd finished only weeks ago. It was a fall scene of the lake with Jackson and his dad fishing.

Both fishermen wore colorful plaid shirts and waist-high waders as they cast their lines. You could almost feel the cool, crisp air of the fall morning. Aunt Willa had brought the photo out of her room one day to show Lauren. "Aunt Willa—I love this photo! May I borrow it to paint from?" She really didn't like to paint from photos, but this one was an exception.

"You may have it if you'd like." She had smiled and said, "I have better than the photo." She laughed at Lauren's expression and said, "I have that entire day right here." She'd tapped a forefinger to her temple. "Jackson was about fifteen years old at the time."

She hadn't shown the painting to Jackson, with one thing after another happening, she'd forgotten all about it until now. It would definitely go and probably be one of the first to sell, since Nicolas favored her small works.

Not planning on going out again, she opened the garage door and eased the Range Rover inside.

Aunt Willa was coming from her suite; a set of rooms just off the kitchen, consisting of a large sitting room, bedroom, and generous sized bath-dressing room combination.

"Hi, Aunt Willa—you'll never guess!" Lauren plopped the picnic basket on the bar.

"Probably not," she said and paused by the bar.

Lauren hurried around to where she stood. "Jackson's agreed to go with me."

"Oh, good, he wised up. I'm happy to hear that. He needs to get away for a few days—that's wonderful!" She hugged Lauren.

"Yes, it is and I'm happy." She glanced at Jackson's aunt. "But he put conditions on going. He made me promise not to accept any commissions or com-

mitments that I might get offered, if they required
traveling back and forth to Europe."

"That's a bad thing? You said you'd pretty much
decided not to travel as much anyway."

Lauren bit her lip and glanced down for a moment. "Well, I did, but if something really big came
up. . . ."

"A husband, a daughter, and a new baby are
pretty big, too." She linked her arm in Lauren's and
led her to the morning room. They sat opposite each
other in the big chairs by the windows. "How did
Jackson make you promise that anyway?"

Aunt Willa's words startled Lauren. "He wouldn't
have agreed to go if I hadn't promised, or that's the
way he made it sound."

Aunt Willa smiled. "But you didn't have to promise."

Lauren swallowed the frustration that rose along
with the volume of her voice. "But he wouldn't have
gone!"

"Agreed, you might have had to go to Italy alone,
but still it was a choice."

Lauren flung her hands out. "Brooke was excited
about the trip until her dad said he wasn't going. And I
wanted her to go." She got to her feet and stood at the
windows, her arms folded across her chest.

"Do you think you may later regret making the
promise?" Aunt Willa raised her brows. "Because if
you do, it's not too late to reconsider. Besides, Jackson
wasn't fair not to give you some time to think about
it."

"Oh, well, no. I didn't need time to think, if I had
told Jackson I needed time, he would have been okay

with that. But I would have done almost anything to have him go with me—"

"Ah, almost anything, like agreeing to a promise you didn't want to make?"

Lauren turned from the window and glanced at Aunt Willa, too late she saw that she'd been caught. She strolled back to sit in the chair facing Jackson's aunt. "Thanks. I guess it's too late to complain now."

Aunt Willa gave her the same look she sometimes gave Brooke. Thank goodness, the phone began ringing. Lauren grinned at Aunt Willa and jumped from the chair and made a dash to where her phone lay on the bar. It was Clair.

"Hi, girlfriend!"

"You sound chipper and breathless, anything going on?"

Lauren laughed. "No, nothing, I was chatting with Aunt Willa. What's on your mind?"

"I just booked a flight to Italy for Drew and me. We'll see you at the exhibit."

"Ohh, I'm so glad! I hated to nag you about it, but I was sure hoping you'd go."

Clair exaggerated a sigh into the phone. "Miss the event of the year—the one showcasing your work?" She laughed. "I feel as if we haven't spoken in weeks; we need to have lunch."

"Yes, I feel the same way. We haven't had a chance to really talk about Caroline and Charlie's evening together—I'm glad they hit it off, but I want to hear everything." She hesitated. "Clair, remember when Max and I were in New York?"

"Of course I remember, what about it?"

Lauren glanced toward the morning room, hoping Aunt Willa had dozed off and couldn't hear the conversation. She lowered her voice. "I never got to tell you about that, or that Jackson and I have been bickering back and forth ever since . . . oh, it's a long story, but Max is going to be back in town soon—"

"Yes, she's already booked a room and she sent a message saying she would love to see me while she's here."

Lauren paused. "Oh? She didn't tell me that, anyway, she met a man, the owner of a gallery, and they've been corresponding ever since." She gave a rueful laugh. "It turned out that the man was a friend of Jackson's."

Clair said, "It is a small world."

"Yes, really! I'm sorry for rambling, but I'd wanted to ask you to make a point of seeing Max while she was staying in the hotel, but it looks like my intervention was unnecessary."

Clair laughed. "Max doesn't strike me as a person who needs much looking after." She was quiet for several seconds before saying, "I'm checking my calendar. Why don't we plan a lunch date? Maybe Max and I could drive out to Valley Ridge while she's here. We could have lunch or an early dinner."

Lauren's relief at Clair's thoughtfulness reminded her again of the blessing Clair had been in her life. "You're so sweet to do the driving, I appreciate it. You name the time and I'll be available."

"We could invite the guys too, if you'd like."

"As far as inviting the guys, I'll leave that up to you."

"I'll ask Drew what he thinks." She laughed. "Since Max's new friend is a friend of Jackson's, she might like to bring him, too."

The idea of Simon Lankford showing up startled Lauren, she *still* hadn't told Jackson how that all came about.

Clair's voice sounded hesitant when she said, "Or, would that be a problem?"

"No, of course not—"

"Probably better if it was just us?"

"Oh no, it really doesn't matter at all to me."

"Okay, we'll see. I'll let you know when the date is set."

They ended the call and Lauren rose from where she'd taken a seat at the bar. She had better make a point to speak with Jackson—and soon!

Moving toward the morning room, she peeked around one of the fat columns that marked the entry to the room. Aunt Willa remained in the big chair, her feet on the ottoman with her ankles crossed. And totally relaxed, she snored softly.

Lauren crept past the door and quietly took the stairs one at a time. The possibility of Simon Lankford coming to dinner kicked her brain into gear.

The picnic at lunch had turned out with better results than she could have imagined. But they couldn't have dinner in the park. She had to come up with another good idea.

Brooke was sleeping over at Allison's and it wouldn't hurt Aunt Willa to take a night off from preparing dinner. Lauren bit her lip and envisioned a quiet dinner in their bedroom sitting area. All their favorite finger foods and pajamas should set the mood.

She would tell Jackson everything; he'd be glad when she quit talking.

She glanced about and rearranged the chairs, drawing them closer together and angled more to the windows; to catch the evening light. Lauren startled when she glanced out and saw Aunt Willa meandering through the herb garden—no, no, no! She headed to the stairs and flew down—half way—then hurried the rest of the way as fast as possible without running. She hurried out to the yard. "Aunt Willa! Wait up."

Jackson's aunt turned and frowned into the sun as she waited to see what Lauren wanted.

"I wanted to catch you before you gathered herbs for dinner. I thought since Brooke was staying over at a friends, I'd have a light dinner for Jackson and me in our room."

"That sounds lovely. I'll cut some flowers and bring them up for you."

"Great! That would add the finishing touch, thank you! You'll have a free evening, too."

Aunt Willa smiled. "I may see if Thelma would like to have dinner out and see a movie."

Lauren nodded and smiled. "That sounds like fun."

If only dinner in their room that evening proved as successful as lunch in the park had."

# CHAPTER THIRTY-THREE

# Evening Alone

Lauren and Aunt Willa were in the den when Jackson arrived home. His aunt was waiting to have a few minutes with him before she left to meet Thelma for their Friday night on the town.

Lauren was simply waiting. She'd dressed in the pale, periwinkle blue pajamas he'd once told her looked pretty with her violet eyes. All his favorite finger foods had been prepared and were already upstairs.

All Jackson would have to do was shower, slip into a pair of comfy sweats or pajamas and relax. The evening was planned to the last—

"Penny for your thoughts, dear." Aunt Willa chuckled.

Lauren caught the gleam in Aunt Willa's eyes and grinned. "Well, if you're thinking dinner in our room is a romantic candle-lit occasion—it's not!" She raised her brows. "This is business."

Aunt Willa laughed heartily. "Poor Jackson, he won't know what's hit him."

Giving Jackson's aunt a sidelong glance, Lauren sighed and became serious. "Actually, I believe he will appreciate that I've made time for a conversation that is way overdue."

She bit her lip and considered confiding to Aunt Willa what she and Max had gotten into while Max was in New York. She gazed directly at Aunt Willa for several long seconds, and in those seconds, the truth of her feelings for this kind and wise woman filled Lauren with emotion. She had become more to her than just Jackson's aunt. "Aunt Willa, I hope you've never minded that I call you Aunt."

Jackson's aunt tilted her head slightly. "I'm delighted that you call me Aunt." They laughed, and Lauren reached to touch her hand, as she did so, Aunt Willa clasped Lauren's in return.

"You're more like a girlfriend," Lauren said.

"I'm so glad you feel that way, and the feeling is mutual." Aunt Willa nodded once more. "I thought Jackson was lucky to get you from the very first."

Lauren gave Aunt Willa's hand a gentle squeeze and released it, saying, "Thank you for that." She smiled. "I think I heard the garage door."

"Yes, I think you're right, he's home." She lifted her brows. "Good luck, dear."

Lauren murmured, "Thanks." Silently they waited for Jackson to make an appearance.

He walked in, stopped just inside the doorway and shoved both hands into his pockets. "Well, if ever I saw two felines that looked like they just caught the canary."

Lauren and Aunt Willa turned to each other at the same instant and raised questioning brows. Lauren said, "We're innocent, no canaries."

He continued to gaze, a smile hovered on his mouth. "I don't smell food cooking, are we dining out?"

Aunt Willa stood and went to Jackson and giving him a hug, said, "Thelma and I are going to dinner and a movie." She patted his arm. "I think you have dinner plans, also." She smiled and left the room. Gone only a few steps she called back, "I'll see you at breakfast in the morning."

Jackson didn't move as he called over his shoulder, "We'll be there!"

Lauren rose from the couch and sauntered toward Jackson, she didn't miss the glance that swept the periwinkle pajamas—it was luck that she'd remembered he liked them.

Jackson remained in the same spot with his hands deep in his pockets. He looked down at Lauren as she walked close and slipped her arm through his.

"What are my dinner plans?"

She tiptoed and kissed his lips. "We're having dinner in our room." Lauren smiled up at him. "And I'm going to answer your questions and tell you everything that we haven't had a chance to talk about the past few weeks." She liked the expression that lit his face as he wrapped his arm around what used to be her waist.

"I'm ready for that, lead the way." They strolled to the stairs.

"I thought you might want to shower first—"

"No, I don't. I'm hungry—for food and talk."

She laughed and leaned her head against his shoulder as they took the steps one at a time with his arm firmly around her.

*\*\**

At first Lauren was anxious as she and Jackson settled into the chairs with the food and tea close by. Jackson returned thanks as they held hands.

Afterwards they each prepared a plate and Lauren poured tea. They chatted about the gallery and Lauren told him she'd called Allison's aunt and given her their phone numbers in case she needed them.

Jackson popped a grape in his mouth. "Did I tell you I'll probably get to make it to Brooke's lesson?" He followed the grape with a bite of white cheese.

"Oh, she'll be so happy! I'm glad, too, honey. It's important to her that you're involved in what she's doing." Lauren smiled. "I can't wait for her to know she's going to Italy." The promise she'd made Jackson crossed her thoughts like a small dark shadow; she quickly brushed it aside. "Guess what I did this after-noon."

He munched a bite of cold ham. "I can't imagine. Did you celebrate a quiet evening?" He grinned.

Lauren pursed her lips. "No, but I thought about it. I told your aunt how much she means to me."

"Oh? That was thoughtful. I'm sure it pleased her that you shared your feelings."

He gave her a tender look, which encouraged Lauren to explain how much she'd come to love his aunt and to think of her as a friend as well as an aunt.

Jackson nodded and said, "I've no doubt she feels the same way about you."

"She said she did." Her cheeks warmed as she remembered the moment they'd shared.

Jackson perused the food tray once more. Lauren wasn't very hungry and presently silence lingered between them. They'd covered the small talk and everyday topics and Lauren suspected Jackson was ready to move on to the more serious subjects he expected they'd discuss. With his plate recharged and his tea refreshed, he settled into his chair once more.

"Where do you want to start?" He looked at Lauren.

She knew what he meant. "I'll start with the first letter from Max."

He kept his eyes on his plate. "Probably the best place." He waited patiently as Lauren explained about Max. How she was something of a sleuth and that even as a child she had a way of stumbling into strange and mysterious situations. Jackson uttered not a word, but he rolled his eyes.

"Do you want to hear this?" Lauren spoke firmly. He grinned and mumbled an apology.

\*\*\*

An hour later, almost to the minute, she smiled and said, "As you see, we came to no harm and everything turned out fine, and we met Simon."

Jackson made an exasperated sound and shook his head. "The fact that you came to no harm was not the point—you girls didn't know at the time that Simon was a decent guy, Max *thought* he was a *diamond smuggler!* I can't imagine that a diamond smuggler would be someone to mess with—they have a lot at stake." He glared.

Lauren eyed him back. "I'm sorry. But it's past and I can't undo it, and I learned a lesson." She gave him a moment to think about it. "Can't you be glad that it was your friend Simon and not some bad guy?"

"Of course I'm glad." He hesitated before speaking again. "Did you like him? What about his gallery?"

Lauren relaxed. "I did like Simon, but we just spoke for a few minutes. And his gallery is very nice, not so much as yours and Matt's." She smiled. "Remember, I was left wandering about the gallery waiting for Max to give me a signal. I couldn't really check things out."

Jackson chuckled with her over that as his eyes strayed to the food tray once more. Absentmindedly, he said, "Sounds like Max liked old Simon too."

"Uh-huh, she did—does." She smiled as Jackson raised his eyes from the tray where he was busy making another plate.

"What does that mean?"

"It means they've been corresponding ever since that day." Suddenly Lauren was hungry. She moved to the table with her plate. "Remember that last letter I got from Max?"

He finished making his plate and settled into his chair again. "I remember you started to say something about it, but something happened and it was forgotten."

"Well, she's coming to New York next weekend to spend some time with Simon, and learn more about a project he's involved with."

"Jackson's eyes grew wide. "Don't tell me she's going with his gallery and not us?"

She laughed. "I don't know about that, but the project Simon's involved in is a charity of some kind, she wasn't clear on that." She shrugged. "That's the mystery as to why he buys her bronze horned toads, along with art objects from other artists as well. They're put in some kind of charity auction, I suppose."

"Sounds interesting. We'll have to have them out some weekend when she's in the city." He filled his mouth, savoring the flavor. When he could speak again he said, "You know, kill two birds with one stone."

"It may be sooner than later. Max has already booked a room at The Belmont, and has plans to see Clair while she's staying there." Lauren had Jackson's full attention as she spoke between bites of food.

"Are they coming out?" He sat his empty plate on the tray. "Next weekend?"

Lauren nodded. "Possibly."

Jackson ran his hand through his hair. "Good, I'd like that. I'll have an opportunity to warn old Simon about poaching my bronze artist."

"She's not your bronze artist, yet—not one piece of Max's work is in the gallery." Lauren Laughed at Jackson's pouty face and proceeded to stack things on the tray. "Let's carry all this down and then we can relax and watch a move—would you like that?"

He began to help put things in the large sturdy basket they used to haul things up and down the stairs. "Yeah, I'd like that, if you'll pick the movie."

Lauren gave an exaggerated groan. "You know I hate picking the movie."

He shrugged. "Well, you don't like what I pick either." He grinned. "You have to pick."

They trudged downstairs, Jackson carrying the heavy stuff and Lauren the lighter load and when they reached the kitchen, he said, "Did you carry all this upstairs by yourself?"

"I did, but in small loads at a time. I knew you'd help bring it back down." She smiled.

After the kitchen was cleaned and everything was put to order, they strolled to the stairs with their arms around each other. As they started up, Jackson said, "What happens if we can't decide on a movie?"

Lauren raised her face to his. "I hadn't thought that far ahead, I guess . . . just go to bed and read, or something."

"Well, I'm feeling mighty picky, there may not be a movie that interests me tonight."

# CHAPTER THIRTY-FOUR

# Much Ado

Monday morning arrived in the whirlwind that all her days had become. Lauren woke early with packing on her mind. She began mentally sorting wardrobes for the three of them almost from the moment Jackson agreed to go. He had assured her he could do his own packing, and for that matter, he recommended that Brooke should pack for herself, too.

Lauren admired his confidence, but she'd rather he arrived in Florence looking the part of the handsome businessman he was, and Brooke, the pretty little girl her dad was proud of and with neither of them wearing limp corduroy and faded jeans.

She had nothing against corduroy, or denim, just not for this occasion.

So much had happened the past week, Lauren's thoughts were still playing catch-up. Clair and Drew had come out on Friday to spend the weekend in their cottage. Max and Simon Lankford drove out the next day on Saturday, and Lauren persuaded them to spend the night and attend church on Sunday. The lady who helped Aunt Willa with the housework had worked extra days preparing the guest rooms for Max and Simon. She'd done most of the cooking and serving, too.

They had enjoyed having guests in the house. Jackson and Simon had spent hours talking business and reminiscing, and the days had passed quickly.

"Why are you up so early? I thought you might sleep in this morning after a busy weekend." Jackson frowned.

"I'm too excited to sleep in." She sat on the side of the bed. "I feel like Brooke when we told her you were both going with me after all."

"She's only ten, she can still jump and squeal and get away with it." He grinned.

Lauren laughed. "I know. You do realize this is the week of the exhibit." Her eyes followed him across the room. "You look handsome."

"Thank you." He finished tucking a white shirttail into dark gray slacks and his black loafers gleamed. "I do realize it's the week. The work also starts at TechRom today. We may be meeting with several of the staff, we're not sure, but I thought I'd be prepared in case."

"I'm glad they moved it up those few days so you could be in on the first of it."

"Me, too. Good old Matt, he keeps me covered." Jackson laughed and leaned over and kissed her. "Come have coffee with me before I go." He pulled her to her feet.

Lauren grabbed her robe. When she tied the belt, she noticed she'd expanded another couple of inches.

"Jackson, the days are flying past, the baby will be here before we can get the nursery ready." She suffered a panic moment.

"Don't worry about the nursery until we get back from Europe." They reached the bottom of the stairs. "Clair, Ally, and Aunt Willa have all offered to help you."

"I know, but I wanted to do most of it myself."

They found Jackson's aunt already browsing her paper. "Good morning. There's breakfast casserole and hot yeast rolls."

Jackson poured two cups of coffee, handing one to Lauren, he proceeded to prepare himself a plate with the casserole and carried it to the table.

Lauren cradled her cup of hot coffee and wandered to the windows and stood gazing out. "The gardens lose a little more of their color every day." She turned. "Aunt Willa, is it just me or do the days seem to be rushing past?"

"It's not just you, dear. The days are rushing past."

"Have you given any thought to the Christmas party? Should we be working on the guest list? Maybe I should—"

"Lauren! Listen to yourself. Stop worrying—right now—I order it," Jackson said.

She laughed. "I do feel at times that my mind is running crazy."

After a while, Jackson carried his plate to the serving bar. "There will be plenty of time to start the nursery and plan the party when we get home from the exhibit." He walked to where she stood and took the cup from her hand and placed it on the table near her chair. "Sit here and enjoy your coffee." He shook his head and glanced at his aunt. "It's her nerves." He re-filled his cup and sat opposite her in his chair.

"Oh, Jackson, I've never been nervous in my life."

He eyed her several seconds. "Neither have you ever been pregnant before, nor had a big exhibit in Florence, Italy, or had to plan a nursery, or oversee riding lessons—"

"Okay, I get it. You may be right." She cut her eyes to Aunt Willa. "I do have a lot of changes going on."

"What about riding lessons?" Brooke straggled into the morning room and dumped her backpack, and note folder on the floor by the door.

Jackson looked in her direction. "Nothing much, just that you did a great job with your first lesson last week."

She grinned and went to get her milk and cereal. "My teacher said I was natural in the saddle. Allison said that meant I had a good seat." She looked over her shoulder at Jackson. "Do you know what that means, Dad?"

"Uh-huh, I would think it means you sit light in the saddle and have good balance."

Her eyes lit up. "That's what Allison said, too. Not exactly the words, but it meant the same." Brooke concentrated on the bowl of cereal for several minutes. "Allison's been riding since she was six-years old."

Lauren went to refresh her coffee. "Anyone else?" She held the carafe aloft; they declined. She strolled to the table where Brooke was finishing her breakfast.

"You have to miss your lesson this week. I reminded your instructor."

Brooke nodded. "I know, she told me to have fun on the trip. So did Miss Flowers. She told the whole class that I was going to Europe." David Holt asked where that was and made everyone laugh."

Lauren sighed. "Does he really not know?"

Brooke giggled. "He knows! David's real smart, he just likes to make people laugh."

"Oh, does David make good grades?" Lauren asked.

"Uh-huh, straight A's."

Lauren looked across the room at Jackson and smiled. He motioned for her to come, so she squeezed Brooke's slender shoulders and strolled to her chair next to where Jackson was sitting. Taking a seat on the edge of the cushion, she said, "What?"

"Have you told Brooke that we've made arrangements for her to skip classes the day before we leave?"

Lauren glanced at the table where Brooke was inhaling her cereal and put her hand to her face. "I completely forgot!"

"She will only go to school today and tomorrow of this week." He nodded in Brooke's direction. "She's finished eating, let's tell her."

Lauren nodded. "Brooke, your dad has something to tell you."

Depositing her dirty dishes on the serving bar, she went to her dad's side. "What, Dad?"

"You'll be missing school the day before we leave for Italy. That makes just two days of school this week."

"Really?" She narrowed her eyes and counted. "That's just today and tomorrow that I have to go to school!"

She jumped from the arm of Jackson's chair and streaked upstairs to get her calendar. Moments later she thundered back down the stairs. "I don't go back to school until October."

Lauren cut her eyes to Brooke. "That's right you won't go back until the fifth. We'll get in late on the fourth."

She jumped up. "Six whole days!"

Aunt Willa had been quiet all morning, so they all looked when she spoke.

"I bet you'll be begging to get back to school before it's over."

"Nope, I wouldn't care if I never went back!"

Aunt Willa laughed. "Just mark my words."

Lauren hugged her robe closer. "As soon as we get back, I'm getting onto the baby's room. I want it finished by Thanksgiving."

"It shouldn't take too long to get it finished," Aunt Willa said. She glanced at Lauren. "That is if you don't get overloaded with work after your exhibit."

Jackson lowered his paper a bit and looked over the top at his aunt.

Lauren crossed her arms over her chest. "I've already told Nicolas that I was taking a break until after the baby is born."

The newspaper rattled, and Jackson's face appeared. "You've already told him?"

She nodded. "Uh-huh, weeks ago."

Aunt Willa got to her feet. "Claude and I plan to get the flowerbeds ready for winter." She went to the serving bar and refreshed her coffee. "The month of

October is always the busiest month of the year." She glanced at Lauren. "It goes in a wink. I'm glad we're having a quiet Thanksgiving and doing the big party at Christmas."

Lauren nodded. "Oh, me too. That'll be fun."

Jackson looked at his watch. "Brooke, are you ready to go? It's about that time."

"Yes, sir." She jumped up and ran to the door where her school things were piled on the floor. "Max said she was coming back at Christmas and her sister is coming too." She jerked on her backpack. "I can't wait for Christmas to get here."

Lauren and Aunt Willa exchanged glances and Lauren said, "Christmas will be upon us before we're ready for it."

Jackson got to his feet. He pulled Lauren up and kissed her nose, then her lips. "Take it easy today and none of that worrying about the nursery—promise?"

"I promise." She walked to the door with him as Brooke straggled ahead with her load of school things.

After they were finally out the door, she and Aunt Willa carried things from the morning room to the kitchen and straightened up.

Later, she went upstairs to her closet and pulled down luggage for herself, she got Jackson's Luggage, then on to Brooke's room and retrieved hers also. She carried them into a guest room and lined the bed with the three large suitcases. Hopefully the physical act of packing would divert the panic attack that threatened.

\*\*\*

They were finally through boarding and on the plane. Jackson recalled the last four days and the hectic pace the house had been in, and it hadn't eased up until now, as they buckled themselves into the comfortable wide seats in first class. Jackson laid his head back against the headrest and sighed. "This feels good just to sit." He glanced across at the girls. He was glad to be there with them.

Lauren smiled. "Agreed, it *does* feel good. I'll probably fall asleep once we're in the air."

"I'm not going to sleep, I'll be too busy taking pictures of everything. "Brooke giggled and aimed her One Shot at Lauren. After looking through the view-finder at her dad, Brooke lowered the camera. "Dad! Act like you're having fun."

Jackson immediately closed his eyes, lolled his head and pretended to snore. Brooke and Lauren both laughed while Brooke snapped shots of her dad as he clowned.

Jackson opened one eye. "I'll get even when I catch you sleeping with your thumb in your mouth."

Brooke's eyes narrowed. "I don't sleep with my thumb in my mouth." She turned to Lauren. "Do I?"

"I've never seen you sleeping that way."

Suddenly the engines roared, the plane began to move slowly, it seemed to taxi forever; then it picked up speed as it rumbled down the runway and after a few minutes, with a great thrust of power that forced them against their seats, the plane shuddered and lifted into the air.

Lauren tapped Brooke's arm. "In a few minutes you'll see the Statue of Liberty, you may want to get a photo of that."

Brooke pressed her forehead to the window. "I do want a picture . . . I see it! There it is!"

"Better get your picture—quick!" Lauren was laughing as Brooke became lost in the scene and appeared to forget her camera.

"Oh yes!" She jerked the camera to her face.

Jackson peered through his lashes at the girls and forced back a smile. Brooke's Statue of Liberty would be a pin dot in the photo, but Brooke would be satisfied with it. Lauren was obviously thrilled to have them all on the plane together. And to think he almost missed it. They were scheduled to arrive at Florence Airport, Peretola, late evening. A taxi would be waiting to take them to their hotel.

The next several days promised to be exciting, but Jackson wondered what changes the excitement filled days might bring to their lives?

# CHAPTER THIRTY-FIVE

# Goodbye Italy

Lauren marveled how a body as exhausted as hers was could continue to function. She guessed it to be like hunger pains, ignore them long enough and they go away.

And no matter how hard she tried, she couldn't ignore Nicolas Conti's voice and the conversation they'd had the last evening of the exhibit.

She played the words over and over in her head like a favorite CD.

Guiltily she raised her eyes to Jackson.

He'd quietly and patiently fixed Brooke's seatbelt when she whined that it wouldn't fasten. Not given to whining, Lauren guessed that Brooke's fatigue was speaking. Once Jackson got her buckled in the seat she fell asleep as soon as the plane lifted into the air. And now Jackson sat slumped next to the window gazing out the small porthole.

"Are you completely wiped out?" She smiled when he turned and nodded.

"Yeah, I guess I am. You?"

Lauren nodded. "Me too. Clair and Drew were wise to stay an extra few days at the villa and rest up." She sighed. "I'm tired, but very pleased with the way everything turned out." She met his steady gaze. "Comments were good."

"Yes, they were, and so were your sales." He compressed his lips and nodded again. "I'm proud of you."

She held his gaze. "Thank you." After a pause, she said, "It meant so much to have you and Brooke there."

"I'm glad. I'm glad we were there for you. It was enlightening." He nodded once more and continued to hold her with his piercing gaze. Lauren shrank from the gaze and glanced down at the magazine in her hand.

She might believe he'd heard the conversation between her and Nicolas if she didn't know better. They had been alone in Nicolas's private office, except for his secretary, when they were talking.

She raised her face. "Enlightening?"

"Uh-huh." He turned to peer out the small window once more.

"What . . . what does that mean—can you *enlighten* me a little?" She gave a small laugh.

He glanced back, but now his eyes just looked tired and weary. "Nothing really, just that I got to observe you in a whole different light—the way most other people see you."

Lauren laughed. "You almost make that sound like a bad thing."

He expelled a long breath and rubbed his hands over his eyes, saying, "I didn't mean to sound that way."

She had come to know Jackson so well that any nuance of change in his emotions became like extended feelers to her own emotions.

He was not himself. She racked her brain to remember anything that might have happened to distress or worry him, but she drew a blank.

Throughout the time they were in Florence, Jackson had appeared to genuinely enjoy meeting many of the people who appreciated her work and owned her paintings.

Lauren had thought he was having a good time. He and Nicholas hit it off from the start. She supposed Jackson, like Brooke, was worn out.

She sighed and laid her head back on the headrest and closed her eyes.

The drone of the plane's powerful engines soon got inside her head and she surrendered to the much-needed sleep . . . *Nicolas excitedly informed her that one of their top government officials had enquired about commissioning Lauren to do portraits of his family . . . she laughed delightedly, saying, "Wonderful, wonderful, but suddenly Jackson appeared across the large crowded room, he was shaking his head and glaring . . . no sound came from his lips as he formed the words "You promised . . . you promised. . . ."*

Lauren jerked awake, knocking the magazine she'd been holding to the floor.

She glanced at Jackson. His head lolled against the window where it had slipped from the small pillow on the headrest. Brooke was sound asleep, curled into the wide seat. Lauren reached for the bottled water in the cup holder built into the console. She twisted the top off and drank half of it.

Jackson mumbled in his sleep and stirred long enough to shift his head back to the pillow. Lauren studied his sleeping face. Would he ever forgive her for accepting the commission? Thankfully, the man was happy to wait until after the first of the year to get started. Lauren hoped to work it out with Jackson by then.

A flight attendant spoke in a soft voice, "Miss, would you like something to drink?" She smiled and glanced at the sleeping pair.

Lauren smiled back and shook her head, and indicated the water she was drinking. She retrieved the magazine from the floor, but was soon bored with it.

She put her seat back and tried once more to sleep. She'd always found the flying time passed more quickly, and she arrived home feeling better if she slept the hours away.

The nap had lasted no more than an hour when she roused at the sound of Brooke and Jackson whispering. Brooke was having fun with her dad and forgot herself and giggled out enough to awaken Lauren.

She raised her seat to the upright position and reached for the light blanket provided by the airline. "Ohh, it's gotten cool in here." She tucked the blanket around her shoulders. "What are you two laughing about?"

Brooke giggled and said, "We're playing tic-tac-toe and Dad beats me every time—it's no fun not to win."

"Yes, your dad is good at games. It's hard to win with him."

Jackson glanced up from the notepad they were playing on. He did the same direct gaze as before. "Oh, I don't know, you're pretty good at games, yourself."

She tilted her head and frowned. He'd said that in a way that made it sound like a barb. Either something was wrong with Jackson or her guilty conscience was making something of everything he said. "Jackson, did something happen—"

"Lauren, would you mind calling an attendant, please?" He looked straight at her, knowing he'd interrupted. "I'm hungry. How about you girls, aren't you hungry, too?"

"Uh-huh, I am," Brooke chimed in.

Lauren pressed the call button and gave Jackson an imploring gaze before she said, "I wonder what lunch will be?" While they waited for an attendant, Lauren chatted with Brooke. "How many photos have you taken so far?"

Brooke rolled her eyes. "Probably hundreds! Dad had to change the first card and put in a new one." She picked up her camera and tried to find the number of images left. "I never can remember which button it is, oh, there!" She studied for a minute and looked up, distress filled her eyes. "I just have eighty-one more pictures to take."

"That's a lot of pictures—"

"Nooo! It's not very many!" She looked at the back of the camera again as if staring at the number might change it.

"But you got most of what you wanted on the flight over, didn't you?" Lauren smiled encouragingly. "And you photographed the people at the exhibit."

"Well. . . ." She happily forgot the camera when the attendant showed up with their dinner choices.

"The food is pretty tasty to be airline fare. I couldn't eat at noon when lunch was served."

"Oh, why couldn't you eat lunch?" Jackson asked.

"Still excited over everything, I guess." She smiled. "Maybe that's why this tastes so good now."

"Uh-uh, the lasagna *is* good!" Brooke was cleaning the small tray.

Jackson kept his eyes on the plate of food. "It's not bad."

\*\*\*

The dinner trays were picked up, and one by one they each made the trek to the tiny bathroom. Lauren reset her watch and began to study the screen that continually displayed the flight information. According to it, they should arrive in New York around twelve-thirty a.m. Then the drive to Valley Ridge would make them arrive home at two-thirty a.m.

"Lauren, am I going to school tomorrow?" Brooke yawned and wallowed in her seat as if it were a bed.

"I don't think you'd be any good in class. You'd be sleeping with your head on your desk most of the day."

"Good, I'm tired." She settled into her seat with a book in her arms.

"Mrs. Flowers is not expecting you back until you're rested."

"Oh, I remember now, and Mrs. Flowers may want me to show off my pictures to the class." She yawned.

Jackson looked up from the magazine he was reading and met Lauren's eyes, they grinned. And in almost the next moment Brooke was asleep.

They were in the last leg of the journey, that point in time in air travel that Lauren begins to get anxious for it to be over. She was ready to be home. It was dark and the attendants had asked everyone to pull down the shades. Squinting to see the time, she didn't hear Jackson at first because he was trying not to wake Brooke.

"Lauren—" He leaned forward.

"Yes?" She leaned toward him.

He whispered, "I'm going to call for coffee, would you like a cup too?"

She nodded. "That sounds wonderful!"

Jackson pushed the button and in moments an attendant appeared and he ordered.

Lauren watched Jackson's interaction with the attractive flight attendant and thought for the hundred thousandth time how lucky she was to have found him.

Even if he got upset over the commission, Jackson loved her and he would forgive the broken promise.

# CHAPTER THIRTY-SIX

# Home Comforts

Jackson and Matt stood at the desk studying the layout of the office that belonged to the new president of TechRom. The new president happened to be the son of the past president and a super nice guy. His office was the last to receive its artwork, and his office got the most pieces.

It was a huge office and required at least five large canvases and several smaller ones, and then the job would be finished.

Jackson straightened his back and ran his hand through his hair. "It's been nice having a free rein in selecting the art work for the job."

Matt grinned. "We know what we're doing; they know that and that's why we have their trust and why they're pleased with the job we've done."

"Yeah, I know." He sighed. "I'm actually ready to be finished with this project."

Matt nodded. "I've noticed you've lost some steam. It has taken a lot of time and gobbled October right up. I can't believe how the month has flown by. This is the twenty-seventh—"

"Don't remind me, please." Jackson gazed at the layout again, but he wasn't seeing it. Today made twenty-three days since they'd been home from Europe and Lauren hadn't yet confided that she been offered an important commission of three large portraits.

"Yep, a few more days we'll be into November and then December." Matt clapped Jackson on the shoulder. "You'll be teaching that little boy how to fly fish before you can get turned around twice."

Jackson grinned and pushed his hands into his pockets. "I'm looking for a child's fishing rod for his Christmas."

Matt laughed. "If you find a source, get me one too, for Eli."

They exchanged glances at the sound of laughing and talking. Matt said, "Ally was bringing some papers by for me, it's probably her and Maggie."

No sooner had he finished speaking when Maggie knocked on the door and pushed it open. "You guys have visitors." She chatted a few minutes and then said she had to get back to work.

Jackson sat at the desk and glanced at Lauren. "Don't you have an appointment with the doctor today?"

"Mm-huh, I do." She wandered over and placed her cheek against the top of his head.

Matt hugged Ally and thanked her for the envelope she handed him. "While you girls are here we should have lunch at the club—what do you say?"

Ally smiled. "I'm free."

Lauren looked at her watch. "I have to be at Dr. Stinson's office in an hour and a half. Does that give us enough time?"

Jackson patted her arm she'd draped around his neck. "Sure it does. Matt and I don't need to linger over lunch anyway, let's head that way." He got to his feet.

Ally took Lauren's arm as they walked to the door. "You can tell me about the finishing touches you've added to the nursery—and did Brooke get the drawings of the dogs finished?"

Lauren laughed. "Yes, she did, they're being framed as we speak." She shook her head and gazed at Ally. "Thank you for allowing us to copy your idea. Brooke would have been devastated if we hadn't used her drawings in her little brother's room."

"Not only did I not mind, I was flattered you and Brooke liked my idea."

"Come on girls, out the door, we've no time to waste." Jackson informed Maggie on the way out that they'd be back soon. And later in the club restaurant, seated around the large table that practically had their names engraved on it, Matt shuffled his menu on top of Ally's and said, "I don't need to look at that, I know what I want."

Ally nodded. "Me too." She didn't even bother opening the menu.

Jackson smiled to himself, remembering when Ally used to study a menu forever before making a decision, and it had driven him crazy. She and Matt were good for each other.

He glanced up to see Lauren looking at him a half-smile on her lips and a question in her eyes. He'd better get with the program. "Ah, yes, I'll have my same old usual and iced tea."

After the waiter had taken their orders, they relaxed while waiting to be served. Ally said, "How often are you seeing Dr. Stinson now?"

Only once a month, but I think that's supposed to change the next week or so."

Jackson perked up. "To once a week?"

"Oh, probably every two weeks for the month of November, then every week the last month." Lauren glanced down. "The last couple of weeks I've really gotten a lot bigger, and I watch my diet."

Jackson raised his brows. "Not sneaking extra chips when you're alone in the house?"

She rolled her eyes. "You know how careful I am."

Matt changed the subject, saying, "Lauren, have you gotten a lot of inquiries for commissions since the exhibit?"

Jackson gave her a sidelong glance and held his breath, anxious himself for her reply. Lauren cast a furtive glance in his direction.

"Um, not really. Nicolas put the word out that I was taking a break . . . for a while."

"Better prepare yourself, I'll bet you get covered up with inquiries. That show gave you a lot of exposure and some really good coverage. The exhibit is still getting good reviews." He laughed. "You know how it is, it'll all hit at the same time."

Jackson watched as she laughed and tried to act like she didn't have a care in the world. But he knew Lauren well enough to know when she had something on her mind. He had to guard his mouth every minute of the day to keep from blurting out that he knew about the job she'd been offered—and had taken— behind his back. When did she plan to confess she'd broken her promise to him?

***

After dropping the girls back at their vehicles and sending them on their way, Jackson and Matt went back to work assembling the collection of canvases for the job at TechRom.

They wrapped and loaded the paintings into the back of Jackson's Range Rover.

Matt looked at his watch. "It's past middle of the afternoon, and I could use a coffee break, how about you?"

"Sounds good, we've about got all we can get in this load."

Matt agreed. "Let's have coffee and then run this out and unload. We can take the remaining large canvas and the smaller ones over tomorrow."

"Yeah, sounds good."

Matt glanced sideways at Jackson as he'd been doing off and on all afternoon. Jackson wanted to confide in Matt, but he held back, his pride maybe, the downfall of many a man.

He followed Matt to the break room. "I'm curious, Matt, do you and Ally ever misunderstand each other? You know, discover you want different things?"

Matt furrowed his brow. "Well, probably, how do you mean?"

"Well, you want one thing and then you find out she wants another, but you thought all along that you both wanted the same thing?"

Giving it a moment's thought Matt said, "Yeah, we do that. As an example, I liked my recliner, I thought Ally did, too, but come to find out, she hated it."

Jackson laughed. "Not quite what I had in mind— so, she finally told you she hated it?"

"No, she kept arranging pillows on it and hanging fluffy throws on the back of it, you know, things I had to find a place for when I went to sit in my chair."

Jackson laughed. "Like camouflage?"

"Yeah. Once I realized what she was doing, I asked if she'd like to get me a new chair." He laughed and poured their coffee. "My new chair arrived in two days."

Jackson sat at the table with his legs stretched out, his ankles crossed. He chuckled. "Do you like your new chair?"

"Oh, yeah. It's comfortable and it does look a lot better than the old one." He shrugged. "And more importantly, Ally likes my chair too."

Jackson sobered and plowed his hair. "Lauren and I seem to disagree on more serious issues than chair styles." He sighed. "She keeps things to herself, that I feel she should share with me. I never really know what's going on until it accidentally comes out, or as if an afterthought, she mentions it."

Matt said, "And that bothers you. What does she say when you confront her?"

Jackson folded his arms across his chest. "Typical comments are that she didn't think about me wanting to know, she forgot to tell me about it, or she didn't want me to worry . . . the list goes on."

"Those are all reasonable answers."

Jackson gazed at Matt. "I wish Lauren and I were as in-tune as you and Ally seem to be."

Matt sipped his coffee and eyed Jackson over the rim of his cup. "People are different, couples are different. You had the opportunity to be with Ally, but that didn't happen because the magic you feel with Lauren wasn't there with Ally, and the magic is important."

Jackson puzzled for several seconds. "Yes, it is. I love Lauren, it's just. . . ."

"A personality is made up of many parts, when you marry, you accept the whole package. It's like the Bible, you accept the whole, or none, no choosing and picking favorite parts and throwing out the rest."

Jackson nodded and sat quietly. Matt got to his feet and refilled their cups.

"Thanks." Jackson waited until Matt had sat back down at the table. "Lauren was offered a commission that any artist would consider a turning point in their career." He gazed at Matt. "She doesn't know that I know. Nicolas's secretary let it slip."

"Why would she care about you knowing? I'd think she would want you to know."

Jackson looked at his legs and feet stretched out in front of him. "Before we went to Italy I asked her to promise me she wouldn't accept any work that would take her back and forth to Europe, because of the baby and . . . you know."

Matt sighed. "And she promised?"

"She promised."

# CHAPTER THIRTY-SEVEN

# First Snow

A fire crackled in the fireplace, large snowflakes drifted past the windows, a tray on the table beside her chair held every conceivable aid and comfort a cold could want. And Lauren sat swathed and covered like an invalid. She wailed, "I don't have time for this!" Her scratchy voice lifted to the rafters.

"Come, come, wailing about time doesn't change it or grow more of it." Aunt Willa set a cup of steaming hot tea on the table. "I'll clear some of this out of the way." She began to remove some of the magazines and games that Brooke thought might entertain the patient.

Lauren patted the tender skin of her nose with a Kleenex. "But I *don't* have time to be sick . . . there's so much to do."

Aunt Willa sat in Jackson's chair across from Lauren and cradled her own cup of hot tea. "I assure you there's nothing to fret about. Everything that needs doing will get done—"

"Thanksgiving is one week from today!"

Nodding, Jackson's aunt said, "All that's left to do is roast the turkey, and I'm having that done in town. You're looking for things to worry about."

Lauren gazed down and ran her hand over her stomach. "I still have a full month at least before the baby comes." She raised woeful eyes. "How can I get any larger?"

Aunt Willa's eyes were sympathetic. "Are you sure it's a full month?"

Lauren nodded slowly. "Today is the seventeenth of November and Dr. Stinson said somewhere around the twenty-second of December." She looked at the covered mound once more. "By then I may have to be dragged about—" She looked up at Aunt Willa's burst of laughter. "Well, look at this!" Lauren pushed the throw back and she and Aunt Willa gazed, mesmerized by the size of her stomach.

"Well, let's work on the plans for the Christmas party and take your mind off things."

Lauren covered herself and arranged the throw back in place. "I'm so glad we're having a quiet Thanksgiving. Did you invite Thelma to join us?"

"Yes and she accepted."

They spent the next hour going over details of the party in December and how many guests would be staying overnight to attend church services the next day.

"I don't like it when Christmas falls on Sunday." Lauren laid her head back on the chair and gazed out the windows.

"No, me either." Jackson's aunt rested her hands on the lap desk she was using and turned her gaze to the windows also. "The snow is beautiful, and I like watching it fall." After a few minutes she stirred herself, saying, "It wouldn't hurt to go over the guest list one more time just to be sure we haven't forgotten anyone."

Lauren nodded. "No, it wouldn't hurt anything to be sure." She smiled to herself. Poor Aunt Willa. The Christmas party was planned down to the smallest detail.

The guest list included everyone they knew, so there was no danger of anyone being left off. Aunt Willa wasn't concerned about the party; her goal was to distract Lauren from the miseries of her cold.

"Thank you, Aunt Willa, for bearing with me. You always go above and beyond friendship. I can't imagine how I would have managed this big house without you." She laughed. "Jackson would have already fired me."

Aunt Willa chuckled. "I think he's thought about firing me a couple of times."

"No, he would be lost without you." Lauren shook her head. "Jackson's told me how you took charge and cared for Brooke when he was overwhelmed by grief over Jenna."

"Yes, that was a bad time." She sighed and stood. "But times are good for Jackson again, thanks to you, dear."

Lauren looked up at Aunt Willa. "I hope so."

"Don't be silly, of course you make him happy." She peered at Lauren's teacup. "Would you like another cup?"

Lauren shook her head and blew into a fistful of Kleenex. "I think a nap might feel good about now."

"A nap is a good idea. I'm having another cup of tea and finish these cards I hope to get in the mail to-day."

Aunt Willa headed to the kitchen and Lauren set-tled deeper into the chair, pulled the blanket up to her chin, yawned and closed her eyes. Her mind wandered to how unhappy she was going to be if her cold lin-gered into Thanksgiving.

It had hit with a vengeance just the day before, so it might possibly linger . . . *Max called and was shout-ing over the phone that they couldn't make the Christ-mas party, they'd been snowed in with a blizzard, Clair and Drew couldn't make it and neither could Charlie and Caroline. Lauren searched for Jackson and found him walking in deep snow, snow so deep Lauren struggled to pick each foot up. "Jackson, no one is coming to our party, the snow is so deep they can't make it." Jackson's eyes were sad, he slowly shook his head back and forth, "They know—they know you broke your promise. . . ." He turned and walked away . . . she tried to run after him, but her feet wouldn't move through the snow. "Jackson, wait! I'm sorry, I'm sorry. . . ."*

"Lauren! Lauren, dear, wake up." Aunt Willa stood over her gently shaking her shoulder.

"Oh, that was awful! I had a bad dream." She straightened her blanket and looked at Aunt Willa.

"No one could get to the Christmas party because of a bad winter snowstorm."

Aunt Willa laughed. "That is a bad dream, and it may come true, after all the planning we've done." She smiled. "In New York, a bad snowstorm is always possible and no amount of planning can change it when one hits."

"I'll be very unhappy if that should happen and cause Max and Whitney to miss coming to us again." Lauren sniffed. "This is going to be the perfect Christmas."

Aunt Willa sealed another envelope. "We won't even entertain the thought of severe weather. Would you like some orange juice? It might help your throat."

"Um, maybe another cup tea, please, with extra honey? That seems to help as much as anything."

"Yes, of course, I'll be right back with it." She retrieved Lauren's cup and hurried into the kitchen.

Lauren put her head back and closed her eyes. Jackson's sad face and the words he's said in the dream came back. A flash of anger swept over her. It wasn't fair of him to ask such a promise—why had she bothered with the exhibit and show in the first place if she wasn't allowed to reap the rewards of all her hard work? She brushed away the fact that Jackson hadn't twisted her arm. But he wouldn't have gone. . . .

"Here's a fresh cup, dear, it'll help ease your throat." She went back to her chair and took up the lap desk once more.

Lauren sipped the hot, fragrant tea and watched Aunt Willa. "How many cards are you sending out this year?"

"Hmm, somewhere around a hundred, maybe a few more." She sealed another one. "Are you sending out cards?"

"Oh, probably next week, maybe tomorrow if I feel better." She said absentmindedly, "Mine are mostly to clients." She sighed deeply and took another sip of her hot drink as her thoughts wandered.

Aunt Willa rose from her chair and went to the fireplace and poked at the fire, she added another couple of logs from the wood-box. She glanced at Lauren as she sat back down in her chair. "You've been sighing every few minutes the last hour. If you want to talk, I'm happy to listen." She had picked up her pen and started on the cards once more.

Lauren set the teacup on the table and laid her head back. "Oh, me, where to start."

"The beginning is always a good place."

Lauren lolled her head sideways and gazed at Aunt Willa. "Remember the promise I made to Jackson? An unfair promise in the first place."

Aunt Willa nodded. "Yes, I remember. I believe we talked about the choices you had."

"And, if you remember, I had very few choices because it was important for Brooke to go. And Brooke *wouldn't* have gone if I hadn't made that promise."

"I don't know why you're fretting over it, everything worked out like you wanted it too, didn't it?"

Lauren continued gazing at Jackson's aunt. "Something happened that I haven't told Jackson about, and I'm running between feeling rotten about it and being angry with him."

"Does Jackson have to know about it?"

Lauren nodded. "Uh-huh, eventually." She looked away from Aunt Willa and stared out the windows at the falling snow. Her breathing tightened and her face grew warm at the very thought of telling Jackson what she'd done. He would never trust her again.

She felt the tears welling and she didn't want Aunt Willa to see her crying. "Too much tea, I'd better run." Kicking at her covers, she scrambled from her chair and headed to the bathroom.

After a cleansing cry, she washed her face in cool water and detoured by the kitchen and grabbed a bag of sour cream chips and on her return, boldly waved the bag in front of Aunt Willa. "I haven't had chips in ages, and I need comfort food."

Aunt Willa laughed. "What's the old saying, 'Drastic times calls for drastic measures'?"

Lauren smiled. "Agreed." This was indeed drastic times for her conscience, her integrity, her loyalty to Jackson and her old fashioned sense of fair play. The only thing she could do was to confess that she wanted to do that commission and apologize to Jackson for breaking her promise.

But the time had to be right.

And finding the right time might prove to be like finding the needle in the proverbial haystack

# CHAPTER THIRTY-EIGHT

# Winter Storm

December marched toward the middle of the month, and with a sky as gray and cold as a winter day could get. A severe storm threatened the entire state.

Lauren gazed out the windows of the morning room while she waited for a call. She hoped the storm would hit and be gone before Christmas. She'd returned from Dr. Stinson's office to see that Nicolas had left a message.

She listened twice, hesitated a moment, and erased it.

He had asked her to return his call, as they needed to discuss dates of when she might expect to start work on the first of the portraits for the family in Italy. The commission consisted of the father, mother and one daughter.

Nicolas could have at least waited until after Christmas.

They had already determined that each canvas should be no smaller than forty by forty-seven inches.

Several life sketching sessions would be followed with a photography shoot of each subject in preparation to starting the actual painting.

Lauren had not been sleeping well lately and she was tired. She'd called Nicolas back as soon as she listened to his message—when he didn't answer her call, she left him a message and said she'd be waiting.

What was keeping him?

Her head begin to throb, and she wished the call would hurry and come through so she could take care of it and get comfortable. She might even get a short nap before Jackson and Brooke got home.

Lauren turned from the windows and eased into her chair, she hadn't gotten her strength back since that awful cold that lingered for two weeks. She was barely feeling human at Thanksgiving, and was once more glad they had decided on a quiet holiday with Thelma as the only guest.

Clair and Drew, her dad and Caroline had celebrated the holiday with Drew's family. Matt and Ally went to her parents for the day, along with Matt's family who'd been invited to share Thanksgiving dinner.

Lauren wistfully gazed at the phone, willing it to ring.

Her thoughts drifted to her doctor visit earlier in the day. She had told him last week that she couldn't possibly go until late December to deliver this baby.

And today Dr. Stinson agreed that the baby seemed further along than the middle to late December due date he'd first thought. He had smilingly suggested she'd be wise to prepare a little early just in case. When she asked him how much earlier he thought it might be, he'd shrugged and said anywhere from a week to ten days. She reached for her phone and looked at the calendar and muttering to herself, "Today is Friday, December ninth, so . . . a week earlier than the twenty-first due date would put it somewhere in the middle of next week—"

Lauren jumped when the landline began ringing. Oh, why hadn't she put the receiver near her chair before she sat down!

Nicolas refused to call her on the cell phone.

Lauren struggled to her feet and waddled toward the phone. "Hello." She smiled and carried the portable phone back to her chair. "I'm moving slow these days." The conversation lasted a good forty-five minutes before they said goodbye and ended the call.

With that taken care of, Lauren went straight upstairs and put on her warmest pajamas. She browsed the collection of books she planned to read someday, selected one, and slowly made her way back downstairs to sit by the fireplace. She pulled her favorite throw over her legs and feet and settled in to read, knowing it would soon put her to sleep. She hadn't read long before the book drifted to her side and she slept soundly.

The sound of the garage alert woke her with a start, at the same time the water she'd drank just before Nicolas called urgently needed to be eliminated.

Lauren threw the coverlet to the floor and swung her feet to stand, too late, she felt her foot catch in the soft fabric, she screamed, fought the air for balance and pitched headlong. Darkness closed in—

Voices above her moved in and out, some she knew and some not. Once she recognized Jackson and

Dr. Stinson that was all that mattered. She drifted off again to blessed nothingness. Weird dreams ran on endlessly, and she dreamt that Dr. Stinson was talking to her, but she couldn't wake to answer him and then thankfully they all went away. . . .

\*\*\*

"Are you awake?" Jackson sat in a chair by the hospital bed. "You've had a long rest."

Lauren stared at Jackson seconds before the memory of her tripping rushed back. Her hands went to her stomach, her flat stomach. "The baby—"

"The baby's fine. He's doing great." Jackson moved closer to her. "He's a little early, but Dr. Stinson said he would have been here by this time next week anyway."

"Oh, thank you dear God." She whispered. "At my last visit Dr. Stinson told me he suspected I might deliver earlier than he first thought—when was that? How long have I been here?"

"You saw the doctor yesterday, Friday. You've been here since yesterday evening. It's 9:40 a.m. Brooke and I got home at five-thirty and Aunt Willa came soon after."

"Oh, your poor aunt! I'm sure that scared her."

"Of course it did, we all went to the hospital. After Dr. Stinson came out and told us you had suffered no injuries, but it looked like the fall had started your labor. Dr. Stinson was worried about a concussion since you blacked out. He thought you might have hit your head."

Jackson rubbed his hands over his eyes. "Aunt Willa and Brooke stayed until the doctor came out to tell us the baby was in good health."

"He really is healthy?" Lauren wiped her eyes.

"Uh-huh, weighing in at six and a half pounds and eighteen inches long." Jackson held her hands. "It didn't hurt him at all to arrive when he did." He gazed tenderly and wiped the tears off her cheeks. "It nearly scared me to death though when I stepped into the kitchen and heard you scream and fall." He shook his head. "I don't ever want to go through that again."

Jackson smiled. "Brooke stayed calmer than I did. She took one look at you lying passed out on the floor and didn't say a word, just flew to the phone and called 911 and told them exactly how to get there." He grinned. "She impressed me."

Lauren cried and smiled with pride. "Oh, our Brooke, she's so grown up."

Jackson sighed. "Yes, she is. I'm proud of her."

"Me too." Lauren squeezed his hands. "When can I see him?"

"I imagine as soon as Dr. Stinson makes his rounds, he'll give the okay."

Lauren wrapped her arms around Jackson's neck. "I love you—I wish you could *really* know how much I love you."

\*\*\*

Jackson got to his feet and pushed the chair out of the nurse's way as she bustled into the room. She approached the bed and placed a tiny, mummy-shaped bundle into Lauren's arms.

Jackson had forgotten just how tiny babies are. Lauren gingerly held the bundle close, and looking into the nurse's eyes, she said, "I'm terrified I'll hurt him."

The nurse laughed and adjusted the blanket away from the tiny, pink, scrunched face. "Nah, he's tough, you won't hurt him. He probably won't even wake up!" She laughed.

Lauren bent close and studied the small face and head and gazed up at Jackson. "He is healthy and perfect!"

Jackson had dragged his chair back close to the bed as soon as the nurse left. "You didn't believe me or Dr. Stinson?"

"It wasn't that, I just had to see for myself." She kissed the small downy forehead. "I couldn't bear it if he'd been hurt." Lauren drew him closer. "When can Brooke come see him?"

Jackson glanced at his watch. "I called Aunt Willa and told her about—"

A soft knock sounded on the door and it pushed open a foot and his aunt peeked in. "May we come in?"

"Yes, ma'am." Jackson stood and went to the door. "You girls come in and see what Lauren's got."

Aunt Willa allowed Brooke to approach the bed first. Lauren patted a place on the covers next to her.

"Can you believe it, Brooke, all the planning and work to make a nursery and now he's really here?"

"Wow, I can't believe it!" Brooke sat carefully on the bed, her eyes fastened on the baby's face. He opened his eyes as if returning his big sister's scrutiny.

"He looked at me!" She whirled. "Dad, the baby looked at me!" She turned back and bent to kiss the little forehead. "He's soft, like the horses muzzles."

Everyone laughed and Aunt Willa moved closer. "He looks like you did as a baby, Jackson."

Jackson huffed. "You remember what I looked like when I was a baby?"

She huffed back. "I was fourteen when you were born, of course I remember."

A short time later, the nurse quietly entered Lauren's room. "I hate to break up the fun, folks, but baby must return to the nursery. You can view him through the nursery window, if you'd like." She went out carrying their baby as if he was an unbreakable package.

Brooke's eyes widened, she watched the nurse disappear and the door shut behind her. "She's rough with him!"

Lauren laughed, reaching for Brooke's hand. "She knows how to handle babies, it's her job."

Lauren shook her head. "I hear you kept your cool when you saw me passed out. That's the second time you've rescued me."

Brooke nodded. "Uh-huh, I remember the bridge. We practice what to do in emergencies at school."

Jackson said, "Well, I can see that you pay attention to the teacher. I'm very proud of you, Pumpkin."

"Thanks, Dad." She jumped off the bed and went to check out the flowers Lauren had received. "Here's one from Clair and Drew, and one from Italy, N-i-c-o-l—"

"Nicolas." Jackson finished for her. "How did he know? I didn't call him." He glanced at Lauren.

She smiled, and looked pleased. "Clair probably called him. How sweet to send me flowers."

Jackson got up and wandered to where Brooke continued reading cards. "Here's Ally and Matt's, and Maggie's. . . ."

Aunt Willa rose from her chair and hugged Lauren. "I'm just grateful you're healthy and fit." She sighed. "I hate I wasn't there when it happened, I might could have helped."

Lauren returned the gesture of affection. "I'm an adult, I shouldn't need someone to stay with me every hour of the day. I was in a hurry and still half asleep and just tripped. Things happen."

Jackson turned, but he caught himself just in time to keep from blurting out, *Yes, things happen, accidents happen, but when you make promises to get your own way, then break them casually and deliberately . . .* he quickly turned back to reading cards with Brooke.

Aunt Willa walked over and admired the flowers for several minutes. She draped an arm around Brooke's shoulders "We better go. We'll come back this evening at visiting time for another peek at the baby."

Brooke ran and hugged Lauren goodbye. "I hope I get to see him this evening."

Lauren said, "We'll make sure you see him."

Jackson walked Brooke and Aunt Willa to the car, mostly to get out in the fresh, cold air and clear his head. Huge snowflakes were beginning to fall, filling the sky with its drifting beauty. He watched with upturned face for several minutes before heading back inside the hospital.

He'd promised himself not to mention the job in Italy. He'd continue to wait and hope Lauren confided in him of her own will, but with the baby's arrival, it was getting harder to keep quiet.

He'd not break his promise, even if he had to tape his mouth.

CHAPTER THIRTY-NINE

# Christmas Perfect

Lauren came home from the hospital with Joshua Colin Montgomery on the twelfth of December, two weeks before he was due to be born.

They'd been home nine days. He was a healthy, contented baby. Perfect in every way. Lauren and Aunt Willa busied themselves decorating the house while waiting for Joshua to awaken, be fed, and go right back to sleep. The days passed swiftly.

The day before Christmas Eve, Lauren and Jackson stood gazing out the windows of the morning room. "The gardens look beautiful covered in snow."

Jackson's arms encircled her. "I doubt we can possibly have the Christmas party."

Lauren nodded. "I know. Max called. They're having a hard winter with lots of snow in Colorado, too." She turned and pressed her face against his chest.

"As long as we're together with the children and Aunt Willa, we'll have a good Christmas."

He kissed the top of her head. "Agreed." They wandered to the big chairs and settled in. Winslow and Winnie were lying near the fireplace, but they relocated to be at Lauren's feet.

"Let's give them a brush. They're not sure about the baby." Lauren went to get dog brushes and tossed one to Jackson. She sat on the floor and began grooming Winslow.

"They'll need extra attention for a while." Her cell phone rang.

"Hi, Clair." Lauren continued brushing with one hand.

"We can't make the party, and I hate it. Drew's disappointed, too."

Lauren sighed. "Not to worry, it can't be helped."

"Will Max and Whitney try to come, do you think?"

"Oh, no, they're snowbound in Colorado."

"Maybe we all needed a quiet reflective Christmas," Clair said.

"Could be. Whatever, I'm going to enjoy it and be grateful." They chatted a while and ended the call. "That was Clair. They're staying home."

Jackson nodded. "I don't blame them, I wouldn't ask anyone to get out in this." He finished brushing Winnie. "We may start a new tradition of celebrating quietly at Christmas."

Lauren gathered the brushes. "I'd probably like that just as well."

Aunt Willa entered the room. "Is this weather supposed to break anytime soon?" She got comfortable in her chair.

Jackson lifted Winnie to his lap. "Nah, supposed to go through Christmas day." The room fell quiet until Brooke came in complaining that riding lessons had been canceled.

"Be glad for the poor old horses." Jackson said. "Anyway, lessons fell on Christmas Eve, they had to be canceled."

"They have indoor arenas, Dad," She said and wandered out again.

The baby monitor sitting on a nearby table gave a mouse squeak, they all smiled and Lauren headed for the stairs. "Brooke! Baby's awake if you want to see him." She called as she passed Brooke's room.

Lauren followed closely as Brooke entered the room with Joshua in a protective grip. "We thought it might be nice for the baby to take his bottle in here by the fire." Lauren sat on the floor and held him in her arms; she and Brooke took turns holding the bottle.

Lauren put him on her shoulder and patted up a big burp. They all laughed like it was a big accomplishment. "I'll make a place here on the floor. It's warm and we can watch him."

"I'll watch out for him." Brooke quickly grabbed a baby quilt and spread it on the carpet. The evening passed slowly. And the snow continued.

*** 

The next morning Lauren stuck her head in Brooke's room. "Christmas Eve gift!" She hurried away feeling like a child and headed down the stairs. Baby Josh was already downstairs in his bassinet with Jackson and Aunt Willa. The buffet consisted of Aunt Willa's Traditional baklava, curried eggs with sourdough biscuits and jam, and a choice of hot drinks. Tradition in the Montgomery home was a large breakfast and gift opening on Christmas Eve morning while still in pajamas and robes.

Brooke straggled in. "Why didn't you wake me, Dad?"

"I thought you'd like to sleep in since you stayed up last night." He hugged her. "We wouldn't start without you." He brushed her hair away her eyes. "You can be the hander-outer of gifts."

Her eyes brightened. "Let's do presents first and then eat."

He nodded. "That's usually what we do."

Aunt Willa said, "I'm getting my coffee first."

"Me, too." Lauren went to the serving bar for coffee. "Jackson, coffee?"

"Yes, thanks." He glanced at the baby. "He's sleeping right through the noise."

"Hmm, he's a good baby." Lauren set Jackson's cup on the side table.

Brooke crawled around under the tree searching out the names. "Hurry, everybody, I can't wait!"

Jackson took a hot sip of coffee. "Okay, we're ready."

Aunt Willa got the first package, then Lauren, then Brooke laid one aside for herself and one for the baby, last she handed Jackson his. The process was repeated until a short while later the tree was bare and colorful wrapping paper, bows, and gift bags littered the room. They admired the gifts from each other and enjoyed the fun. Brooke had opened the baby's gifts for him, a fishing pole and a book of nursery rhymes.

Jackson and Brooke made a game of gathering the litter into a trash bag and Jackson carted it to the garage.

Finally, the smells of breakfast pulled them to the serving bar. "Breakfast looks delicious." Lauren was suddenly starved.

"I hope it is. I wasn't sure about the eggs, are they still hot?"

"They're warm enough."

They sat at the round oak table in the morning room enjoying the food, chatting and thanking one another for their gifts.

When it grew quiet at the table, Lauren said, "As for tomorrow, I think we should still dress in our Christmas outfits and go ahead with the formal dinner as planned, even though it's just us."

Jackson glanced out. "Good idea. There'll be no getting to church in the morning."

Aunt Willa said, "Yes, good idea, Lauren. We worked hard for this party and we can still enjoy it."

"I'll still get to wear my new dress," said Brooke.

Gathered around the table, they renewed the Christmas spirit, and the day passed pleasantly.

\*\*\*

On Christmas morning, the world outside resembled the setting for a perfect holiday movie. Snow topped the trees and covered the gardens, and it continued to fall. Lauren felt in her bones that this was going to be the best Christmas ever.

Phone calls began coming in early with friends wishing them a Merry Christmas.

It was the next best thing to being together as they shared text images of the snow, their gifts, and each other opening packages and carving their Christmas turkeys.

Ally sent pictures of Eli's first Christmas. Max and Whitney called. Whitney sent images of deep snowdrifts, and pictures on the ranch of horses huddled in loafing sheds.

Jackson insisted everyone pile on the floor in front of the fireplace and they took a family photo to share with friends. Joshua slept in big sister's arms in the photo.

Brooke scrolled through Whitney's images of the cows and horses in the snow, and mourned. "Ohhh, poor animals!"

Jackson's brows went up. "And you wanted to have riding lessons."

"But, in the *arena*, Dad!"

Aunt Willa and Lauren served lunch at one o'clock. The four of them sat around the beautiful, festive, Christmas table. The large table was set with Jackson's grandmother's best china. Jackson gave thanks for the food and the many other blessings they enjoyed.

Afterward, Jackson folded his napkin and laid it by his plate. "I've never tasted better roasted turkey."

Aunt Willa laughed. "I can't take credit for the turkey. I had it done in town, but my help and I did the baking and candy making."

By late afternoon everything was cleaned and back in order with tons of leftovers to freeze. Jackson commented that Joshua hadn't been awake an hour all day. He began to worry that something was wrong.

Lauren laughed. "Nothing's wrong."

Aunt Willa said, "He's growing. Sleeping is his main job." She got to her feet. "And I'm going to my room and join him in that occupation."

Brooke jumped up from the carpet and said, "Me, too. I want my pajamas on. It's dark and it seems like bedtime."

"Have a good nap, girls." Jackson watched them as they left the room together. He walked to the windows and motioned for Lauren to join him. He took her in his arms. "Did you have a good Christmas?"

"Lauren leaned against his chest. "It has been a perfect Christmas. Thank you for the book. I'll treasure it."

Jackson laughed. "It's just a beat-up old book. But I'm glad you're pleased."

"It happens to be a rare, out of print, signed, first edition."

"I'm glad you know what it is, because it doesn't look like much to me."

Lauren snuggled. "It's a beautiful book." She hesitated. "I want to talk, Jackson."

"Okay."

Lauren glanced at him, he voice was guarded, his body tensed. She smiled. "Don't worry, it's nothing we're going to argue over."

"Good."

She took his hand and led him to the fireplace. They sat on the floor. She took a deep breath. "I was offered a commission. I really wanted to accept . . . I did accept it."

"Lauren—"

She quickly put her fingertips over his mouth. "Let me finish. I accepted the job, knowing I was breaking my promise to you and going against my own principles." She focused on the fire for several moments. "I'm sorry, I just wanted it so badly."

Jackson ran his hand through his hair. "How could you consider a job based in Europe, flying back and forth with an infant to care for—"

"With today's technology, I could do it. Not easily, but I could do it with just one trip—two at the most."

Jackson got up and threw a log on the fire. He wandered to the windows and stood with his hands pushed deep into his pockets. He paced and stopped and paced again. Finally he came back. He dragged Aunt Willa's footstool close to where Lauren sat on the floor.

He eased onto the footstool and took her hands. "I won't fight you on this anymore, I know what a good opportunity means to an artist. But, I don't like it, and I may not be very patient." He sighed heavily. "You'll do a good job, I know that, and thank you for telling me."

Lauren stared into the fire. "The day I fell, I had a long talk with Nicolas." She looked up at Jackson. "He's a very nice man."

Jackson made a disgusted sound, but said, "I know."

"I told him I was giving up the commission; he said he wasn't surprised."

"You're . . . what?" Jackson frowned.

"As much as I wanted to do the job, I couldn't choose it over you—I tried."

Jackson got to his feet and pulled Lauren up, too, his arms tightened around her. "You *have* turned it down? Definitely?"

"I have. Definitely."

He released her, but his hands moved to her shoulders. "You let me agonize over being selfish? Knowing you weren't taking the job . . . why?"

Lauren sighed. "I had to know *I* turned it down, and not because of you. You needed to know that, too. I didn't want either of us to someday wonder, *what if?* This way, I can never blame you for holding me back, and you can never accuse me of loving my work more than I love you."

Jackson laughed and hugged the breath out of her. "But what if I had failed the test."

"I have faith in you." Lauren said, "Oh, and you have another Christmas gift." She went to the backside of the huge tree and removed a package and brought it to him.

Jackson shook the package. "No rattling parts." He untied the green satin bow and tore the paper off. He stared at the small painting of him and his dad fishing in the lake. "Oh, Lauren, I love it! I remember that day as if it were yesterday." He looked up from the painting. "Thank you! But I thought it sold at the exhibit?"

She smiled. "Clair told me you were having a fit over it. I'd forgotten you'd never seen the painting. I had Nicolas stick a red dot on it, and I sneaked it home."

A tiny cry sent Lauren hurrying to the bassinet, with Jackson following her. Baby Josh stretched and squirmed. She picked him up and placed the sweet smelling bundle in his father's arms.

Jackson strolled to the windows. "You won't re-member it son, but this will be your best Christmas ever."

Lauren leaned against Jackson as they gazed out the windows upon Christmas's winter wonderland.

"Isn't it like nature? We planned what we thought would be the perfect Christmas. But Mother Nature canceled our plans with snow from Heaven, and gave us truly the best Christmas ever.

With the baby nestled between them, she tiptoed to kiss Jackson, and whispered, "Merry Christmas, my love."

~ The End ~

Mary J Hicks is the author of three novels and numerous short stories. If you like a clean story with a bit of romance, you might enjoy her series, A Valley Ridge Romance.

Mary's short stories are fun, easy reads about human nature. Mary lives in a quiet country setting in the Red River valley, a setting she finds conducive to her life of writing and painting.

Learn more about the author and follow her on her website at: **www.maryjhicks.com**

Mary's books are available on Amazon.

# I thank you...

I **give thanks to my Lord** always, for loving me. Without Him I could do nothing.

Thanks to my brothers and sisters and their spouses.

**Words are little things** to express my huge debt of gratitude to my daughter, Gayle, for her tremendous help, thank you, dear.

**Many, many thanks** to my sister and neighbor, Ruth Allen, for reading every word and helping me work things out—and doing it in a kind, patient manner.

***

**And to the two beautiful ladies** who grace the cover of my book, Erin and Dovie Banta, for modeling with grace and patience, thank you!

***

I enjoy hearing from my readers.
marehicks4@gmail.com

OTHER BOOKS
in the
Valley Ridge Romance series
by
Mary J Hicks


Trespassing On His Heart ( Book one )

Love's Tender Heart ( Book two )

\*\*\*

A Volume of Short Stories

The summer Boarder

www.ingramcontent.com/pod-product-compliance
Lightning Source LLC
Chambersburg PA
CBHW030400180626
46812CB00005B/1859